TO THOSE
WHO HAVE
LOST

To Those Who Have Lost

Text copyright © 2022 by Quincy Lee Clark

All rights reserved.

No part of this book may be used or reproduced in any manner whatsoever without written permission except in the case of brief quotations embodied in critical articles or reviews.

This book is a work of fiction. Names, characters, businesses, organizations, places, events, and incidents either are the product of the author's imagination or are used fictitiously. Any resemblance to actual persons, living or dead, events, or locales is entirely coincidental.

For information contact:
https://www.quincyleeclark.com

Cover design by Maxim Mitenkov
Editing by Emily Klopfer
Book design by Quincy Lee Clark
Formatting template: Derek Murphy

ISBN: 978-1-7386763-0-9 (paperback)

First paperback edition: July 2023
10 9 8 7 6 5 4 3 2 1

To my mother, who taught me to never dare stop fighting for what or who I love

Nothing contributes so much to tranquilize the mind as a steady purpose—a point on which the soul may fix its intellectual eye.

Mary Shelley, *Frankenstein*

Chapter 1

Moira

UNDER THE COVER OF NIGHTFALL, the seemingly endless sprawl of the city ahead appeared to be nothing but a candle's flame attempting to hold off the otherwise impenetrable darkness. I spared a glance back over my shoulder to the rotund, middle-aged man climbing the steep knoll behind me, and let out a sigh. "We camp here for the night, and maybe we'll get there by tomorrow afternoon if we're lucky."

"When you told me to follow you, I wasn't expecting…" He swallowed loud; he was panting like a dog. *Pathetic.*

I looked ahead to the flickering city lights and drawled, rolling my eyes, "Let me guess, you forgot to drink water again, right?"

"*Listen you bitch—*"

"Okay, Qasir, we've been through this plenty already. I didn't force you to come with me." I took a deep breath, frustrated, and said, "You were the one that came to me—*remember?*" I didn't bother glancing back towards him and instead kept my focus on the city before us. I had never seen a city quite so large or so bright before…frankly, it was as if the people there never slept.

His breathing came closer, approaching my right side, and eventually quieted down beside me.

About *fucking* time.

I rolled my eyes—

I was on the verge of strangling him just to keep him from distracting me from the unsettling, beckoning view the knoll posed of the city—miniature from this far away, but still so…

Overbearing.

"Fine," he finally acknowledged. "I did come to you, but you never told me the trip would be so…" He paused. "Difficult."

I shook my head, exasperated and quite literally at my wits end, and spit, "I told you that the difficulty of the trek would be entirely dependent upon *you* and what *you* wanted. If *you* didn't want to put in the work, then you should have asked for someone else to do this for you instead of wasting my time with your stupid complaints."

I glared back to silently curse the decrepit dirt path we had painstakingly walked on for the past two weeks straight. It veered north, back into the valleys that would ultimately lead to the circus where we first crossed paths.

There were times when I *truly* regretted my life choices.

But, whatever.

At least I wasn't a complete failure.

At least *I* could climb the stupid little hill we were now both standing on without nearly cacking off in the process.

I slowly dragged my head towards the lights once more, and an invisible flame licked up my spine in response. The city itself seemed to be summoning my presence.

Strange.

The flicker had never been so keen to have me follow its designated path before.

I asked, "Do you know where we are exactly?"

"You told me to trust you." I felt Qasir straighten beside me. "To follow you to the edge of oblivion, yet you don't even know where we are or where we're headed?" He was seething. Apparently, he didn't want to so much as *try* to be civilized with me anymore.

It didn't matter—all I knew was that if I didn't crawl off to bed for some sleep soon, I would inevitably end him for keeping me awake. Even if he was practically double my size.

"Did I say that I didn't know which way we're headed?" I gave him a second to respond and cut him off as he opened his mouth. "No, I don't think so. I know *exactly* where we're going." I nodded to the direction of the sprawl just a day's trek away, and the flicker dancing over my spine quieted, content with my decision to continue onward into the sand. "All I was asking was if you knew what they called this place. If you don't want to tell me, that's fine. You're probably too dim-witted to know anyway."

Qasir growled at me.

I couldn't say I blamed him.

After having virtually nothing to do besides analyze the man for two weeks straight, I'd become quite adept at knowing what would make him tick—a priceless jewel on a boring trip; yielding great entertainment value—for me. Without it, I wouldn't have been able to enjoy myself.

All those weeks ago, I'd been told to lead him to whatever he desired most in the world. I had no choice but to follow through on my…promise to do just that.

Despite despising damn-near every step of the way.

Taunting and teasing him only seemed reasonable to me. Occasionally pissing him off kept me on the straight and narrow— as in, it kept me from abandoning him without food and water on the road we had been walking.

To make things worse, I couldn't even have a decent conversation with the man either. It didn't even matter that I was trying to *help* him. He desired more than anything to be a man of status. Just like almost every other man I'd stumbled across in my time here. So, naturally, he couldn't even deign to speak to me with any shred of respect. Who was I, after all, but a *woman* in his eyes.

A means to an end.

Even if this "means to an end" knew more about the way things were than he ever would.

That little fact became clear to me on day three of our little "trip" together. Because of Qasir's obscene appetite we were already running low on supplies, so when we stumbled across an inn with a couple of houses nearby and a tavern, I'd asked him if he could be a decent human being and cover the cost of what we'd need in order to continue the journey. A simple request on my part. I wasn't capable of covering the cost of the goods anyway. The ringmaster still made sure of that.

He'd agreed—by some miracle—but insisted that first, he would be the one to deal with the merchant who we were to purchase some bread from—that was fine—and second, that I wouldn't be allowed to stand beside him while he bargained because he couldn't have a "foreign cunt" like me around while he performed his transactions.

I unwillingly obliged and observed him from afar during the affair. It killed my pride to do so, but I wasn't going to let my pride starve us both into early graves.

Even so, the thought was tempting.

As I'd watched, I noted that he'd kept flaunting his pitiful coin satchel around for everyone nearby to see throughout the entire exchange. Clearly, his insistence to deal with the haggler was only for his selfish—

Qasir's voice interrupted my thoughts. "The city is called Neosordess."

The gruff voice knocked me out of my stupor, and I grinned to myself. "Thanks for saving me all of the trouble." I tucked a strand of hair behind an ear. "At least your pea-sized brain knows *that* much."

He kicked a rock off of the hillock we were upon—the only indication of how much I was aggravating him, but remained pointedly quiet, like he was withholding something.

"Come on, out with it." Curiosity got the better of me.

"With what?" His innocence was palpably fake.

"Qasir," I drawled, "there's no point in wasting our time. Unless you don't want us sleeping on something half-decent tonight?" He was still carrying the weight of our sleeping arrangements on his back after the day's journey, so I feigned interest in his well-being, stating, "If I still feel like I got kicked by a horse because you didn't set up camp the other night, I can only imagine how a man of your age must feel, especially with the added task of lugging around that heavy bag *all* day." A well-deserved, pointed jab in his direction—

Evidently, I couldn't keep up the charade for very long.

I too had been carrying some supplies on my back, but nothing of real substance. I wouldn't describe myself as weak; however I wouldn't say that I was particularly well-suited to manual labor either.

I shook my head, strands of midnight hair falling into my eyes, and grimaced. I was truly shocked that I'd wound up here literally trying to convince a *stranger*, that it would be in *his* best interest to keep following me, even though I would almost be guaranteed no real *significant* benefit from doing so.

It would be one thing if we'd both desired the same things in life. Hell, after three years of pulling stints like this, I wasn't even sure it was worth it to keep hoping for that day to come—the day in which I would venture across someone who had a similar aspiration to me in mind.

But nope.

Instead, I'd led close to fifty men in the past three years to *their* desires: fame, fortune, power, women...I probably should have given up entertaining the idea as soon as it popped into my head. But still the thought lingered. *Maybe I wasn't alone.*

Even if it was an impossible wish anyway.

No one would *ever* have the same desire as me.

I should have spent my time more productively; figuring out what I could actually carve out of this meek existence, instead of holding onto the hope of returning to everything I used to be.

Another one of the many, *many* regrets in my life.

I glanced down to the ground at my feet and nearly sobbed in relief upon noticing that it didn't merely consist of rock like the majority of our earlier chosen campsites. This site was relatively flat for once, and even had some grass to help soften it. There was a *slim* chance that I'd have a decent night's rest. But that would only happen if I could ignore Qasir's obnoxiously loud snoring.

I swore. I was a lot more patient than people gave me credit for. A month with a brute like Qasir had been…insufferable, especially considering the fact that he hadn't yet placed down his damned backpack so I could get some sleep.

I'd had enough of his bullshit for one day.

Staring at his back and the satchel still waiting there, I snapped, "You know what, just pass me my bedroll. I don't need you to do shit for me, and if you want to put your back out again just because you're being too stubborn or lazy, then that's your own prerogative."

He glowered as he dropped his satchel with another string of curses thrown at me, then said, "Tonight will be the *last* night I camp with you, or even see your smug face." He untied the leather holding our supplies while kneeling in the dirt. "I don't even care if you follow through at this point with your end of the bargain— it's probably a load of shit anyways." He tossed the remnants of his food to the side of the hill, then quickly found the bedrolls he'd been searching for. "He's a liar…always has been. As if a young thing like you could lead me to anything—I know that my brother may think you're something *special*, but he has forever been a moron. A lying moron at that."

He snapped his fingers in my direction. I guess he'd expected me to keep looking at his haggard face, creased with age—no doubt a result of his *charming* demeanor—while he spoke. I rolled my eyes, then shifted them away from the bedroll, back toward him, and waited for his next wave of *exhilarating* conversation to come crashing down on me.

"Listen girl—the only reason why I haven't used my dagger on you yet, is because you're still supposed to be useful to me. If he has lied to me about you, don't think that I won't use you as a way to send a message to him." His eyes, a dark ochre in colour, echoed the promise that laced his words. Frankly, that may have been the first time they'd ever looked so menacing in my presence, but then again, I could have been wrong.

It was more likely that it was simply the first time I'd bothered paying attention to them for more than a fraction of a second to notice their cruelty.

Even so, it was difficult to keep the retort from jumping off my tongue. He'd literally just said he didn't care if I fulfilled my end of the deal or not, but I bit down hard and held the comment in.

The foul coppery taste of iron in my mouth made me want to gag, but I kept my face neutral and didn't shy away from his gaze when I swore, "Qasir, I will not break my bond to you." I exhaled through my nose before continuing, "I will keep it even if it's not in my best interest to do so." I paused again, this time contemplating what to say next, when I conceded to my intense need to sleep. "Can we please just set up the bedrolls now? I want tomorrow to come as soon as possible and sleeping seems like the only way that that's going to happen." I threw my arm out towards him, hoping that he would just toss me the bedroll and waited.

To my surprise, he did just that, and I couldn't help but grunt as I caught the surprising weight that came with my sweet salvation.

He chuckled quietly. "Pathetic—" a sneer, "worthless girl. No wonder why he has you working in the circus—you're clearly of no use in the real world."

I dismissed his insult. The fact that he had even bothered with my services in the first place told me enough about how "useful" he was. *He* was the pathetic one. I dropped the bedroll to the ground first before I was able to shrug off the small satchel I'd been carrying.

A thud as the burlap sac hit the earth, and then silence.

Let him believe that he'd wounded me.

Let him believe that his words even mattered to me.

He would never amount to anything anyway.

I made sure to position my bedroll as far away from him as the little mound would allow and drew my gaze towards the luminous city on the horizon once more, lips twitching upwards as I listened to his struggle perhaps ten feet away. Grunts and curses and more grunts.

Such a charmer.

I prayed that Qasir wasn't exaggerating, and that tonight *would* be last of which that would require me to listen to his intolerable sounds.

A night without him would be amazing.

I smiled to myself as he quieted down, imagining just that, and lay down upon the makeshift bed. I'd been right—it was a hell of a lot more comfortable than almost everywhere else we'd slept for the last four weeks, and I nearly moaned as my muscles finally relaxed.

I tore my eyes from the bright lights accompanying Neosordess, as he'd called it, and stared at the few stars twinkling overhead, flickering in acknowledgement of my attention. "Thank you," I whispered only loud enough for me and the stars to hear, "for keeping me sane and for reminding me of who I once was." I shifted my gaze back down to the city again and closed my eyes to shut out its light.

One more day.

Just one more day.

Chanting this prayer silently to myself helped me find oblivion's sweet embrace, and I was finally allowed to drift off into the dreamless sleep I yearned for.

Chapter 2

Moira

THREE TIMES.

Three times in the past hour I'd been forced to halt our journey to Neosordess. Qasir knelt over his knees a few steps ahead of me, gasping for air, and wiped at his brow which was now drenched with sweat.

"Hurry up—you're wasting my time with your stupid breaks."

No one could be slower than the old buffoon.

"We're almost in a desert…" He gulped down his remaining water. "I need these breaks to keep from collapsing." Sweat appeared to be drenching every crevasse on him, and his skin had taken on a reddish hue, accompanying the darker brown that was there prior—a sunburn then.

"Listen, if we can pick up the pace even a little bit, we can make it to the city before sundown." I chucked my cannister of water in his direction and stated, "Drink and rest for a few more minutes. But no more breaks until we reach the city."

The desolate land surrounding us allowed for a gust of wind to throw a lock of hair into my eyes and I cursed myself a fool for not throwing it into a braid or something when I had the chance at dawn.

Qasir shot a questioning look my way—probably a result of the incoherent ramblings that found their way out of my mouth, but quickly found the water cannister at his feet to be more interesting. He then asked, "Why is it that you're perfectly fine—free of even a sunburn, while I'm over here on the verge of dying from the heat? Hell, you even have your black hair down. Isn't that supposed to make you warmer?" He took another swig of water and stood tall enough for the sweat to begin its descent down his shirt once more.

Repulsive.

"Maybe it's because *I'm* not shoving my face full of food every chance I get." I paused, "And besides," I fingered the lock that grazed my cheek, then tugged it behind an ear, "the colour of my hair has nothing to do with it. Your hair is on the darker side of things too…what's left of it that is."

Qasir guzzled down the rest of the water that remained in my cannister, lobbed it back towards me, and glared.

I glanced to where it had landed at my feet, then began trying to make designs in the hardened, cracked earth beside it with my foot as I continued, "As far as a serious answer to your questions though Qasir, I'm not entirely sure myself. The heat just doesn't bother me, I guess. It never has." I bent over so as to retrieve the now empty container, and silently implored that we wouldn't need any more water.

The city was still easily another hour or two ahead, and that would only be the case if Qasir could pick up his sorry ass and quicken his damned pace up a bit.

I waited another five minutes for him to catch his breath then declared, "We leave now."

It was perhaps the most pleasant conversation we'd ever had.

※

Lucky for me, he did manage to pick up the pace slightly—enough to ensure our arrival before nightfall.

I faced the city slowly taking shape before us and stared in awe at its sheer size. I refrained from the urge to halt entirely and made sure to keep my feet walking forward. Last night, I was under the impression that it was mere sprawl, but now I could see one monstrosity of a building towering above all else; breaking through cloud cover that the other buildings couldn't even touch. It was *unnatural*. I could barely hold back my disgust at the sight of its artificially luminescent face.

"You think it's bad from out *here*?" Qasir chortled. "You haven't even *seen* bad. We're still on the north side of the river that bisects the city—"

"You're telling me *this* gets worse?" I held in my grimace as I stumbled on the ground I was walking on.

"I don't know—do you like criminals and mad men?" He took a deep breath but managed to keep up the hastened pace. "Because as soon as you cross the Aspitha...girl, you would be lucky if you survived for five minutes. On the other hand, the northern side might offer you some peace; it's said to be a holy place."

Despite the uneasiness that came to replace my wonder at the reverence of which Qasir spoke of the north side, we continued our hike towards Neosordess. Light radiating from the distant monolith became more apparent even with the immense distance still separating us from it.

And despite my intense need to get some answers on what exactly he *meant*, I remained quiet, contemplative; perfectly content to continue the trek there in silence.

※

After another hour or so, we reached the northeast wall separating the city from the wasteland surrounding it. The wall was not what I'd imagined considering Qasir had said it was the barrier for the northern "holy" side of Neosordess from the outskirts we had just hiked for days.

I was surprised I hadn't noticed it earlier.

Slate-grey and constructed of some sort of cinder block or brick, the wall was perhaps twenty or thirty feet tall—not counting the merciless barbed wire fence preventing anyone from climbing it, nor the armed guards' stations positioned every so often, with two on each side of an automated gate that would allow us access into the city.

Holy place indeed.

We were halted by other armed guards in another distinct area before the gate; separated from it by a chain link fence before we were both searched.

A man in a uniform matching the slate-grey of the wall performed my "obligatory" pat-down as well as Qasir's, finding the dagger he'd been carrying on our expedition. Yet the guard returned it to him, no questions asked.

I gawked, "What's the point of searching us if you aren't even going to remove our weapons after you find them?" The question leapt off my tongue before I could regulate my behaviour, but the guards performing the security check of sorts remained dead silent.

With their absent responses, nor mere acknowledgement that I'd spoken, I threw a quick glance Qasir's way to gauge his thoughts. He didn't seem even the slightest bit alarmed. "Qasir." I hushed. "What is this?"

He only shrugged, before striding forward to the next checkpoint. Mutely, I bit down onto my tongue, yet again drawing blood from it before I clenched my hands into fists at my sides and threw invisible daggers at his soaked back. *Fine* then—I would have to wait.

A job was simply a job, and as soon as I was done leading Qasir to his wildest dream, I would definitely not be staying here any longer than necessary—even if Neosordess actually had a *holy* side.

What a load of bullshit.

The following checkpoint had even *more* armed guards than where we first came in, all dressed in the same dreary grey as the others, and I found myself uneasy as a man, no older than thirty, opened his mouth to speak. "How long do you plan on staying in the city?"

"I don't know." A short, terse answer, but he wrote something down on the sheet in front of him, nonetheless.

His focus didn't shy away from his work as he asked the next. "Why did you come to the city?"

"Because I saw the lights." Another terse, albeit dishonest answer—

More writing.

"Have you been to the city prior?"

With the latter, when I'd told my inquisitor that I'd never even heard of Neosordess until a day ago, he then asked me an unexpected follow-up question. "Would you like someone to be your guide in the city for the duration of your stay?"

"No." I quickly declined the offer.

Regardless of having a man like Qasir at my side, I still figured that I'd best be alone with him instead of bringing some creepy guide along with us. I could handle my own.

Or at least I could *most* of the time.

And it wasn't as if the guide would be of help to me, even if I needed it...even if Qasir did decide to pull a fast one and throw me to the wolves for whatever reason, surely the guide would never bother trying to hear my side of the story. I would simply be sentenced for whatever it was he pinned on me, and that would be that.

The guard's face held its blank stare as he wrote on the page for another moment, then broke into the most...uncomfortable smile I'd witnessed—effectively shattering the tremendously awkward silence building between us, "May He welcome you."

Qasir and I were finally granted permission to enter the expansive city before us.

I was just grateful that he'd managed to keep up the pace we'd set earlier, and that consequently we made it through the gates well before nightfall.

Alabaster sandstone starkly replaced the slate grey of the wall, making up each of Neosordess' buildings, and each was lined with elaborate glass fixtures, probably originating from the desert that seemed to be slowly creeping towards the city from the south. The buildings seamlessly merged with the landscape, and people flooded the streets in bright colours.

Almost peaceful, except for the hushed whispers, careful smiles, and quickened footsteps that suggested otherwise.

The man's empty words echoed through my mind—

May He welcome you.

What was that even supposed to mean? I shook my head to clear it of the intrusive thoughts forcing their way to my mouth and scowled. The whole exchange had set me on edge.

But no matter. I had a job to do—I had to focus.

We manoeuvred amongst all the too-quiet people and a few large, humped creatures carrying what looked to be saddlebags, before I remembered that I had to reorient myself so I could see where we were in relation to Qasir's desire. I looked inwards briefly to my flickering dancer and paused our stroll, placing a hand on Qasir's shoulder so that I would sense only his desire.

It was surprisingly difficult.

My little flicker felt the desires of the people passing us by, and it took all of my concentration to have it home in on Qasir alone.

The flicker that was no more than a whisper the night before, became a frantic waltz upon my spine—twirling and impatient and, of *course*, leading me and Qasir towards the southern side of the city, across the river. Fortunately, it was also leading us in the general direction of the towering behemoth glowing ahead. I wasn't all *that* disappointed with the flicker's decision; the tower intrigued me, and perhaps whoever "He" was would be found there too.

I pointed towards the monstrosity and said, "We go that way until I say otherwise."

"Seriously?" Qasir scoffed. "The Pillars of Messiah? Only He and His disciples are allowed to even get close to the premises."

Qasir was delusional. Pillars?

"What do you mean, *pillars*?" From where we were standing on the northeastern side of Neosordess, I could only make out one pillar piercing the sky, and that alone was enough to make my stomach churn.

Qasir drawled over the noise of the people rushing around us, "Silly girl. Two pillars break the clouds here in Neosordess— Legacy and Virtue." He pointed towards the visible pillar, and stated, "That one on the Eastern side is Virtue. Both Legacy and Virtue become one though closer to its base, but together the Pillars of Messiah represent the two fundamental principles the Messiah brought forth upon His ascension into power. Legacy is said to represent the eternity of the work He and His disciples do for the people of Neosordess. Virtue is said to be righteous and proves to the people every day, that He does what is best for their society. The Messiah built it in the city's exact center so He could look over all of His people, and so that all in His city would remember who their ruler is."

May He welcome you.

"So, you're telling me, that this "Messiah" as you called him, built that," I pointed, "when he came into power?" I shrugged. "It doesn't seem like he cared about the people all that much..."

Everyone that hurried by us seemed to be in good spirits, but the dancer flickering on my spine suggested that it was a facade, masking an oppressed people incapable of speaking out against His totalitarianism. My little flicker sensed a real, desperate need that seemed to radiate off of each and every one of them. With the smiles plastered on their faces, I wondered if they even realized it.

Qasir glared at me, unimpressed with my observation and barked, "Are we leaving now or not?"

I considered saying no just to taunt him; however, I'd made a promise to him and his brother—an oath of sorts—and I could not, *would* not, break another oath, no matter how much I mentally railed against it at times.

I didn't deign him a response, and instead began weaving in and out of the relentless flow of bodies that seemed to be scurrying away from the southern side of the city, more and more with the sun's steady descent towards the west.

As the sun's light faded further, night's heavy blanket began falling over the city. Glowing signs made from the glass fixtures I'd noted earlier fought against its weight; radiating only the brightest colours, the lights seemingly mimicked the people who had flocked northwards only minutes earlier. Admittedly, it was almost pretty.

The Pillars of Messiah was the only building that seemed to do otherwise—it shone with only the brightest white light and was domineering; casting its light to the point that the other, more beautiful, and soothing lights of the people seemingly faded away.

Night had fallen over the city in earnest when we'd reached the border gate of the two pillars.

Standing under it, I could only bring myself to gaze at the blinding, uncomfortable light for a moment—it was *too* clean. I tried ignoring the unholy light, but it had already burnt its image into my mind. Red and green dots spotted my vision and wouldn't fade even after I closed my eyes.

Qasir had been right about the protective measures put in place to thwart our access to the Pillars. Yet more armed sentries stood guard aloof, ready to protect their Messiah from any external threat. Chain link wrapped itself around the bident's base, and more barbed wire rested above the perimeter.

Mercifully, my flicker urged us away from the behemoth to the bridge linking the two halves of Neosordess. Holy or not, the Pillars was not a place I wanted to stay nor admire.

I began stumbling towards the bridge perhaps a city block or two away, still blinded by the lights, when I came to realize that Qasir was still gawking at the Pillars of Messiah. He held a grin conveying nothing but admiration for both the structure and the men shielding it. That man was fucking *laughable* in my opinion. He was practically in a trance.

I turned where I stood to the flicker's protest, and approached him slowly, "Weren't you the one hurrying me along earlier?" I waited, but he didn't seem to care that I'd even spoken—*surprising*—so I asked instead, "Do you want to reach what you actually desire, or are you content to just stand here staring at this eyesore all night? Because if the latter's the case, I would be more than happy to abandon you here."

He dragged his face away from the unbearable Pillars towards me, then glowered. The extremely bright light accentuated every pore and scar on his face made his already bulbous nose appear swollen, pitted, and reddish. I had to glance to the paved road beneath us to prevent myself from retching at the sight.

As if the man could get worse.

I asked again, arms crossed and tapping an impatient foot, "Are you ready to leave now?"

"Am I not allowed to enjoy a great part of my history?" I dared a peek upwards to see him scan me head to toe before he sneered. "Never mind, an ignorant woman would never be able to understand what it's like to believe and appreciate something as perfect, as holy, as His greatness, and the disciples."

"Qasir, we haven't even seen the Messiah or His disciples yet; what makes you think they're so great? As far as I can tell, the *Messiah* and His stupid dis—"

"You fool," He shifted his eyes towards the guards standing watch at the Pillars and snickered, "those men there *are* the disciples. The men that greeted us as we made our way into the city are also His disciples. You're more oblivious—"

"Enough Qasir." I made to grab him by the worn tunic he wore and attempted to drag him onward—it didn't work. He was easily another head taller than me and was far too out of shape for me to even move him an inch. I conceded and let him go.

"Girl—you can't force me to do anything I don't want to do, and I can assure you that the disciples will be of no help to you either…"

Right—figured as much.

He continued, "But I will continue, if only to get rid of you sooner." He gestured to the bridge with a hand and remained in place until I took a step towards his fate.

I grit my teeth.

Just a bit longer.

Chapter 3

Moira

STEPPING ONTO THE BRIDGE to escape the unholy, holy north side of Neosordess was not nearly as satisfying as I'd thought it would be on the trek there. No guards watched to see who crossed and when, unlike every other "border" that existed in the city. Instead, it remained vacant—absent of even the lights that decorated both northern and southern sides of the city like a shroud.

Water underneath the bridge ripped at the shore like a rabid animal, crashing against the rocks scattered throughout its turbulent surface over and over again, whilst rapids drowned out all sound and gobbled up any surviving light from the city that made its way to its black edge.

I took another step further and looked over my shoulder to Qasir who still seemed hesitant in taking even that first step onto the bridge. I didn't understand why—the bridge was made of solid concrete or something and had a four-foot-high barrier preventing people from absentmindedly falling into the violent water beneath.

Unless he was worried that he would fall through.

I chuckled noiselessly to myself as the idea sprang into my head. Smiling, I faced ahead once more and continued onward towards the southern side of Neosordess, stopping only halfway to peer the drop into the water below…another *terrible* idea. As I gauged the dangerous rapids monopolizing the whole waterway beneath, my mind spun, envisioning how it would feel to fall—then how it would feel to be swept away…

Spinning and weakness and more *spinning*.

I hated the joys of vertigo.

Ever since arriving to this unknown place, the water soothed me; reminding me of a peaceful, not-so-painful time—but here, in this metropolis of too-pure light, everything felt wrong.

The height. The water. The city. The people.

I slowly backed away from the ledge, being particularly careful not to fall over, and quickly reached the bridge's other side. I sighed, practically heaving on my euphoria—I'd survived.

But my solace was short-lived. This southern side was said to be worse than the north—or at least, Qasir wholeheartedly believed that to be the case. I took the breather to understand the layout early, to have an escape plan for myself ready if needed. To my right, more whitewashed sandstone buildings made up the majority of the infrastructure; however, larger, more industrial buildings idly watched me in the distance, and I could only assume they manufactured certain goods—factories then.

Additionally, my right was cloaked in a near-invisible smog. With the night's darkness pressing in upon the city, I couldn't be certain if instead the fog was a trick of the city's heavy lighting or simply a consequence of my oh-so-helpful dizzy spell. But, as a metallic, sulfur-ridden scent forced itself down into my lungs, I all but suffocated and knew that I hadn't been deceived into thinking a veil hovered above the factories in the distance.

I could only hope that Qasir's desire didn't lay there.

But, if that was what it would take to be rid of him, I would *gladly* suffer through the stench.

Directly ahead and to my left, those same whitewashed buildings were unkempt and the light fixtures marking them were spotty—only a few here and there were strewn on the horizon. It was *exactly* the sort of squalor I'd want to live in if I wasn't instead made to live out my days in a grimy circus tent.

As if.

As if these people would choose to—

A person wailed in the distance, pleading for someone to help them, and I kept my face neutral through their screams.

They weren't important to me.

No matter what my flicker wanted me to think; to *do*.

I felt Qasir approach my side and didn't bother glancing back as he murmured, "I told you girl. There's a reason the people were fleeing from the bridge when we first arrived." He chuckled. "Monsters live on this side of the water." Whatever. I'd dealt with my own fair share of horrors in my life. I just never felt the need to scream through them.

The person's death knell rang in the distance, and I couldn't bring myself to feel anything…except maybe impatience. He or she was ultimately responsible for his or her misfortune, just as I was completely responsible for my own.

Closing my eyes, I ignored the crashing water of the Aspitha, emptied my head of their final pleas, and zoned in on the flicker that was now tentatively leaping in pleasure at the fact that we were getting close to our destination—though I could sense it wasn't exactly happy that I'd chosen to ignore whomever he or she was.

I dismissed my little dancer's bad attitude.

My flicker wasn't the only one disappointed in me.

A memory flashed: possessive hands pressed in on me, forcing my head to a naked groin—I discarded the thought, and made a scathing sound before opening my eyes.

Even before I was found useful for my "supernatural" ability, I hadn't been left to suffer. I'd been saved from nothing less than torture and a probable death and…and if I was in another world, I would have rescued them, stepped up to the plate—paid the good deed forward. But I wasn't *in* another world, and I couldn't bring myself to fuck up this job. I was getting sick and tired of my damned flicker's moral compass, especially when it knew that I didn't even possess the strength necessary to stave off anything or to save anyone.

Including myself.

Staring straight ahead, the flicker made no inclination as to which way I had to go. I ground my teeth and shifted my head ever so slightly to the right, but it still didn't stoop to give me any *real* response—just the same dance it had been doing with my eyes closed. I brought my head back to centre and gazed ever so slightly to the left before I felt it.

A scorching pain pulsated outward from where my flicker had danced only seconds earlier, and I knew, I *knew* that that was where Qasir's desire could be found. I grinned at my secret little dancer, nodding my head towards the dying lights barely dotting the main strip and said, "We go this way. It should only take an hour for you to finally reach what you desire most." At least *some* certainty came with the years I'd wasted and the pieces of myself that had been stolen away from me.

"How are you so sure?"

"Because I am."

He stepped in front of me, cutting me off, and threw a mocking smile over his shoulder. "Well girl, it has been a pleasure."

I scoffed. "Don't get ahead of yourself. I'm the only one who can actually lead you there." I took a few hastened steps ahead so I could reach his side.

Refusing to stop for me, Qasir instead continued into the wavering streetlights.

What an *asshole*.

I retaliated, halting my steps altogether whilst pretending to pause in contemplation of…I wasn't exactly sure. I smiled to myself and tapped a finger on my chin for good measure. Dramatics aside, I couldn't give him the pleasure of chasing after him.

Qasir whirled towards me and demanded, "Now what's your problem?"

"Well, it's just that, without me, you could very well end up getting yourself killed..." A brief intermission as I sidestepped some choice words. "It only works if you follow *me,* you know, not the other way around. But if you want, go ahead. I'm sure you'll be just fine because I'm so *useless*, remember? I mean, it's okay with me. I'll just have to relay this whole incident to your brother so that I don't get in trouble for you taking off in this...*lovely* city." I raised my eyebrows for an added effect. "Just be careful of the *monsters*."

He took a visible breath before merely dipping his head in response. I went again to pass him by, but he threw out an arm to prevent just that. "You *swear* that this isn't a trick, and that I'll reach what it is that I desire most, as long as I follow you for the next hour?" His whisper sent a chill down my spine, dampening my dancer's invisible flame.

I tilted my head and stared into his dark ochre eyes. "We've already been over this. Yes. I swear it on my very existence." Before he could respond, I ducked under his outstretched arm and continued by, not caring what obscenities he mentally threw my way as a result of my display.

The further we trekked into the southeast, the more disturbing our surroundings became. The lights that were once frequent to the north were now erratically lighting the main strip, and more sobbing erupted from back alleyways we'd passed, but I kept my chin high. Those people would either live or they would die—fate always had its way. And I couldn't convince myself to begin meddling with it.

Despite the infrequent lighting, the stars still didn't make an appearance in the night sky above us. It was as if the stars themselves were too afraid of whatever demons supposedly dwelt here to show their faces. I couldn't comprehend why—stars, unlike those who were suffering and broken in the darkened parts of this city, were immortal. They didn't need to worry about surviving. They just *were*.

Free.

Just as I once was.

Qasir and I had to jump over pieces of broken glass that littered the streets from bottles and lights, and the wind scattered trash and sand through the tunnel of sandstone houses as we endured. Among those in the alleyways, I witnessed people injecting foreign substances into their arms, and others sleeping with cardboard boxes—their only sources of protection.

At some point, I'd heard a commotion down a side alley and found a lecherous geezer with a young woman writhing against a decrepit sandstone structure. I'd quickly whipped my head from the image to give them some privacy—but clearly, they couldn't care less if people knew of their arrangement or not.

We passed others on the journey too, some who reeked of booze, and others so scrawny it wasn't even apparent if they ever bothered eating.

The only blessing that came with the further we went on our trek into the land of sin, the more the stench of the noxious smog to the northwest seemed to dissipate. But Qasir had been right; Neosordess' character seemed to disintegrate the further away from the purifying light of the Pillars we got.

A while later, I felt the flicker become a frantic mess, indicating our close proximity to whatever it was Qasir was destined for—or I so desperately hoped. Slowing my pace to a crawl, I examined our surroundings again, and noted that the shoddy quality of the lights had improved only slightly. Careless, winking fixtures exposed what seemed to be a cluster of kiosks to our left, catching my attention immediately.

A few people manned the tables.

Odd.

Especially considering how late it was and the fact that no one else was even visible on the main strip; no one was in their houses, no one was in the street…not to mention, their goods were nothing of real use; one vendor sold old cloth, and another sold pottery or something. Certainly no goods that would warrant being up this late at night to sell.

I peered behind the vendors and noticed a staircase of sorts leading down beneath a derelict building. It was rundown to the point of no-return, with broken windows on each of its five levels. A solid portion of its roof had caved-in, and debris from its broken sandstone beset the street below.

Without looking to Qasir in confirmation, I walked towards the vendors at the kiosks.

Music.

There was *music*.

Each step brought me closer to music; a wild thing of heavy bass, with little rhythm to dance to. Under the usual circumstances—if those circumstances even existed—it was nothing my little dancer would typically show any interest in; however, it spun to the untamed beat and grew more fervent as we drew closer.

I didn't bother smiling at the rugged dealers at their tables as I strode by, instead focusing on the staircase and the music luring us into the shadows. More coloured lights broke through the looming darkness, flashing from just beyond the doorframe the stairs stopped at. Like fireflies.

What *was* this place?

I didn't let myself contemplate that idea as I took my first step down into the beckoning dark. It was unsettling; the bass from the music caused the unsteady metal staircase to vibrate, and certain steps were non-existent, having rusted away after years of neglect. The railing accompanying the staircase also wobbled and provided little, if any, support—not helping my already watery legs. I couldn't help the relief that flooded me as I noticed the staircase was only twenty or so steps down into the pit.

TO THOSE WHO HAVE LOST

My torture ended swiftly.

Chapter 4

Moira

IT WAS AN ALTERNATE DIMENSION. The music which had been nothing but a throb only so many feet from the doorway, had somehow transformed into something so overpowering that it became difficult to focus on our other surroundings.

I revelled in the dulled senses that came with the beat, letting the pounding, demanding tone of the music fill and soothe my weariness; wiping away my exhaustion as if it were no more than a cobweb shrouding my body, my mind.

My eyes finally adjusted to the gloom, unveiling a hallway that veered off in two different directions. To the left, there was a spiral metal staircase supposedly leading to the first level, and to the right, an archway. Unsurprisingly, the roaring music originated from the latter, and multicoloured pink and green and blue spotlights reached just beyond the arch into the hallway. The arch was surreal with its lights and deafening noise, and I couldn't help but notice the dark figure leaning leisurely against one of its columns—a daunting image.

My flicker leapt in excitement with even that slight glimpse into the room beyond the archway, acting like a butterfly, fluttering its wings all over my back.

Jittery little thing.

Qasir's desire would have to be close—just as I'd thought.

It wasn't a surprise that I'd clearly have to look elsewhere to find my own. My damned flicker was a gift, but it never led me to what *I* wanted, nor what *I* desired. It was practically useless with its forever *altruistic* tendencies.

A shooting pain lanced through my back into my chest, and I instinctually arched into the pain as its flame consumed me. Very well. Maybe the flicker wasn't *useless*, but it certainly was a pain in my ass.

I shook my head as I snapped back into reality and looked over my shoulder to find Qasir's face cascaded in shadow, condemning me...silently berating me. Whatever. Like he had any right. I fought my annoyance and growled. "Follow me, and I'll tell you where to find it."

He grumbled, barely audible over the music. "Fine."

I took this as my cue to start towards the arch, and cathartically rolled my eyes when he was out of sight. Frankly, I couldn't bother caring what Qasir thought about any of it. I was just doing what his brother insisted for me to do for him anyway. Maybe if he was going to be such an ingrate, he shouldn't have accepted "help" from someone with my skillset at a circus.

Risible old man.

The coloured spotlights immediately greeted us upon stepping through the arch, along with a sweet-smelling smoke I could only assume was opium. The room continued mostly to the left; to the right, there seemed to be only a spot for the stranger to stand, and a blackened wall appeared straight ahead of where we stood.

To the left, I could see that couches of the darkest colours were strewn all about, and people lounged on many of them; some smoking large pipes, others with women dancing naked above their smug faces.

Ultimately, the room was larger than I'd initially thought. It possessed high ceilings and was an irregular L-shape; meaning that when we stepped into the arch, we were in the short and narrow corridor of the L. A grander, more open room actually existed to the left of the corridor, and sparkling balls made of hundreds of little mirrors reflected variegated lights all over the place, giving the illusion of a light source being present when stepping into the corridor just beyond the arch.

In the rear of the large room, straight ahead of the smaller corridor, a man stood behind a bar serving drinks and food. A stage was to our left against another wall which backed onto the hallway we first encountered; a pole was centre on-stage, and dancers used it to swing their grotesque bodies every which way. In front of the stage were more couches where more people watched the night's entertainment, throwing their wallets at those they deemed worthy of their affection. And to the right of that against the opposite wall, more tables were strewn about, seemingly used for gambling purposes rather than the exploitation the other couches seemed to offer.

Wider, taller bodies than my own blocked my view of the rest of the space, and I had to get onto my tiptoes in order to discern what the wall opposite us had. On the furthest wall from the entry was a large mezzanine of sorts, overlooking the chamber and everyone within it. It wasn't fancy at all by any means; however it was clearly where the one in-charge kept watch, for a figure clothed in shadow lounged on an improvised throne, a henchman standing three feet away from him.

Of course, it was when I glanced *there* that my little dancer threw itself into a samba. Qasir would find his innermost desire there: power. I nodded. Such a predictable vulture.

I began weaving in and out of those draped across various couches, and dodged those who tried to pull me aside, assuming I was part of the nightly entertainment, as I continued towards the far mezzanine. The backpack I was carrying jostled against the inebriated bodies I passed, and I struggled with the urge to just tear it off of me. It was an unnecessary hindrance at this point; carrying nothing but a few empty containers that had only a day or two ago held some food and water for the trip.

Lights bounced off the walls and onto the faces of those who swayed to the music, and the haze of opium smoke hindered my attempts at really taking a good glimpse of who exactly watched us from above.

With the mezzanine quickly approaching, I noted the lack of stairs leading upwards from where we moved inside the chamber. Of course. *Of course* our only access to my flicker's target was the staircase we passed when we were in the hallway. I took a deep breath only after I'd clenched my jaw with enough force to pierce my already injured lip. But it made sense; easier to guard a singular entryway if you were supposed to try and keep a certain individual safe.

I didn't hesitate as I turned to the person closest to my right while pointing towards the looming mezzanine above, and asked, "Hey, who is that?" I needed to better assess the situation. Perhaps I'd read the scene wrong and Qasir wanted something else entirely.

I really hated the subjectivity that came with the flicker.

The woman startled, laughed, and said, "Him? You mean Kieran?"

"If that's who is sitting on the chair, then yes." I didn't bother with niceties—the woman was clearly an employee of this…establishment. Judging by her flimsy, almost see-through clothing and garish makeup, I assumed she'd much rather be talking to someone she could take to bed—or to a couch for that matter. I held in my grimace as the thought crossed my mind.

"Then yes, Kieran is the one on the throne. He's the one in-charge of this space. You know, *I* heard that in order for him to come into power he had to actually like take out the previous guy… I can't remember his name…" She paused and tapped her hand on her arm. "Ah-ha! His name was Victus or something like that." I caught the scent of opium on her breath, and it was very obviously interfering with her memory.

"So, that guy up there, Kieran. He "took out" the other leader so he could take the throne for himself?" I looked over my shoulder to Qasir and noticed he'd curled his fingers into fists, agitation turning his knuckles white. I returned my line of sight to the woman in front of us and listened to see what other information she'd willingly offer up without prying.

"No one knows too much about Kieran, but his second in-command is pretty popular. He usually asks me for *special* favours after a long, hard day of helping to look after the place." She shifted her stare to Qasir who was still behind me, and asked beneath lowered lashes, "How about you sweetheart, you interested?"

Qasir didn't deign responding, and instead kept his eyes glued on the mezzanine. Huh. Perhaps he was finally beginning to comprehend my line of questioning—

The woman merely smiled, gazed at me, and said, "Tough crowd. No matter. If he wants to talk to Kieran, he'll have to go up that staircase in the hall. Kieran doesn't like getting in on the action like everyone else here. I've always thought him a little strange considering he runs the joint. Why'd you ask about Kieran in the first place again? I don't think you actually said."

I lied, "Just curious—it's my first time here. You see, a friend told me to come if I wanted to get any action, and I just wondered what *he*," I nodded towards the mezzanine once more, "did here." She couldn't know anything about Qasir's arrangement with me. I couldn't have her recognizing my gift—

I was *the Moira* after all—the woman from a faraway, mystical land who was capable of leading anyone to whatever it was they sought for. I knew very well how she would react to the truth... It would be the same way that others had reacted after Qasir's brother, Salvador, had disseminated the knowledge upon learning of my otherworldly capability.

Her big mouth would probably act to fuck us both over.

The woman shrugged, "Like I said, Kieran just runs the place. He doesn't engage in any of the activities we offer here, despite the many freebies I know he's been offered—myself included." She blushed. "Anyways, I get where you're coming from as I've been there myself." The woman then quizzically peered behind me and asked, "Was that older man with you?"

"He is with me." I cocked my head in confusion. "Why?"

"Because he seems to have taken off. Maybe he found someone else to be more of his taste." She paused, raising a painted eyebrow. "He definitely looked hungry for *something*."

I whirled around. *Fuck*. Qasir was no longer behind me. He'd essentially become invisible for all the sprawl of the people throughout the chamber. Without dismissing myself or thanking her for…for her lack of discretion, I hurried towards the bar at the opposite side of the room, closest the arch, and strained my neck as high as it could possibly go. Hundreds of people gathered in this crumbling pigsty. I wouldn't be able to find him.

A thought struck me: Qasir might very well have taken off to the hallway staircase after that woman mentioned that *that* was the only access to the mezzanine.

Fuck this job.

Squeezing through the mass of dancing, writhing bodies, I left the chamber, headed into the darkened hall, and sprinted through the hallway in an attempt to reach him before he could do anything extremely foolish. He was *so* impatient. I hadn't even told him that he could find whatever it was he desired there. He must have arrived at *that* conclusion after what that damned worker said.

"Where are you going, doll?" The man leaning against the archway earlier called after me, but I hurdled past him.

I nearly missed the staircase leading upstairs and tripped over my feet instead; grabbing the railing to both save my own skin and to not to pass it by altogether. Fucking Qasir—if he would have just *listened* to me…

These stairs resembled those used to enter the establishment: metal, well-used and probably responsible for the likes of fifty different illnesses. Another platform laid at their summit, with an entrance supposedly leading onto the chamber's mezzanine. My legs protested.

Still, Qasir was nowhere to be found.

Great, I thought. Just what I fucking needed.

I ascended the stairs slowly, legs aching with the movement, catching my breath after practically sprinting to reach them. Too many steps later when I finally reached the landing, I was *almost* capable of breathing normally. The breath wheezed out of my lungs, and I held onto the railing.

No harm in staying on the sidelines to first assess the situation Qasir had gotten himself into, and no point in rushing in there when I had no idea as to what exactly I'd be rushing into.

I peered through the doorway and saw a very familiar balding head as he parted the curtains strewn about the chamber ahead of me. He slunk towards the throne, hiding behind different pieces of fabric I'd assumed could be used to cordon off the space from the damn-near bordello below.

Illuminating parts of his face were the coloured spotlights, and where they didn't reach, shadows created a stark relief across his features.

I stood idly by and watched.

If this was what Qasir wanted to do so much, I wouldn't stop him—he'd been granted (temporary) access to my services, not the other way around.

He crept over to a space hidden just behind Kieran and his second in-command before drawing the ugly dagger he'd been carrying earlier.

If Qasir failed—oh *no*.

I opened my mouth and took the first step to leap in his way, but in my attempt to do so, my little dancer burnt me. Scalded me, really. It was determined to *cook* me from the inside out and I couldn't breathe. My breath wheezed out of my lungs again and I desperately held onto my sides to keep from collapsing.

Clearly, I was *meant* to watch.

And my flicker thought it *wasn't* a pain in the ass?

I clamped down on my tongue and breathed through my nose. So much for my little dancer's moral compass. Jackass. I was just trying to protect my *own* self-interest. But nope. It couldn't let me do that. My flicker couldn't be bothered to save me, nor itself for that matter.

Agonizing seconds seemed to drag on forever before my flicker calmed itself enough for me to stalk forward through the curtains a few steps. If I was meant to watch this unfold, as my flicker *obviously* wanted me to do, I at least wanted to see what was going to unfold between them. I needed some decent entertainment anyway. I just prayed the *entertainment* didn't result in my untimely demise.

Although, that would be fitting considering my luck—or lack thereof—as of late.

I'd kept my eyes solely on the potbellied silhouette of Qasir ahead of me, but as I broke through the next curtain, I could finally distinguish some of Kieran's features. The off-kilter lighting radiating from the glass fixtures on the ceiling of the chamber made everything appear distorted.

But even so, Kieran was beautiful.

Not the brute I'd expected with what that hag down below had said about him murdering the previous leader. But then again, she'd also said that she'd tried to seduce him…

I could see the appeal now.

His hair appeared dark and was cropped short, exaggerating the fact that he was obviously blessed with facial features that could easily bring both women and men to their knees. Exuding only confidence, Kieran held a power stance in the chair, like it was, indeed, a throne. He draped himself over it in a careless yet somehow not careless, tactical way—an ankle crossed over a knee. I admired the sheer arrogance of the gesture. He held a wine glass in his hand that he swirled intermittently—bored—and a broad sword that he kept within drawing distance at his side.

It took more effort than I'd like to admit to remind myself not to gawk at the murderer on the chair, and to instead focus my attention on Qasir's movements behind Kieran's throne. While I'd been staring at the beauty that was Kieran, Qasir had seemingly moved, and was now only a few feet away from Kieran's back.

Beams of light struck Qasir at uneven angles and bounced off the dagger he now held, ready to assassinate Kieran.

A miracle.

It would take a bloody *miracle* for Kieran to come away unscathed—Qasir had the upper hand, and I implored that he kept it that way.

Kieran didn't seem to notice anything amiss and continued lounging, half-empty wine glass still in hand. It was strange—part of me almost yearned to warn him of what I was sure Qasir was going to do. Hell, Qasir didn't even deserve the power Kieran held while he sat in that chair. But that desire was infinitesimal compared to my own survival. The old man was *disgusting*, rotten even, to his very core. However, I couldn't move. I couldn't—*wouldn't*—risk my life for either of the men standing before me. I kept my feet planted where they were. Besides, I had a feeling that even if I'd decided differently, that that would have only made the whole situation way worse and way more complicated than it already was. Best to sit idly by and watch, just as my flicker wanted me to do.

I wondered; would Kieran even know what had happened to himself if Qasir were to indeed plunge the dagger into his back? Would his second beside him even do anything to avenge his life, or would the tall, uncomplicated man, simply bow to Qasir? And would the people down in the chamber below even notice that the man sitting on the rickety chair was not the same person, but instead an imposter to Kieran's stolen throne? I shook my head and continued watching them from the sideline.

Reluctance practically eddied off of Qasir as he seemingly assessed for the perfect moment to strike—almost as if he was second guessing his ability to actually follow through on attaining his greatest desire. He was wasting precious time.

Funny, considering that he was so willing to threaten me with the bloody dagger. Perhaps he was reconsidering because Kieran *had* in fact killed before; or because Kieran, unlike myself, was a man—a threat to Qasir's seemingly bottomless ego if he were to fail.

Then, as if my thoughts had summoned him into doing so, Qasir struck, thrusting through the curtains he was perched behind and lunged at Kieran with the dagger.

Good riddance.

Chapter 5

Moira

THE GRACE AND FLUID EASE with which Kieran moved was like the most beautiful of waltzes.

I'd never seen another man move as he did. As if having seen the attack coming, he simply dropped the wine he was carrying in one hand and unsheathed his sword with the other practically instantaneously—a blink and I would have missed the movement. I was awestruck as he twisted off the chair he'd been lounging on only a second before; so quickly that his darkened trench coat flared behind him on an invisible wind, and parried Qasir's dagger in such a manner that one may have mistaken Qasir for a child having only picked up a weapon for the first time.

Qasir, in what appeared to be shock, dropped his dagger into the puddle of wine and shattered glass now on the floor, and stumbled backwards.

How was that possible?

I wasn't exactly proficient when it came to combat strategy; however, I was almost certain that Kieran had successfully executed the *impossible*.

Kieran didn't sheathe his blade.

Instead, he remained poised with his sword outstretched towards Qasir and stalked forward—a predator homing in on prey.

I stood there at a loss for words. Qasir would not be let off with a mere slap on the wrist.

I had to get off the mezzanine—quickly—before someone suspected me of being an accomplice in Qasir's miniature coup. I was too close to them. I was such a *fool*—I should have held further back...like any *sane* individual would have. Now I had no choice but to wait for them to be distracted. Fuck. No need in drawing any of their unwanted attention to myself.

"Who are you?" Kieran's voice was quiet, yet it carried itself above the booming music and was laced with a lethal venom I'd become far too familiar these last few years for my own liking. Even still, my little dancer trembled in his voice's wake.

"Qasir." Qasir's voice shook and was no longer filled with the arrogance I'd grown accustomed to on the trip here. "My name is Qasir Rahat." He began backing up further and raised his hands, palms facing outward towards Kieran.

He was halted by the blade of Kieran's second at his back.

I was in desperate need of leaving. If they saw me...

My breathing became ragged.

I was going to die if they caught me.

But I was stuck—a statue, frozen in place by their interaction.

"So." Kieran drawled. "Why are you here?" He sheathed his sword, no longer needing it now with his second keeping a steady eye on Qasir from behind.

"I was brought here and told to get rid of you..."

Oh no. I shrunk behind the curtains only slightly obscuring me from their vision.

"By a woman..."

"A woman?" Kieran's voice sounded skeptical.

I needed to leave.

Why couldn't I fucking *move*? A reaffirming, tingling sensation radiated from my spine and I suppressed a laugh. My flicker was going to be the death of me.

"Y-yes...she has pitch-black hair, and the bluest of blue eyes—"

"Where is *she* then?" Kieran's impatience was unmistakable, and it seemed that he could barely stomach Qasir—relatable—and his pathetic attempts to smooth over the fact that he had tried to kill him a minute earlier.

This was the distraction I'd been waiting for. But still I remained, at a standstill—my little dancer had somehow pinned me to the mezzanine, and I silently fought for the freedom to escape. An inert eternity passed before I "won", finally willing my legs to skulk towards the doorway at my back. If I could continue backwards on silent feet, with the darkness and the odd lighting on my side, then perhaps I would be able to bolt down the stairway into the hallway, up the next stairway leading out of the establishment, and into freedom's embrace.

"She should still be h-here. The last I saw of her, she was down there." He pointed below to the vacant spot just before the mezzanine. Of course Qasir would use me as the scapegoat for his actions. What an *asshole*. I should have known that his damned desire was only going to cause me grief after stumbling into this...cesspool of a city.

The clicking of a tongue. "Well, Qasir Rahat, if we can find her, perhaps I will let you live."

Fuck—I had to move faster.

If my little dancer wasn't such a drama queen, I'd have already been well on my way out of the city.

I twisted to the stairway, but the stupid curtains hindered me from doing so, effectively wrapping around my ankles, and making it so that it became a feat in itself not to trip and give away my position. Three sets of footsteps steadily approached; however, a few more feet and I would be out the door and out to the freedom of the night.

One set of feet suddenly came to a halt, and I heard Kieran beseech, "Derrik, would you please be able to turn on the lights?" The spotlights then disappeared, and I was encased in complete darkness. Shrieks erupted from below the mezzanine as the music too was silenced.

Then, as if summoned, blinding white lights replaced the dark and I was exposed; no longer hidden from those who were hunting me, and my eyes needed a moment to adjust to the sudden brightness. A sense of urgency swept over me, and I no longer cared if I made noise. If I didn't escape, Kieran would almost certainly kill me; Qasir's damning testimony would be enough to have the job done. In a place like this, I wouldn't even be surprised if Kieran made a spectacle of it for the patrons below.

I lurched forward and again heard the sound of their footsteps pursuing me. I tried running faster but the maroon curtains still gripped at my heels, throwing me off-balance. This place clearly rarely saw any true light like this, because if it did, they would, or should, have been replaced years ago. Cobwebs and opium smoke clung to the fabric and—

I stumbled, barely catching myself from a fall that very well could have allowed them to catch me.

A calloused hand then wrapped itself around my bicep, and I shrieked. I'd thought they were further behind me. There *had* been close to thirty feet separating us when the pursuit began—I didn't realize I was so slow.

Useless.

I turned my face slowly towards my captor, and gasped.

Kieran leaned over me ever so slightly, and I couldn't help noticing that he was even more beautiful than I'd thought. I would have been lying if I'd said that a part of me was not grateful that my death would be at the hands of this man instead of those of Qasir...or his brother for that matter.

His face was by no means rugged; however, the intensity expressed in his eyes made his face striking, even with his otherwise delicate features. Even in the starkly white lighting, his skin tone was warm, a golden honey in colour, and his eyes...

Goddamn, his eyes.

"Surprised?" Kieran's smile did not reach the glaucous orbs which had captured my attention. I stared—not in fear, but in awe of the eyes of a predator. Against his complexion his eyes were piercing; stolen from the forest itself. They were the lightest green of wood moss and glittered with the challenge I presented. That was expected. I mean, he assumed I'd led Qasir there to kill him.

"Qasir," Kieran looked back over his shoulder to the man who was now smirking like a cat in my direction, "is this the woman you were talking about?"

"Yes." No hesitation from Qasir as the word flew out of his mouth. Fucking *asshole*. Even after *everything* we'd been through together...the bickering, the insults. I understood why he did it: better he blamed me for his own failure than admit any responsibility for his actions.

Kieran's voice was anything but warm as he continued, "How could this meek little..." He cast an assessing glance back to me, "*girl*, force you to do anything?" He looked towards the arm he still held a firm grip on, then released it. "She's lucky that she can carry that lonesome sac on her back." He paused briefly, as if contemplating his next move, and I instinctively straightened to my full height. Kieran still had almost half a foot on me, so it did nothing to make me feel safer, but I couldn't let it show that his insult was perhaps truer than he knew. Kieran gave me what appeared to be a knowing look, then turned back towards his second and Qasir.

He strode towards them, shoving the curtains aside as he went. And rather than stopping at them, he merely swaggered onward back to the throne he'd been sprawling on only a few minutes ago.

Typical male arrogance.

But to my surprise, he didn't approach the throne to sit. He instead went behind it, traipsing through the sticky wine he'd unintentionally spilt there, and reached down to pick up Qasir's dagger. He weighed it in his hands, appearing contemplative once more, then waved the dagger towards Derrik. "Show Qasir to the railing," Kieran ordered, nodding to the mezzanine's ledge that overlooked the disgruntled partiers below.

Qasir fought off Derrik's initial advances, and stuck his finger out at Kieran, bellowing, "You said that if we found the girl, that you'd let me *LIVE!*"

"I promised to do no such thing," Kieran muttered while examining the dagger once more. "*Perhaps* is what I said, and I'm certain the girl can vouch for me."

Qasir couldn't hold his own against Derrik for long; Kieran's second was heavily muscled and was very capable of restraining both Qasir and his attempts to kick and swing, all the while shoving him at the rail as directed. Derrik then kicked in the backs of Qasir's knees, forcing him to collapse upon the concrete floor we all stood on. The crack of the knobby bones on the floor echoed through the level, and Qasir screamed, "*YOU PROMISED!!!*" He wept and still flailed his arms, trying to wrench free of the stone-faced man holding him in place.

Kieran, still grasping Qasir's blade, only stalked towards the mezzanine.

"Please, I'll take it back, and you will never see me again," Qasir bargained. "I'll even work here if it would make you happy. Just *spare* me."

Neither Kieran nor Derrik acknowledged that he'd even spoken. A guffaw broke through my lips, and I shot a hand to my traitorous mouth. Kieran only glanced to me, unimpressed.

Did I *want* to get myself killed? Why couldn't I just keep *quiet*? I was such a fucking fool.

A disappointment.

It was a horrifyingly beautiful sight—horrifying because Kieran obviously held a great deal of control and felt he could exert it whichever way he pleased, yet beautiful—Kieran clearly had no intention of keeping Qasir alive. After what I'd seen of the man, I was ecstatic that was to be the case. Granted, Qasir wasn't the *worst* individual I'd dealt with on these sometimes lengthy expeditions, but the thought of him just roaming around like he'd done nothing wrong—I was all but elated that there was at least some justice in this lonely, awful place.

Kieran only lifted a hand when he reached Qasir's side, and the crowd below, still waiting for the night's entertainment to begin again, all went silent as if willed to do so. Only Qasir's pleading broke the silence. Then, Kieran's quiet, silken voice filled the space. "This man I've brought before you tonight just tried to plunge a dagger into my back." He paused, "I have no problems with those who try to challenge my right to rule; however I expect a *proper* challenge. Stabbing me in the back proves no strength nor worthiness for that matter—"

"IT WASN'T MY FAULT!!! THE GIRL FORCED ME!!!" Qasir's pleas became so profound that they managed to interrupt Kieran's monologue. He must have thought that this place was a *democracy*—if the crowd went to his side, he'd be saved from the fate to be bestowed by Kieran. Clearly, the meaning of the Pillars fell onto his deaf ears; there was no democracy here.

Kieran merely continued as if Qasir was nothing more than a pestilent bug and I had to bite the hand still resting at my mouth to prevent yet another risky outburst from escaping. "As I was saying," Kieran waited once more, regaining control from Qasir who'd now succumbed to the inevitability of the situation and helplessly wept in Derrik's grasp, "this man is a disgrace—a coward. And apparently, he is incapable of taking responsibility for his actions, further demonstrating his cowardice."

Kieran glanced towards me again, did the slightest, practically indecipherable nod, and before turning his head back to those loitering in the chamber.

I was so confused. Did he somehow sense that I'd held in my laughter and approve of my restraint? I shook my head.

"Cowards are of no use in this world, nor in any other, and I would *never* allow one into our ranks here, so I shall ask, Qasir Rahat. Do you have any last words?"

Qasir whipped his head around to face me and gifted me with the most belligerent smile I'd since witnessed. "You said that you'd lead me to what I desired most—to my brother's behest or not." I silently pleaded that no one in Neosordess understood the reference. "I didn't want this. I didn't want to die." He took a deep breathe and chuckled, "You failed in your promise to me." He then spit, not a foot away from my feet. "Oath breaker."

I kept my face neutral and held his damning stare.

This oath wasn't broken because of *me*.

Kieran, to my relief—oblivious—stepped in, obstructing Qasir's view of me and jerked Qasir's head forward, so it faced the crowd once more. I moved to better position myself so I could see Qasir's side profile.

With the white lighting, his bulging nose and haggard face were just as pronounced as they were under the Pillars of Messiah.

I wanted to see it.

I wanted to see him finally get what he'd deserved all along.

I wanted to witness the spectacle Kieran was going to make of his demise. The thought of him dying made me anything but upset; I was almost giddy.

Oath breaker. It wasn't my fault he was completely incompetent of following the instructions I'd given him. *Follow me, and I will tell you where to find it.* A *child* would have done a better job of just—

Kieran suddenly grabbed a handful of Qasir's balding hair with one hand, then whispered something into his ear, before slowly dragging Qasir's own dagger across his throat.

Blood rained down upon those below, and some screams erupted from the crowd—different from the occasional hollering that had previously echoed through the space whilst the bass drummed, and the partygoers danced.

I just stood and watched as Qasir tried to staunch the blood with only his hands, gulping like a fish as his face grew unnaturally pale. Pleading eyes turned to me, and I blinked.

I wouldn't feel guilty for the man.

This was his fate.

He was the one responsible for his actions.

He groggily shifted his head back to face the rail at eye-level just ahead of where he knelt, then slumped over, eyes flickering opening and closed. Qasir lost consciousness and fell forward, slamming his head off the rung on the mezzanine's railing, before sliding off into the people still gathered in the chamber. I heard the sickening thud that accompanied his body hitting the stone floor not twenty feet below and flinched ever so slightly at the sound.

"Not used to seeing people die in front of you, I imagine?" Kieran was watching me, gauging my reaction to Qasir's (in my opinion) timely death.

I avoided the question, and instead asked, "You don't seem too bothered by it yourself. Do you do that," I nodded to the direction of Qasir's lifeless body, "often?"

Kieran chuckled, before stating matter-of-factly, "Believe it or not, it's not as frequent as you'd think." He took another second to assess me, the *accused*, before he said, "Why is it that you came closer when it was obvious that I was going to kill him? Are you *insane?*" I didn't bother commenting. "Maybe Qasir was onto something when he used you as a scapegoat. In the Messiah's name, you even *laughed.*"

A quiet smile lit up his striking green eyes; bright and full of light, as if to spite the death he'd just committed. It was unnerving. I didn't have the time to respond before he turned to Derrik, who was once again standing guard at Kieran's side, and mumbled, "Do what needs to be done to make the people happy. Leave the body for a bit; it will serve as a message to anyone else who has any funny ideas."

"Sure thing, Kieran." The nonchalant way in which Derrik addressed him only made me question Kieran's character more so than before, but it didn't matter. I wasn't safe. Kieran had just murdered the man I'd been with for a month, and as far as I was concerned, he could still very well be contemplating how best to kill me too. Even if I was innocent of Qasir's actions.

The blinding white light disappeared, replaced by a sudden darkness solely split by the many coloured spotlights strewn throughout the establishment. The music also returned, vibrating the mezzanine we were standing on, and acted to successfully turn the chamber below into the frenzy it had been prior to Qasir's execution.

Good.

I'd be able to sneak out and leave before anyone noticed my whereabouts. I began doing just that, sneaking away back towards the doorway leading off the mezzanine, but I was halted by a familiar firm grip on my upper arm.

"Going somewhere?" Kieran peered down at me; his full lips curled into a cruel smile.

"I was trying to leave." I attempted to shrug away his hand but was incapable. I wished this body wasn't so meek and pathetic and fucking *weak*. I stared at him in horror as it dawned upon me, "I am not your prisoner."

The rank stench of a former cell crept into my nostrils, and I had to control my breathing. *Come one, come all, the Moira of your dreams shall deliver you to your any one heart's call.*

I couldn't be his prisoner. If I was his prisoner, I'd never go home and…

It was foolish to believe I'd ever return.

But I couldn't…I couldn't give up on that dream.

I'd been working towards that sole goal for five years. I couldn't believe that I'd wasted that time looking for a way back home for nothing.

Kieran scrutinized my gaze for a moment before speaking. "Consider yourself a temporary guest instead." He paused. "I just want to figure out a few things first about you before I let you go."

"Just ask me what you want to know *now*, and I will answer your questions. Please don't keep me here any longer than necessary. I-I…" I paused, gathering my thoughts, "I need to leave here."

"Why's that?"

"It doesn't matter." I wasn't divulging *that* information to him. I'd only met him maybe ten minutes earlier—he was practically a stranger. Not to mention, he was the stranger who'd executed the man I'd travelled with for almost a month. I was frankly pissed that *that* much time had come to pass in the first place, and that during that time, I'd actually come to know him...very well.

Kieran shrugged. "And that is why you are staying here until I say otherwise." He nodded to Derrik, "Take her upstairs to the cells. Give her food and whatever else she needs." He then faced me once more. "Sleep, and we'll talk once you're rested."

"I don't need to sleep—I've had plenty," I lied.

Cells.

I knew I was a prisoner.

I thrashed against the memories that plagued my consciousness again. I could practically smell the reek of animal manure as it melded with the other more alluring scents of popped corn and caramelized candies of the circus. Then there were the gawking faces, and the greasy, greedy hands ceaselessly goading through the bars as they all sought to touch my unnatural pallor—

Whatever.

He merely gave me another knowing look, let go, then strode back towards the throne he was perched on earlier.

What did he *want* from me?

The music no longer held off the heaviness of my eyelids and I felt a yawn dawning on me; the adrenaline from earlier finally seemed to be waning. I refrained from the urge as I heard Kieran kick away the shards of his broken wine glass.

His lackey then gestured with a hand towards an alternate area; shrouded in curtains behind Kieran's throne, supposedly leading higher into the safety hazard. I carefully followed Derrick's lead because after seeing the feat of strength he'd pulled with Qasir, a man who was so much stronger than me in comparison, I knew I wouldn't stand a chance against him.

After moving a few heavy curtains aside, Derrick uncovered a spiral metal staircase, opposite the mezzanine railing, leading upwards like the others I'd seen, and marched onward. I peered above to gauge how high they went and saw that they were sheared off at the third story. The sandstone of the two uppermost levels had crumbled away, exposing the night sky and utter lack of stars that came with it.

I grimaced at the stairway before me.

Travelling non-stop on foot for almost a full day, made the idea of more leg work not appealing in the least.

I really was tired.

My legs were made of rubber, watery as they had been on the bridge, and the world swayed under my feet. I had to grip the staircase's railing to steady myself. I was so, *so* tired.

A yawn broke through my defenses, and I swore that I heard Derrik laugh at me. "So much for that lie." His gaze raked back to where I still stood gripping the railing, and he sighed. "Only this one time."

Derrik, to my complete shock, then turned and began descending the staircase.

"What are you doing?" I stumbled backward, trying to maintain some semblance of authority in my voice, but it was useless; I was too tired to even care anymore.

Upon reaching where I stood, he knelt, placed one arm under my knee, and hoisted me into his arms. His warmth rushed into me, and I couldn't fight the sigh that brushed past my lips. I managed to gaze at his face briefly as my heavy eyelids fought to drag me into the depths of sleep and noted that Derrik was moderately good looking. Not *my* type per se, but I could see his appeal for others. He had darker skin than I—*surprise*—chestnut eyes, a hooked nose, and he was obviously strong as an ox. However, he had facial hair that prevented me from seeing his jawline, and his hair was a cool shade of brown that did nothing to accentuate his roguish features…unfortunate.

Unfortunate, because I really appreciated what he was doing for me.

He began ascending the stairs once more, and I nestled myself into the stranger's warmth. I didn't care if I didn't know who he was, or what he had possibly done in his life to earn him this miserable title—I desperately needed his warmth to fight off the desert's chill. I closed my eyes after a few moments, and more memories swept by; other hands wrapped around me, cradling me, keeping me safe and guarded from the other men who lurked nearby. Salvador had whispered something into my ear, but I couldn't understand him. His language had been a foreign scramble of syllables and consonants that had taken months for me to even become somewhat fluent in.

I still couldn't believe it. His only brother, Qasir, was dead. I smiled serenely to myself as the truth of those words echoed silently through my mind. To think that Salvador had actually thought he was doing Qasir a favor by lending him my services... I only hoped that Salvador would trust me and understand that I'd fulfilled my end of the bargain—I wasn't to blame for the fact that Qasir had committed suicide as far as I was concerned.

I wasn't to blame for *any* of it.

The intermittent bouncing of our ascent into the sky dragged me away from my thoughts, my memories, and utter exhaustion acted to keep me there. Finally, I fell asleep peacefully in Derrik's arms.

Chapter 6

Moira

I WAS IN THE BOG.

Fluttering lights danced around me, twirling, and spinning, and I yearned to dance with them. But I had a job to do, and if I abandoned my sole purpose, I would be shunned by the very lights I admired.

I stood watch at my post, anticipating the time at which I too could dance free with the lights. My job was an honor, but I couldn't help but feel punished when left to watch for hours on end, whilst many of the others could just be. Liberated from any and all responsibility.

The peach-coloured light radiating from the sun's set only made the job more difficult. Dusk was always my favourite time to just let loose and yield myself over to the flame, but come dusk, the glare off the intermittent pools of still water always made it near impossible to see.

How would I keep them safe while both distracted and blinded?

I felt vulnerable, incapable of guarding them from even the simplest of dangers lurking just below the water's surface beneath me. Not to even mention any of the other threats which would opportunistically descend upon them from the thick bramble of branches and thorns around us.

Unacceptable.

A sudden movement in the brush opposite me across the bog caught my attention.

There was no choice but to drift closer to the site. It was my solitary purpose to defend them at all costs against all *possible* threats. I'd made an oath. And I wouldn't fail them.

The movement stemmed from a young girl—weeping, hands covering her face at the bog's edge. She looked to be crafted from the woods and bog around her; her hair was the colour of the earth's humus, and her skin seemed to emit an inner warmth, like the sun setting before us.

She wasn't a threat to them.

I drifted back to my post further in the bog towards the distant line of trees and stood watch once again.

But there was more movement near the girl.

Maybe something from the depths below had stolen her.

Perhaps she would be meeting the same fate as thousands before her—

Unacceptable; she too needed my protection, and I was a fool to abandon her.

I advanced forward and observed as the sentinel accompanying me also began floating towards the girl. The other cobalt sentry was closer, so I halted my trail entirely and watched the affair from afar.

But again, I let my consciousness drift toward the beauty of the twining flames around me and couldn't help but grow complacent. I'd been hovering inches over the mire for an eternity.

Tonight would be more of the same; nothing. Realization slammed into me as I risked a sliver of my attention to the girl, and I let my flame hiss in indignation. While the other sentinel kept the girl safe, it would be my job alone to keep the royal family safe.

There could be no room for mistakes.

I refocused my attention to the surrounding bog and forest, being careful not to let anything slip us by.

A flash of light in my peripheral and I was back on alert.

Did something happen to them?

I drifted towards the origin of the light and then halted everything.

He'd shifted.

The other sentinel now faced the girl as a man and was lazing beside her in the moss just beyond the reach of the bog itself. He was a complete fool, and he would be punished for his negligence.

She chuckled and wiped at her cheeks.

She was a fool too.

Did she not realize what he was—what we all were?

I floated again to my post and considered my initial purpose. And with each passing second, I decidedly forgot their expressions of happiness as I took stock of the sun which was now nothing but a memory—orange and pinks cresting the horizon before it's glory would disappear entirely for the day.

With purpose, I didn't need love.

With purpose, I didn't need desires.

With purpose, I didn't need happiness.

Satisfied and calmed by my revelation, I returned dutifully to my post and stood watch until my shift ended, then I too was able to waltz with the flickering flames, glad to feel nothing but the freedom of just being once more.

🌳

It was the strangest of dreams, but it left me with a feeling of hope.

Of freedom.

Of peace, at long last.

Keeping my eyes closed, I reached inward toward the tether that latched me to the contentedness and beauty of that dream—I needed to go back.

But I found there to be nothing left but ashes.

Anger burnt its way through me, clearing my head of the disappointment that had ravaged it moments earlier, before it dawned upon me...

I'd forgotten where I was.

I woke up with a start. The sun was blazing high above me, and only crumbling sandstone provided any shelter from the sun's scorching heat.

I rolled off the hard floor I had apparently been dozing on, then remembered my current situation.

Qasir was dead.

I was Kieran's guest—whatever that meant—and I'd been carried up to the cells by Derrik because I was too exhausted to climb the damned stairs on my own. I groaned. I could already tell the day was going to be all kinds of awful.

I wiped at my eyes, attempting to clear my persistent grogginess so as to gauge the layout of the cells. Three of the walls were made of the same crumbling stone as the rest of the building; however, ahead of me, instead of another stone wall, a barrier of iron bars prevented my escape. I crawled toward it and struck the metal with a fist in an attempt to break free, but it was of no use.

The iron bars were free of any rust and held firmly in place. They looked new. Strange that Kieran would decide to first renovate the space where prisoners supposedly dwelled before he refurbished the establishment below. Whatever. These fucking distractions had already cost me.

I needed to get out of here.

I'd escaped the iron that had kept me hostage before—I could do the same again.

"Hello there."

I jumped.

A second after I turned my head to begin searching for another exit from the cell, Kieran appeared out of thin air, carrying a tray of some sort of...*slop*?

"It's food. I know it doesn't look like much, but it's better to eat it than to go hungry."

He smiled, and his glittering green eyes disarmed my retort.

I couldn't bring myself to smile back, and instead asked, "Why do you want me here? The way I see it, I'm the woman a man accused of forcing his hand to kill you. You should have killed me alongside him. I shouldn't be your prisoner." The words left my mouth and were quickly replaced with wholehearted regret.

I *should* have kept my mouth shut.

Kieran merely tilted his head to the side and replied, "Would you like to be dead alongside him?"

"No—"

"Then the way I see it, eat the food here and now, and once that's done, we can discuss my motives." He grinned through the bars separating us, and extended the tray towards me, bending down so it could slide under the iron and through the gap.

Sunshine glinted off his hair; rich brown and curly, despite it being cropped close to his head. "I'll be back in an hour to see how you're doing, so don't try anything stupid." Kieran disappeared as quickly as he'd appeared, leaving me alone to eat my meal in peace.

Maybe I was in fact his "guest." He certainly wasn't treating me like he would a prisoner, other than the locked bars...and the absolute mush he claimed to be edible. I wrinkled my nose. In spite of the cell being a slight improvement to my initial accommodations at the circus, it was still obvious that he treated me as he would anyone else he'd forced into these cells.

My stomach twisted as I examined the slop on the tray. Brown and grey and *disgusting*. I couldn't believe that I'd thought that some of the food Qasir and I'd consumed on the road had been foul...

But Kieran had specifically told me to eat—I used my little finger to scoop up a miniscule bit of the sludge and brought it to my mouth.

Bland perhaps, but at least the food he'd placed in front of me wasn't rotten. A small but welcomed blessing. It didn't matter what it tasted like—I just had to eat. Eat first, freedom later. If I perhaps cooperated, he'd be more considerate of what I wanted: to be free of the cells and then hopefully, to be free of Neosordess altogether.

By some miracle, I didn't cringe as I brought the vile food into my mouth and swallowed.

After eating my meal, which wasn't all that bad considering the circumstances, I laid against the wall furthest from the sun's reach and pondered some more about the plan once given permission to leave this sorry cell.

I knew that one of the first things on my imaginary list would be to discover where Salvador had taken the circus—I silently beseeched that he didn't stray northward...maybe he'd wait for me. I was *the Moira* after all—I practically carried the success of the circus alone on my shoulders.

Upon realizing I possessed such a gift, Salvador firmly believed I was a miracle; preventing the inevitable downfall of Pierserk and all of those who relied upon it with my little dancer by my side. No longer had I been forced to sleep in a cage beside the other wild animals—I was cherished.

With any luck, I would find someone else there desperate enough to ask me to find their greatest desire, and hopefully they would be anomalous from every other person in the last few years I'd taken. Then I would go on yet another quest to find said person's wants. I needed them to want to go back to my homeland. I couldn't be the only one on this planet with that desperate desire.

Home. The word barrelled over me.

I could barely remember what it was like anymore.

For five years, I'd remained stranded in this land without good, without hope, without stars. Seemingly without anyone who could help lead me back. I still found it hard to believe that in a city, in a world, of such light, that such impenetrable evil and darkness could persist to triumph it all.

That couldn't be the case.

Nothing was ever totally hopeless. Right? I was too exhausted to fight the opportunistic doubt that sidled into my mind's eye. I'd learned time and time again, that there were always exceptions to every rule.

And with my luck, I could be *that* exception.

There was a distinct possibility that I was *wrong*.

What if that was indeed the predicament I was in and had been in for half of the last decade? What if I was consequently forced to stay here? What would happen if no one else desired the same thing I did, nor had the same hopes as I? I would be lost here, without real use.

With only Salvador for occasional company.

Tension locked my jaw. Qasir would die in his grave of laughter to know he was right. I massaged my temples. What would I want if going home was no longer an option? Would I want what everybody else had wanted: love, happiness, power, wealth? Could I ever want those...*things*?

With each passing person I helped to find their desire, I'd come to realize that maybe I was the only one discontent with where I was; the only one yearning to go back to the way things once were. But how could that even be possible—there were millions of people. It wasn't like I even chose to come here...

I *couldn't* be the only one.

Right?

Coping with the fact that I'd probably been searching for the impossible for the last five years, and the fact that I'd have to forget all my hopes and dreams and everything in the meantime, made me feel like I could sleep forever. Would there even be a point in staying awake if life only ever brought me disappointment and heartache?

A single tear leaked from my eye, onto the floor, as I silently answered my own question.

No—there wouldn't be.

There wouldn't be a fucking point in anything.

I envisaged this wretched revelation for as long as I could stand, then drifted off to sleep, head still in hand.

A clang on the iron bars startled me awake.

The hour must have been up.

"I'm glad to see that you actually ate what I gave you. Most people would have flat-out refused the offer." Kieran shrugged when I didn't respond, then asked, "Why aren't you trying to convince me to let you go as you did earlier? You can't tell me that you've actually grown attached to the cell." Another pause. "Because that would *also* be a first in my book."

I couldn't convince myself to meet his gaze, so instead I stretched my arms as far as possible in front of me. I hated small talk. It was *pointless* and *useless* and…and it was just another way to waste this dismal life. Why couldn't he just give up with that line of questioning and get on with the real reason I was being held captive above the den below? I didn't feel like talking.

"Well, if you don't want to talk, that's fine. I understand when I'm talking to a wall, so I'll stop." He backed away from the bars, then walked out of sight.

I sighed in relief.

Good.

The last thing I needed was my captor pretending that he cared about my wellbeing.

"Really, sighing at my departure? I didn't think you'd be so happy to see me gone." Kieran returned, carrying a wooden stool so he could sit down to grill me further.

"Fuck my life…" I groaned when he placed it before my cell, then closed my eyes. "If you're going to be insistent, just ask me the damned questions." I just wanted to sleep and forget the thoughts haunting me before my slumber. Maybe my dreams would return me to the beautiful lights.

I heard him chuckle, before exaggerating a sigh. "If only I took orders from you, then maybe you'd have your own way." I didn't hear him move the stool, only the whine of the ancient wood as he sat, and then the sound of a foot tapping, acting to cleave the silence that was beginning to build around us.

I snapped, "Is that really necessary?"

"Personally, I'm fine if this is what you want to do—sitting around in complete silence is such a joy after all... I'll just do my own thing." The foot tapping ceased.

I didn't care. Even the mere idea of his presence was enough to aggravate me. I lashed out. "Don't you have to run that eyesore beneath us? I'm sure the whores and drug dealers miss their main man." The question popped into my head out of nowhere, but I couldn't bring myself to feel sorry about it. Why couldn't he just ask me the fucking questions so that I could *leave*?

I heard the shuffle of his clothing on the stool as he said, "Derrik told me that he's fine looking after Sin's Forum until I'm done with you, so I see no reason to do that yet. Play tough all you want; I'm not leaving until we discuss a few things first."

Discuss a few things? Why did he have to be so cryptic? Pinching the bridge of my nose, I murmured, "Sin's Forum?" I brought my knees to my chest and draped my arms over my eyes to return to the blessed dark once more, then listened to see if he'd respond.

"That's the name of my establishment. I figured that because the Messiah tries to purge this place of all of the dirty deeds one would usually see in a city of this size, and because this is the *only* place those dirty deeds can take place without condemnation, Sin's Forum just made sense." Honestly, the logic behind the name caught me off guard, but I didn't say as much. And of course he didn't bother commencing our "discussion" either.

I peered at him through a gap in my arms between the bars. Was this some sort of game to him? He didn't seem the slightest bit interested in me as he positioned himself on the stool, the length of his trench coat gathered into a heap near his leather-bound boots.

He hadn't removed the jacket; it accentuated his broad shoulders and small waist.

I was growing unusually anxious trying and failing to ignore him.

Did he for some reason decide that he was going to execute me anyway—despite what he'd said about me being his "temporary guest" or whatever he'd claimed that I was?

Staving off the anxiety beginning to gnaw on me, I watched him silently through the gap I'd made with my arms, noting his other features. His full lips seemingly began to silently chant a phrase, over and over—a prayer of sorts. Odd. I didn't take him for a religious man. He certainly hadn't reminded me of the disciples Qasir worshipped; however, I could have been mistaken—*again*. Kieran held his head in his hands, pressing against his eyes with his palms, and…

Then I felt it.

If I'd believed my little dancer to be insistent with the final stretch of Qasir's journey, I was *wrong*.

I was so, *so* wrong.

The usual flicker I felt in my spine matured into a blistering pain; my very skin was melting off my bones.

I couldn't breathe.

I began gasping for air, hyperventilating.

Maybe Kieran had water—I needed to dowse myself with it in hopes of extinguishing my flicker's mighty awakening.

Noticing my anguish, Kieran paused in his ritual, demanding, "What's wrong?"

My eyes widened. I still couldn't breathe.

I couldn't *think*.

Everything was burning.

I needed water.

I grasped at my throat and gulped down any air I could. What was happening?

Kieran rushed from the hall, yelling something unintelligible as he went.

I was going to die.

I was never going home.

Five years I'd spent here, with nothing to show for it.

Choking through the pain, the incessant burning, I began sobbing.

My throat closed up, and my nose offered no relief either.

I was going to die.

The walls felt as if they were closing in on me, trapping me—suffocating me.

I was going to die having never known what I actually wanted in this life. I'd been so focused on a stupid, impossible goal, that it never occurred to me to try aiming for something else, to try *being* something else...something *else* other than a "useless" circus attraction.

I lurched forward into the sun's light trickling through from the ceiling into my cell.

I *could* have been happy here. Perhaps if I'd chosen a different path, escaped the circus, acted for only *myself* for once. But still, a part of me wondered if I even knew what happiness felt like.

The flame burning throughout my body, consuming me, was not quenched by the tears streaming down my face.

My vision blurred around the edges.

Terror struck deep as the world shrunk and tilted and became red all around me.

Then it all went black.

Darkness finally offered me salvation from my little dancer's fury, smothering its overwhelming fire, sweeping away the dread and regret that had ravaged me minutes earlier.

Maybe death wasn't a villain after all.

Maybe my home was on the other side.

"Come on now, wake *UP!!!*"

My eyes fluttered open briefly, only to see Kieran leaning over me, close enough to share a breath, shaking my shoulders in an attempt to rouse me.

I closed my eyes and sobbed in relief.

"What happened to you?" Kieran's gaze was panicked—he was *worried* about me.

I let my eyes drift open once more, then noticed a pitcher of water behind him just before the bars leading to the hallway. I opened my mouth to speak, but no words came. My lungs and my throat ached; I pointed to the pitcher.

He complied, quickly reaching behind himself so he could heave the pitcher towards me.

I went to grab it away, but he halted me with a hand. I felt so weak. Weaker than usual.

A whole, *new* low.

"There's no way I'm letting you put this to your mouth with it being as heavy as it is." Even he could see how pathetic I was. He grabbed a ladle that he also seemed to have brought with him, and gave that to me first, before placing the pitcher at my side.

I nearly spilt the water in my attempt to quench my incessant thirst, and only after I'd nearly drowned myself, coughing as I inhaled most of the water from third ladle, could I bring myself to say something. "T-thank…you." The sound of my voice caught me off-guard; I officially sounded like a strangled cat, and *that* knowledge bothered me more than it should have…all things considered. I carefully lifted my hand back up to my throat to assess the damage, because clearly, I wasn't merely sobbing as I'd thought.

Kieran chuckled at my surprise, then said, "Of course you sound like that. You vomited once you passed out and I had to tilt you on your side so that you didn't kill yourself."

"I *what?*"

That certainly explained the acrid taste and slick feeling of my neck, but…he saved my life? The man who had supposedly murdered everyone to get to where he currently was, perched in front of me…

Words were beyond me as I looked down to the pale robe I'd been wearing for the last few weeks. Just as Kieran said, it was now covered in my grayish-sludge vomit. I grimaced.

"Don't worry, it's not as if the robe didn't need to be cleaned...or burned." He looked puzzled briefly, then asked, "How long exactly *have* you been wearing that?" He nodded towards the now vomit-drenched robe.

"Ever since...I took off with Qasir." My voice still sounded garbled, and my throat scratched.

Kieran gave me a look laced with displeasure. "And how long ago would that be?"

"I guess now," I counted the weeks on my hand.

"Four days?" He interrupted my train of thought.

"Try four *weeks*." Damn. Four weeks without rest, without bathing...

Kieran's eyes widened in surprise. "Four weeks with you, and Qasir couldn't even bring himself to learn your name?"

The question startled me.

Qasir had known my name—he in his infinite wisdom, had just chosen not to address me with it.

"Don't look at me like I'm magic, okay? I just figured that was the case because he kept referring to you as the "girl" or the "woman." It makes me wonder why you didn't just insist on him calling you by your name all of these weeks." His eyes danced with both challenge and something else...understanding.

He would *never* understand me.

He would never understand why I was perfectly content to abandon my current title and all things associated with it.

The Moira.

Oath breaker.

Five years ago, I'd broken that sacred oath. Would I even be allowed to return home? I'd failed in my solitary duty, and...if I could only explain to her *why*, but I could barely see her face. I shook my head to clear away both the memories and the pain that lanced through me.

"Why did you nod to me earlier?"

Kieran cocked his head ever so slightly, "Where'd that come from?"

I inhaled deeply before continuing, "Earlier, with Qasir. You looked to me and nodded. Why did you do that?"

His lips twitched upward. "So you noticed that did you?" A pause. "If you really want to know, nodded to you because I wanted you to know that he wouldn't get away with it; that you weren't going to pay for the price for his actions." At my raised brows, he continued. "Listen, I know that I was *supposed* to take his side, but I really didn't *want* to after he tried and failed to kill me." At least Kieran didn't claim to understand me as I'd expected him to. He leaned back against the bars and tapped a finger on his forearm. "So, don't leave me hanging. Tell me, what is it?"

"What's what?"

Annoyance washed over his features for a fraction of a second, then vanished altogether as his face slipped into cool patience, serenity even; giving me space to breathe without the feeling of being interrogated. "What is your name?"

Why did he even care?

"Why does it even matter to you?"

With my name, he would quickly do the math and would probably choose to keep me prisoner here if he found out that he too, like Salvador, could use me to bring in a small fortune. After all, who in their right mind *wouldn't* use someone like me, with an ability to seek out any desire?

Kieran let out an exasperated sigh, casting me yet another look laced with disapproval, and I mumbled, "This is so stupid. Why do you care so much? Why are you even talking to me right now?" It would be easier to torture the information out of me. I took a deep breath, expanding my chest to its limit, and threw myself into yet another coughing fit, all the while Kieran just sat patiently, watching me, waiting until I was ready. Whatever. Kieran with his pretty green eyes...

Fuck it.

"Moira. My name is Moira."

"Do you have a last name?"

"No."

I could practically see the wheels turning in his mind. He knew who I was—what I could *do*. I waited and counted the seconds for the response I'd grown so accustomed to. *The* Moira? One. Two. Three...

Fifteen.

Nothing.

I didn't show any of the relief that I felt wash over me as I realized he was completely oblivious to who I was. Well, he was either oblivious, or I'd managed to give him too much credit for a level of intelligence he simply didn't possess. It didn't matter. At least I wouldn't have to currently deal with the reputation that had so often preceded me.

I exhaled sharply as more seconds dragged on as still, Kieran had yet to continue. If he wasn't going to do *something* or say *anything* else, why couldn't he just leave me the fuck alone so I could sort through my thoughts?

The most important of which: why did my little flicker decide to go haywire on me? I understood that I hadn't exactly been the most grateful of the dancer as of late; however, it seemed awfully unreasonable for my so-called ally to scald me to the point of nearly asphyxiating on my own vomit just because of that *teensy* error on my part...

Kieran's attention again fixed onto me. "Well, now that that's out of the way, we can talk about what the fuck just happened, and why you came here...*Moira*." He seemingly tasted my name on his tongue, like the finest of wines, then tilted his head inquisitively.

I arched an eyebrow. It was like he could read my thoughts.

I couldn't tell him about my little flicker—even though it was apparent he didn't know *who* I was—he would think I was crazy. In the circus, Salvador vouched for me. I never needed tell people *how* my talent worked. It just *worked*.

That was all that *really* mattered.

I asked, "What were you thinking about," I wheezed, "before my—" More coughing, "episode?"

"I was thinking about..." He looked as if he was going to continue onward, but swiftly halted himself, clamping his mouth shut. "Moira, it's not important. Truly, it's nothing you need to know." He shook his head, then smiled brightly at me. "Now that I've been as open I can be with you, you might choose to bestow that same favour upon me." Kieran inclined his head, then gave me a look that alone told me he was asking his prior question once more.

I ground my teeth before muttering, "That was hardly an explanation. And besides, you'll think I'm crazy." He would keep me locked up here for good.

He grinned, then replied just as quietly, "Maybe." He shrugged. "Then again, maybe not." He readjusted the lapel of his black leather trench coat, his face focused wholly on me; transforming yet again into a mask of pure attentiveness.

The utter intensity of the expression made the breath catch in my throat.

Why was he so flawless?

I hated how part of my body yielded to his beauty, wanting to touch, to taste...

I looked up at the cell's crumbling roof, defeated, then exhaled hoarsely, "Fine."

That man made me...I couldn't let him distract me, nor could I bring myself to watch his face while disclosing part of the reality of my situation. The idea of his disappointment made me feel queasy—maybe even nauseous if I was being perfectly honest with myself.

I closed my eyes, face still to the roof, then whispered, "To answer your first question, I don't know exactly what happened. I have this *gift*, and sometimes it communicates with me. I call it a flicker." It was uncomfortable keeping my head uptilted, so I put my face in my hands instead, keeping my eyes closed so I could almost pretend I was just talking to myself. "For whatever reason, the flicker—which usually feels like a little flame licking up my spine—decided it was going to burn me alive."

"Is your "gift" the reason why Qasir followed you for all of that time?" Kieran's question was careful, curious, and it was clear his intent was to keep me talking without shutting me down entirely.

The fact that he had to ask only clarified my suspicions—I was the closest to anonymity that I'd been in at least the last two years. He truly hadn't heard of *the Moira* before. Unbelievable.

"Yes." I couldn't help but smile as I continued, "Because my little flicker has never done anything like that to me before, I don't know what caused *that* to happen." I swallowed, still fighting against the scratchiness of my throat. "To answer your next question, I ventured into this hellhole because Qasir came to me while I was working in the circus to the northeast of here—past the grasslands, into the mountains. He wanted me to use my gift so he could reach his utmost desire."

Kieran's breathing came to a standstill, and I opened my eyes to see what the problem was.

Shock lit up his eyes, as if struck.

"You think I'm crazy," I sighed. "I knew it."

I shouldn't have said anything. I'd just fucked myself, and any chance of getting out of this damned city, rightfully.

I could have lied.

But *nope*.

Now I'd be lucky if he ever let me out of this cell.

Now I'd be lucky if he didn't hold me hostage and sell my services to those who came to this…

I closed my eyes as I saw the patrons' hands caressing my hair through the bars as they once had—

"Are you serious? Qasir wasn't just rambling…" Kieran barked out a laugh. "You're telling me that you can lead people to whatever the hell they want?" He gave me a skeptical look, not quite believing this small piece of truth I gave him.

"I wish I could say I was joking." My stomach was twisting itself into knots, and I strained against the acid now intent on finding a way upward into my mouth. I refused to meet Kieran's gaze. To meet his judgement.

"Why would you be?" My thought process all but died as I registered his response. I peeked up to where he stood. There, glimmering in his eyes. Hope. "If *I* had that kind of gift, I'd have gotten what I wanted years—"

"I can't." I interrupted him.

"What do you mean you *can't?*" Frustration conquered his calm demeanor.

"I mean, I can't because my gift only works to find the desires of *other* people. Finding my own desire is another story."

I didn't mention that I had yet to find what I wanted—there was no need. Why else would I be stuck in a cell, talking to a man I hardly knew? It wasn't as if I *wanted* this for myself...

Kieran's deportment shifted yet again, but this time it appeared to be pensive in nature. He rubbed his face, drawing attention to both his perfect complexion and the five-o-clock shadow that stippled his jawline. He then stared at the wall behind me. "So, you're okay if I leave the pitcher here? It's almost dusk."

I glanced around the cell—the sun was no longer beating down against the concrete at our feet.

"And I'm sure Derrik will have his hands full if he's left alone..." Kieran gave me a beseeching expression, seemingly full of pain and longing and desperation, before he suddenly, as if he'd merely pressed a button, gave me a radiant smile. "I'll see you soon, *Moira*. Don't miss me too much." He chuckled and raised himself to his feet.

He almost left the cell open; however, to my dismay, he thought better of it, locking it so there was no way I'd be able to escape, before swaggering down the hallway out of sight. Arrogant prick assuming I would miss him at all. There would only ever be one thing I missed, and he was a fool to believe it would ever be him. Or anyone.

I lowered my back down to the stone floor and moaned as it stretched the muscles I'd been straining for weeks straight. Peace from Kieran at last. I closed my eyes against the dimming light of dusk and thought over our conversation in my head.

Was it truly hope and longing and pain and desperation that I witnessed in his gaze upon telling him of my talents, or was I just projecting my own foolish dreams upon him? I shook my head. If it were indeed true, then that would mean he desired something he'd had difficulty attaining on his own. I chuckled to myself; didn't *that* sound familiar. After all, I'd been trying to find someone to help lead me to my own desire…

Wait.

If he wanted something and my little dancer nearly consumed me with its flame when he thought about it…

I gasped.

Maybe he was like me. Maybe my flicker was trying to help *me* out for once. Maybe he could lead me to my—

"*KIERAN!!!*" I screamed his name at the top of my lungs and rose onto my feet in an instant, hoping to draw his attention away from Sin's Forum below. I waited a minute before I called out again. "Kieran!" Still no response. I forced myself to continue, turning my voice rough as I called out over and over.

I heard the sound of heavy footsteps running my way, and a few seconds later, he skidded to a halt in front of my cell. Kieran looked me over with the kind of intensity a general would use to inspect one of his soldiers, and upon seeing I was alright, he demanded, "What's the problem now? I—"

I interrupted him, damning the consequences. "Let me lead you."

Sweat dripped off his brow and he gave me a confused glare. "Excuse me?"

Now that I'd voiced the idea aloud, I was certain this was what my flicker had intended to happen in the first place. I received an assuring caress from it in confirmation of my thoughts.

I smiled before repeating, "Let me lead you."

Kieran wiped excess sweat from his face with a sleeve, then asked, "Why should I do that? You don't even like me as far as I can tell."

"I know you want something," I rasped. "If you let me out of here, I swear to lead you to whatever it is you desire most."

"It's impossible; you're just a girl. As if—" He stopped himself, and distress washed over his features.

"I vow to lead you to your greatest desire. Just free me." I could see an invisible war playing out across his features as he thought over my proposal, so I repeated, "Let me lead you."

He turned his back to me and rubbed his hands through his curled hair. "You would swear your very life to me, all so you can lead me to whatever I desire most?"

I nodded, but upon realizing he couldn't see the movement, I stated, "Yes."

I heard him exhale deeply through his nose, then felt my little dancer begin a fiery foxtrot up and down my spine. It ached so badly, but then, as if extinguished by a bucket of water, it ceased.

"Yes." Kieran's voice cracked through the hallway, and it effectively extinguished my train of thought as well. He faced me and offered me a tentative smile. "Let's shake on it—I'm not sure how honorable your word is." He chuckled, then extended his hand through the bars.

I didn't hesitate as I lunged forward, and firmly squeezed his hand. His hand wasn't as large as I'd expected it to be, but its calluses scraped against my palm as he shook mine. My own still clasped in his, I vowed, "I swear, from this moment forward, I will lead you to your utmost desire. Even if it may seem an impossible task. I will stay true to you and will never break this oath." He didn't need to know that the only reason I'd even offered my services to him was because he could potentially serve my own purpose. But, whatever. The outcome would hypothetically be the same no matter what.

He released my hand, then nodded. "I'll give you the night to get yourself ready for this little trek of ours, and in the morning, we can head out." He bit his lip, deep in thought yet again by the look of it, before announcing, "I'll have to make some arrangements, just in case you do fulfill your promise to me." He smirked, unlocked my cell, then said, "Follow me and I will get you to the bath…you need it."

I couldn't argue with him at that—I felt some of my vomit from earlier slide down my robe and onto the floor in front of me as I stepped through the now open bars. I staunched my disgust and followed Kieran back into the heart of Sin's Forum.

I was even more giddy than I'd been the night before.

He could finally be my shot at finding what I'd wanted for the last five years.

Home—I could be going home, and I was desperate enough to risk it all to return.

I laughed quietly to myself, then descended the stairwell behind him, returning to the soothing darkness yet again.

Chapter 7

Moira

LAST NIGHT'S BATH was like a breath of deliverance, cleansing me of the last five, unproductive years.

I desperately hoped my flicker was right.

Or that *I* was right for that matter.

I couldn't help but believe that it was probably foolish of me to place such faith in a stranger. Realistically, I'd already placed my fate in the hands of nearly fifty others prior to Kieran, so it wasn't like this was some *unusual* behaviour on my part…but he *seemed* different. I didn't think he wanted the same things as all the other men I'd led to their desires. He already had it all in Sin's Forum; the women, the power, the money, the influence…

Maybe he was just greedy.

I shook my head—my little dancer clearly believed him to be different than the others too; never before last night had it launched itself into quite that sort of frenzy with just the wandering of a person's thoughts. Or perhaps my *moral* flicker simply had a plan that I was unaware of for the time being. Whatever it was, I'd learn soon enough. The little dancer always seemed to have its way.

I brushed through my hair with the comb Kieran had left for me on the bedside table and breathed in the fresh scent of citrus that permeated the space. He'd let me stay in a guest room off the main upper corridor for the rest of the night as a result of our little arrangement. He had the decency to provide all the amenities I would need to feel at least partly human again; a bath, a bed...a tangible thread of hope to cling to.

The guest room was perhaps a few doors down from the cell in which I'd been initially placed; however, unlike the cell, it had an almost stable ceiling and a couple of mismatched curtained windows which granted me a perfect view of the Pillars of Messiah in all its glory while I was trying to fall asleep. But upon noticing that last night, it didn't take me very long to close the curtains. I still found that light in particular to be insufferable.

I glimpsed the now opened windows and watched as the sun slowly crept higher over the horizon. Kieran still hadn't visited me yet this morning. I fingered the nightgown he'd handed me after he realized that that shoddy piece of worn-out fabric was the only wardrobe I'd brought for the journey. It was a sage-green, similar to the shade of his eyes, and it was crafted of the sleekest satin. Expensive.

Maybe Kieran was just doing the decent thing by giving me some time to rest after my weeks-long journey with Qasir—but I doubted it. The niceties were probably just to make it so that I wouldn't be dragging my ass around when he finally did decide for us to leave.

After all, saving my life didn't necessarily mean he genuinely cared about me.

I grumbled, but remained sitting there, legs dangling off the bed with the ivory comb nearly stuck in my hair as a result of all the knots that had wound up there on my trek. Kieran had better be my escape out of this decrepit place.

I dropped the comb, before brushing a hand over the fabric clothing me once more. Last night Kieran had thrown out my dishevelled attire before gifting me with much cleaner, more fashionable apparel he seemed to have on-hand for whomever dropped by his room late at night. All of it well-made, and all of it ostensibly fabricated for a different time.

His room was adjacent to mine, furnished in oak and the lightest of blues. When I'd glanced in for only a second as we'd passed it in the night, it had reminded me of calm breezes and clear blue skies.

I forced myself off the bed to walk to the wardrobe at the opposite wall, before donning yet another piece of clothing Kieran had given to me—a lovely two-piece dress, seemingly crafted from the sand surrounding the city, with sheer flowing white fabric for the skirt and a cropped fitted top meant to accentuate my few assets.

I glared at myself in the mirror hanging from the door that led to the hall.

There was a reason men oftentimes mistook me for a girl; I didn't have the curves men associated with womanhood. Slender, not particularly well-endowed, and hips that didn't possess a very womanly physique. At least my face wasn't too dull. My pallor was stark against flowing ebony hair that stopped itself just short of my waist, whilst my eyes stole away from the beauty of my other features.

Whatever.

The dress wasn't meant to make me attractive—it had a purpose. It could probably serve as a head-covering to keep desert sand from whipping itself against my face, or as a shroud to keep cold winds off me from the mountains. Hell, I was sure it could even serve as a sail if need be, to cross an ocean. I didn't even see the point in packing any extra clothing.

I shook my head. I was deluding myself.

It was practically useless.

Not unlike someone I knew intimately.

I spun away from the mirror in absolute frustration. I was to go on yet *another* trip that would lead me to some unknown location with yet *another* man I didn't know. Clearly my little dancer didn't know anything about my safety—or if it did, it couldn't care less about it. I reached for a pair of slippers that were just hidden beneath the bed; satin, like the nightgown I'd worn a minute earlier, but instead of sage they were a cream colour.

A knock sounded on my door from the hall.

I supposed it was time to lead Kieran to his desire.

"Are you decent yet?" Kieran's voice was edged with excitement. I wished I was able to muster the same enthusiasm. Maybe I'd been deluding myself last night too—

As if *he* could lead me back to…everything that had ever mattered to me.

I didn't respond as I continued slipping my feet into the silky material, silently admiring the sunlight as it reflected off them, making them appear more gold than white. The slippers looked and felt as if they had been crafted of liquid sunlight. A near-perfect fit.

Another knock sounded, and I groaned before trudging back towards the mirror and door behind it. Then, upon taking a deep breath, I opened the door so Kieran could come in.

"I see someone is in a great mood." Kieran gave me a smirk that suggested he knew I was in anything but, and I pursed my lips. He closed the door behind him with a thud, and stated, "You can't go back on your word. We made a deal, and now you're stuck with me." His face told me he didn't feel quite as excited as he let on, but I didn't care. It wasn't like we were going to be stuck to one another for the rest of our lives.

I made sure to keep eye contact as I swore myself once again to Kieran. "I know what an oath is. I am not going to break the promise I made you. You will get whatever it is you want by the time we split ways." My throat still tickled with the strain I'd unwillingly put it through yesterday. "I promise."

I just hoped I wasn't helping yet another man to attain something frivolous that anyone with a set could find on their own. Qasir and the power of being a tyrant. The one before him and the sneaky broad that robbed him blind as they kissed—although, that one had (undoubtedly) been entertaining.

Salvador and the success of Pierserk.

I wanted to get what *I* wanted for once, and if it meant leading him to whatever it was Kieran desired in order to do so, I didn't mind paying that price. I was certain that there were others who had been taken from my home. Others who were now trapped here. I'd latched onto that hope blindly for as long as I could remember, and Kieran was odd enough that perhaps he too belonged somewhere else like I did.

I still found it strange that I'd actually been able to choose Kieran as a client—I'd never been granted that freedom before. Salvador had always sold me to the highest bidder...contrary to whether I wanted to help them or not. He'd saved me, so I owed him—he drilled that concept into my head as soon as he figured I understood enough of his tongue.

Qasir had been the only exception to that rule...before now.

I was supposed to act as a peace offering between brothers; Qasir was to be lent me until he found his one true desire, and Salvador was to be given some time and space away from the nagging prick.

I finally understood the appeal of the latter sentiment.

"If you're ready to leave, let's go." Kieran directed his arms to the door behind him, and in doing so, I noticed the very large backpack he was wearing. It too was black, so it blended in with his sprawling trench coat seamlessly, camouflaging it from sight.

I objected and pointed to the satchel. "My stuff better be in there too because I refuse to carry anything like that." There was no way I was going to lug around something on my back that was half my size; I wouldn't even be able to stand, let alone take a few steps.

Kieran gave me a bemused look, then sighed when he realized I was serious. "Of course. What kind of a *man* would I be if I wasn't courteous." He rolled his eyes, then took off back into the hallway.

That would be my cue to follow him.

At least he was courteous like he said—though he could afford to be more modest.

I watched the muscles of his back shift beneath the fabric as we first passed the cell I'd stayed in, before it dawned upon me: he was still wearing the same black leather coat I'd first seen him in. Dust from the desert's sands made it fade closer to his feet, and I could swear that some of the scuff marks were from the day earlier when he'd positioned himself on the stool in front of my cell. And he told me *I* needed a bath?

"Do you ever intend on taking off your coat?" I sneered.

He exhaled deeply, scratching the back of his head as he did so. Pretty sensitive to the minor criticism of his fashion choices if you asked me. "You realize that if we go further into the desert, that coat of yours will do you no good. More of a hinderance, really. It's funny Kieran, I didn't take you for an—"

He snapped, "Do *not* finish that sentence."

"Then why are you still wearing it?" We were now descending the staircase that would lead us to the mezzanine that overhung the epicenter of Sin's Forum. "I mean, sure it's nice looking, but it's not exactly practical."

"Because I want to wear it." His voice carried over the pounding music already filling the space, and he quickened his pace. The archaic curtains which had clung to my ankles only the day before had been shoved aside, clearing the path so we could descend yet another staircase—the one leading into the initial hall Qasir and I'd seen upon entering.

Obviously, he wasn't going to budge on an actual explanation, so I kept quiet. Small talk was too exhausting—the music was too loud, and we were to have a mighty long journey ahead of us anyways. Or at least, I hoped that was true. My true desire would only be found far, far away.

Another minute passed and we were ascending the decrepit first staircase Qasir and I had used to enter Kieran's establishment. The stairs wobbled as we hurried upwards, and I could have sworn I'd even heard a bolt or two fall onto the ground below. Wasn't that safe. Maybe now that Kieran was to be with me, the new person running things would have some sort of incentive to fix the rusting, tetanus-inducing steps.

But it didn't matter.

I wouldn't be coming back here of my own volition any time soon, so why would I care if someone broke their neck on the way down?

The blazing light of day greeted us, and it took all of a moment for my eyes to adjust. We were now beside the vendors lining the outside of his establishment, and today they seemed to be selling linens, candles, and paints. That wasn't conspicuous at all. Nor was the simultaneous nod of their heads as Kieran passed them by. Not quite as conspicuous as it had been the night of Qasir's death, but still.

Some cover *they* were.

He went to continue his trek towards the Pillars in the north, but I rushed forward to halt his shoulder with a hand so he could face me once more. "Where do you think you're going?"

His brows furrowed as he glanced to the hand I'd left there, before slowly peeling each of my fingers off. "Why don't you tell me?" The sticky vestige of my hand still remained, fingerprints marring the immaculate appearance of the black leather material.

Fair enough. "We need to stop so I can get an idea of where your desire lies." I gave him an encouraging smile, and said, "Let's move somewhere a bit more private first so I can give you the instructions without seeming like too much of a lunatic."

He offered me a subdued nod of his chin and we slipped into a side alley no one seemed to pay any heed to. The shade of the alley did nothing to dampen the determination twinkling in Kieran's remarkable gaze as he asked, "What exactly do you need me to do?"

I cringed. "You'll have to think of whatever it was you were thinking of before I had that little episode of mine."

He hesitated at my request, "Won't that cause you to possibly have another episode, Moira."

"Possibly." I shrugged, hair falling over a shoulder with the movement. "But this time I'm prepared for…whatever."

"I don't want you to get hurt."

Well, that was the first time anyone had ever said that to me.

"Just do it quickly Kieran. If you don't start fantasizing about whatever it is for seconds on end, I'll be fine."

Kieran closed his eyes, hiding the amusement that danced there. "Pfft, okay…let me know when, and if, I need to stop."

I waited a second, bracing myself against the coolness of the sandstone to my back, preparing for the surge of my flicker's assault, then said, "Now."

All of my preparations seemed to be for naught.

My little dancer's flames seared my very bone.

Tears streamed down my face as I scoured our surroundings, grinding my teeth as I wrestled against the pain, in hopes of locating where we were to head next. I stepped forward, and the fire in my spine shot through my legs, leaving a tingling ache in its place. Pins and needles threatened them to crumple, and I whimpered. In every direction I looked, the pain radiating outwards from my spine did not cease; however, in a spot to the southwest of Sin's Forum, the pain seemed to become more urgent…more acute.

I screamed against the stabbing, burning—

"Are you okay?" Kieran's voice cut through the agony.

Then, as quickly as it had come, it was gone.

Perhaps because I was prepared for the onslaught of misery and because I hadn't been all mopey and depressed beforehand, I didn't feel the thirst and exhaustion which had accompanied the first time Kieran had thought about who knew what. I ran my hand through my hair before glancing up to Kieran's still confused expression, and explained, "Whenever you think about whatever it is—"

"I can tell you if it would—"

"Listen, I don't care what it is, and besides, it doesn't matter." I continued, glaring at Kieran for his interruption. "Whenever you think about whatever it is," I repeated, "my gift sets me aflame, and I feel like I am being scorched from within."

He chuckled aloud, then turned to face Sin's Forum. "Burning desire."

"What?"

Had he gone mad? From where I was standing, it wasn't funny.

"Burning desire." He gave me a beseeching expression. "Whenever I imagine my greatest desire, you basically catch aflame..."

"I don't care." I didn't care about what he meant.

"Oh, come on Moira. It's a *phrase*. Don't tell me you haven't heard the expression before..." His words faded as the unsolicited words of others toppled over my senses.

Oath breaker.

The insult from my memory echoed into my very being once more and I yearned to rail against it. I would have *never* left. From the little I recalled, I'd loved my old life more than anything.

Her blurry face had to know that.

I would never betray her faith, nor the faith of the—

"We go that way," I said quickly, stopping myself before falling into the fuzzy pictures clouding my mind. I pointed to the direction in which my little dancer decided to push me, and shoved myself past Kieran, who still seemed to be pleading with me. Pathetic that he actually cared about offending me. It was almost offensive how weak he believed me to be. Sickening. I swore, if my little dancer was tricking me about him...

"Fine. I guess that'll just be my nickname for the flicker you feel then: burning desire." He said it with a kind of astonishment that made my flicker content, smug even, for it again began its casual waltz upon my spine. And if my little dancer was going to treat me like this for the rest of our trip...I was going to go certifiably insane.

I exhaled forcefully through my nose, then said, "Let's not waste any time."

We reached Neosordess' western border within a matter of an hour and a bit.

We had to first travel through the industrial region of the city; the veil of the noxious smog I'd noted when I'd traversed the Aspitha with Qasir was thicker than I could have imagined, and it made my eyes water on contact as the stench of burning petroleum stuffed its way up into my nose. Luckily, the border was located only half an hour away from the last factory that we passed, so the smell had *almost* dissipated by the time we'd made it there.

The protocol required for us to leave Neosordess was even more elaborate than the way in; an extra checkpoint was set up so as to keep a physical record of the names and appearances of those who left the city without the Messiah's blessing.

Or at least, that was what Kieran told me.

He'd volunteered that information to me without me asking; he seemed to know the inner workings of the Messiah and His disciples pretty well. *Pretty well*, considering he gave no indication that he followed their religion in any way, as I doubted that his prayers had anything to do with the Messiah. If instead, that *was* the case, my flicker wouldn't have urged us away from the smog and too-bright lights of Neosordess.

I had to admit, it was pretty nice to travel with Kieran; he kept up to my set pace, so I didn't need to go unbearably slow like I had with Qasir, and the occasional pieces of trivia he offered about both the city and the strange animals I'd seen earlier (camels) were entertainment enough to keep boredom at bay.

By nightfall, the conversation had ceased because one) I didn't feel like volunteering any information to him about myself, and two) it was obvious that he was focused solely on reaching whatever it was he desired so much. Kieran was one of the most determined men I'd ever brought along with me in the last three years for these damned peregrinations.

The desert we walked through gave no indication of ending; dunes now stretched as far as the eye could see—an ocean of sand. I couldn't help but draw parallels in my mind as gusts of wind tore at my dress, but there was no water to be found. I was grateful that

Kieran was indeed carrying enough fluids for the both of us; a plastic water bladder hung from his back, and a couple of smaller cannisters could be found in the backpack that was perched beside it.

I only broke our silence after the sun had finally set and the stars were bright high above us. I swung myself around to face Kieran and said, "We should set up camp for the night." The sound of my own voice caught me off-guard—perhaps it had been even longer than I'd thought since the time we'd spoken last.

Kieran also appeared startled, jumping back at the sudden nature of the sound. He groaned, then dropped our backpack in the sand, "Thank the Messiah. I thought you'd never stop."

I furrowed my brow and asked, "If you were so tired, why didn't you bother saying something earlier?"

"Well, I didn't want to hold you back and I also don't want to waste our time." He chuckled, "You also seem to be someone with a bit of a temper, so I didn't want to set that off—"

I started, "You don't—"

"My point." he said, interrupting me, then unloaded the backpack of sleeping bags, food, and our communal water jug. He swigged some water from it before passing it to me.

Great.

I took a mouthful or two or three or four of my own before placing it down beside our backpack. Still, I wanted more but fought the urge as I remembered that we could potentially be without a source of water for a long, *long* time.

And, I didn't want to throw my guts up again.

I sighed, frustrated, as I made to sit down. Sand, sand, and more sand. Surrounding us, the desert's dunes spread far and wide into the horizon. Nothing existed to shield us from the tenacious winds that tore at the fabric of our clothing, and I griped.

Kieran smirked as he finished laying out the two sleeping bags for us to rest on, and of course sand had already found its way into my own bag by the time I tried getting inside. I cursed, "That's it, Kieran. I officially hate the desert." I punched the sand pressing against the side of my makeshift bed and groaned as another gust whipped it back up to hit my face.

Typical.

I closed my eyes to reorient myself and carefully wiped away at the granules that clung to my eyelids, my lips, and my cheeks. Taking another deep breath, I opened them and gazed into the night sky stretching far above us. There were stars. *Stars.* Stars that twinkled and shone overhead, no longer afraid nor hiding from the urban lights that stole away their beauty. I smiled. I didn't realize quite how much I'd missed the stars while I'd been in that…city. If you could even call it that. I cringed.

A yawn broke through his lips, startling me enough that I snapped, "What do you want now?"

"Where are you from exactly?"

Now that question was unexpected.

Kieran continued, "If you were from around here, the sand wouldn't be such a pain in the ass to you."

A flash of lush green and sparkling pools flared in my vision. I briefly closed my eyes again. No. No I wasn't from around here. "I'm from the north." I lied. My home was my sanctuary, and I couldn't, *wouldn't* disclose its truth to anyone here. Nothing of this land captivated my heart. Everything here was as foreign to me as I was to it. Again, if I did—I would be insane.

He grunted.

I glanced to my left and noticed he opened his mouth, surely to inquire further, when thankfully, he thought better of it and rolled away from me onto his side. He whispered, "You know Moira, we don't have to be at odds with each other. You don't have to be so secretive around me."

I didn't want to reply. It was none of his business as to why I wouldn't speak to him.

When I didn't respond, he merely trudged on, unaffected by my asocial behaviour. "Goodnight, Moira," he said. I was surprised he still deigned to treat me like a person at all. He was perhaps the only man I'd met who had thought of me as a person.

Not like it mattered.

I felt my eyes become misty as I tried and failed to think of my home. After five years, I couldn't even see its beauty anymore, only the wisps of its imprint remained etched somewhere deep, in the very core of my mind. I could feel the serenity of barely lapping waves on an overgrown bank, and I could feel the wonderment of the ephemeral flickering lights. There, I knew I had been treated like I mattered. Back home, I had been treated like I was worth something. *Why* did this even happen to me? *Why* was I the one stolen away?

I dropped the subject from my mind, and I had to stare into the night sky once again to calm myself.

My flicker gave me a reassuring caress, and I let that ground me.

I recited a prayer I'd made after my first…*incident* with a client. *Soon*, I would be able to return to where I once was. *Soon*, I would be able to return to *who* I once was.

I had to.

Fire.

I was on fire.

I woke from my otherwise peaceful sleep to find Kieran passed out beside me with the stars still high above us.

I needed water.

I reached between us to the water bladder and clenched my teeth as my flicker sent yet another searing pain down my spine. I quickly heaved the jug above my head and spilt some down my neck.

No relief.

I then brought it to my mouth so I could quench the flame from within, but…no fucking relief. My little dancer began leading into another dance composed of more stinging and aching fire and I panicked. I needed the pain to go away.

I crawled to Kieran and began shaking him "Kieran."

At my touch, he opened his eyes almost instantly, and his fear was a tangible thing as it wiped away all the bleariness that lingered in his gaze from sleeping so soundly.

Then my little flicker stopped.

Relief.

I sighed and fell backward against the sand we'd lain down upon.

Finally.

"What was the problem this time?" I glanced his way and noticed Kieran was giving me a look of reproach as he hissed, "And why did you think it was okay to spill half of our water in the sand?"

I frowned. There was no way I'd used that much. I threw out an arm to the bladder waiting in the sand beside us, and lifted it.

Water sloshed inside, rocking the skin back and forth.

Kieran was wrong. I'd used *more* than half our remaining water.

I stumbled, "I-I am so—"

"How are we even going to make it through tomorrow, never mind the next day!" Kieran rose to his feet suddenly and began pacing.

"It's your fault," I started. "If you weren't thinking about that stupid—"

"I will not be so friendly to you if you are just going to insult me." He stared at me through the darkness, and his moss eyes, which had been glittering in the moonlight only seconds before, became wholly dark.

I closed my mouth and returned to my sleeping bag. I laid down upon it, then swiftly rolled away from the gaze I could still feel lingering on my face. "At least you still have a couple of little bottles left. Besides, if you don't want this to happen in the future, don't think about whatever it is that you want." I mumbled into the sleeping bag I'd raised over my face.

Why did my *gift*—as Salvador repeatedly called it—need to cause me so much distress? My little dancer was *such* a gift...that now we were going to die of dehydration because of it. Cursed thing. I could feel my flicker's disapproval as a single flame twined around my chest before it halted suddenly—

"When I'm *sleeping*, I can't control my thoughts very well." His voice still sounded irritated with me. He sighed, "*If* that happens again, instead of using our primary water source to no avail, you should just wake me."

I didn't respond.

He continued, "I'd much prefer losing a few minutes sleep than waking up to the two of us having no water left in the middle of the fucking desert."

I heard him return to his sleeping bag just as I had, and so I said, albeit a bit gruffly, "Fine."

"Fine." He was still in a "fine" mood.

Whatever. In the morning, we would begin our trek as if nothing had ever happened, and hopefully in exchange, my little flicker would lead us towards some water for what it had made me do.

Otherwise, it would be the one responsible for our deaths out here.

Not me.

I let the sound of the desert's breezes lull me into oblivion's embrace until dawn ripped me away from its comforting arms.

Chapter 8

Moira

THE CLOUDS OVERHEAD provided only some protection against the sun's raging intensity; however, they didn't provide even close to enough to keep us away from our thirst. My tongue stuck to the top of my mouth by midday, and we only had perhaps a quarter of the bladder left.

So much for Kieran packing enough to last us both through the journey. He should have known that *something* was going to go awry—even if it was *my* flicker who had acted in response to his thoughts… Kieran should have known that nothing would ever go smoothly in this world where *everything* that existed was inexplicably wrong. Rationing our water would be our only save and grace to have merely a chance to possibly survive the desert's harsh conditions.

Needless to say, my flicker didn't help us. It only gave me the occasional waltz to guide us through a seemingly homogenous desert. There were no landmarks to guide us. Only a few discrete cacti could be seen littering what looked to be a flat expanse of land before some mountains distantly to the north. Other than that, the desert was a wasteland.

By the time night fell, the need to quench my thirst overwhelmed my every other thought and reason, and I couldn't even fathom travelling like this for another day, let alone as long as it would take to lead Kieran to his desire—unless he just desired to sit down on some random dune out here and in that case...

We'd already guzzled what was left of the other two bottles he'd carried hours earlier, as the sun's incessant rays had made it impossible to even move without first drinking some our liquid gold to fuel us onward. I heaved what was left of the bladder to my mouth before I hastily gulped down the last of my water ration, being careful to keep my eyes averted from Kieran's. I could feel him silently chastising me as I grabbed the sleeping bag that he had diligently carried for me the whole day.

We didn't speak to each other, and I almost felt guilty that I was making him do all the heavy lifting, especially when I noted the sweat that now drenched his hair and fell onto his perfect face when he gave me the roll.

But I was the one doing him a favour.

He was the only man I'd led in the last three years who didn't pay through the nose to Salvador for my services. Still, I wasn't about to thank him for his sacrifice when my flicker began sending shooting flames down my legs again. I growled, "Just because you're pissed with me doesn't mean you have to be a jerk. Kieran, stop doing that." I warned him, keeping my eyes plastered to the bed roll in my hands.

"Stop doing what?" he asked.

I whipped my head to check the surrounding area. I recalled a time—years ago—when the flicker had identified a pack of wild dogs which had circled one of my earlier camps with another client. We'd barely escaped with our lives, and I'd since promised to be more careful, so I checked the sand—the dunes. Perhaps there was a snake or…

Nothing.

Kieran too watched the sand and whispered, "I don't see anything. Moira, what's going on?"

I pivoted toward one particularly high sand dune lying due south of us, when my flicker perked up—apparently reinvigorated, urging my legs to travel to the site. I handed Kieran back the sleeping bag, then began traipsing my way through the sand, gritting my teeth all the while, in order to see what my flicker's problem was.

Kieran called after me, "Where are you going?"

I refused him a response—I didn't *know* where I was going. My little dancer had better decided to help me out for once…

The slope of the dune was steeper than expected, so I began scaling it on my knees.

With each step forward, it became more impatient.

Obviously, it wanted us to continue onward. For what reason, I had no idea, but I was going to find out—even if this all was solely some phantasm of my own making.

Coarse sand found its way under my nails and scraped against my palms, but I plowed ahead. From where I now crawled, a glowing light could be seen just cresting the dune's ridge. I hastened my pace, using all my strength to climb so I could get rid of the flicker's now incessant burning. One hand in front of the other, over, and over and—

There it was; the source of my flicker's frantic tango.

There, seemingly in the middle of nowhere, glowing lights leaked from a single hut.

I sunk forward before hollering over a shoulder, "Come here—I just found a new place for us to rest for the night." At least we wouldn't have to worry about our sleeping arrangements anymore…well, for the night anyway.

I heard the swishing of Kieran's trench coat on the sand, followed by the sound of little rocks falling down behind me on the dune before he finally perched beside me on the mound. I felt more than saw him give me an incredulous look as he asked, "Your "burning desire" told you this?"

I only nodded before rising to my feet yet again.

He laughed, rising beside me, and as his smile stretched across his features, I could see that his lips had become chapped, cracking in some places. "I guess I'll have to believe you when you say it tells you things."

I stepped forward, sand swallowing my slippers whole as I descended the dune. I didn't bother watching to see if Kieran followed suit behind me; I knew he would.

The light leaking from that desolate hut became a beacon in the night, and I persevered against the pain that still raged in my back, urging me forward.

As we crept closer, I could see that the hut wasn't alone; instead, the hut was situated in the midst of an oasis. A spring-fed pond lay a stone's throw from the keep, and a palm grove seemingly protected it against the incumbent sunlight. An inevitable consequence of living so isolated in the desert.

We slowed as we approached the wooden door of the hut, which was conceivably crafted from the palms around us, and I saw two windows—one on each side of the door. The glow of the lanterns from within lit up the space in front of us, so I could also make out that the roof too seemed made of locally-sourced materials: palm fronds. The sides making up the hut itself were constructed of a type of brick—most likely from some sort of clay that could be found nearby.

I heard two distinct male voices from where we stood outside the hut; one higher in pitch, weaker, and seemingly older, and another deeper one that sliced through the room like a knife. The latter voice alone transformed my flicker from a painful tingling ache in my spine to harmless butterflies. I trembled in their wake.

Who *was* he?

I glanced over my shoulder to Kieran and gave him a small nod—my flicker had led us here for another reason besides the water and the sleeping arrangements. The flurry of its invisible wings told me that perhaps my little dancer had something *else* planned for the two of us while we were here.

It would be my responsibility to see what exactly that was.

Maybe it only wanted me to meet whoever had that gorgeous voice…I wouldn't be opposed to the idea.

We snuck toward the hut, and when we reached the front door, I knocked twice. The voices from within went silent. Then, footsteps. I backed away from the door and nearly tripped over Kieran in doing so—I hushed, "For crying out loud Kieran. Watch it." I nudged him forward so he could be the one to meet whoever was to greet us.

"Yeah, *okay* Moira…" Kieran took a step to the door and stood tall, commanding, and relentless. Totally at odds with his response. This man was not the person I'd been travelling with for two days. Gone were his friendly mannerisms and kind words. This was the man who had murdered his way to become Sin's Forum's overseer. This—*he*—was now an albeit attractive version of who I first presumed lazed on Sin Forum's throne.

The creaking wood of the door sounded, and I leaned around Kieran to better see the person behind it. Butterflies skittered this way and that across my spine and I watched as the golden light of the hut spilled further onto the entryway.

The face that emerged was yet another one of beauty.

A much handsomer, more rugged face than Kieran's.

The man standing before us had raven black hair and eyes framed by dark, thick brows that resembled ash. The light and dark grays contrasted one another and acted like coins sparkling against the night sky. In the light gilding the exterior of the keep, it was difficult to discern his exact complexion for it reflected back the gold cast off the candles from within.

"May I help you?" His voice was a caress that worked synchronously with my flicker, causing a shudder to shoot down my spine. I glanced away from him if only to catch my breath as my flicker burnt me.

Fine. The flicker wanted him for some reason.

Kieran spoke, no more than a whisper amongst the dunes, "Hello there." Only the words themselves were polite. "We've been travelling through the desert for a couple of days now, and I was wondering if we'd be able to stay for the night? We'll pay you if need be."

I glared sidelong at Kieran. He seemed to forget that *I* was the one to discover this place and that this was actually *my* idea. Frustrated, I whipped my head back to the glow of the keep in front of us and noted that Kieran was about the same height as the gorgeous man in the doorway.

The man hesitated, then surveyed where I still perched behind Kieran. "You two can rest here the night. Don't worry about a payment."

Did pity shine in those magnificent eyes?

"Thank you," I blurted.

Kieran spun towards me and cast me a hard stare. He ground his teeth as he bit out the sentiment, "Thank you for your kindness."

The man didn't withdraw his eyes from me as he opened the door wider, giving us both enough space to step into the keep. Kieran made to go in first, but the man halted him with an arm against the other side of the doorframe. "Ladies first," he said. He gave me a crooked smile as he inclined his head towards me. Straight hair, landing just past his shoulders, fell into his eyes with the gesture, but he didn't seem to care.

I couldn't help but give him a beaming smile in return.

He seemed decent enough.

Maybe my flicker led me here to give me a little piece of what this life could be like if I tried.

I almost *liked* it.

Almost.

I snuck around Kieran, sidestepping the stranger to the best of my ability; however, the doorframe itself was much smaller than I initially believed it to be. I squeezed by Kieran into the keep, and in doing so, I could faintly make out the stranger's scent.

He smelled of ashes—burning wood.

The scent itself was an alluring blend of burning cedar and birch and walnut.

I stumbled past him into the open room and noticed an elderly man sitting in front of a large hearth. He blearily turned to me and gave a small smile. The old man was so much older than I'd imagined; his beard and head were mostly white, and his skin was wrinkled and blotchy. In his youth, he may have been a handsome man, but at this stage in his life, it was hard to tell. Actually, at this stage he was practically a long-forgotten relic—a miracle that he simply didn't disintegrate into a few stale dust motes, and float away on a wind.

"Hello." I returned his doddering smile and waited for Kieran to follow me into the keep.

I heard some scuffling behind me before both Kieran and the other man stood beside me: the mystery-man to my left and Kieran to my right. I stole a glance at the stranger and noticed he was still observing, no, *examining* me. I furrowed my brow. "What is it you're looking at?"

His face shifted into one of concern, ignoring my sole inquiry as he called, "Waha, I told these people they could rest here for the night."

"I'm not deaf, Sylver." The old man—Waha—interrupted the stranger—Sylver—and continued, "I might be old, but I'm not dead yet!" Even while the man was saying that, I couldn't help but wonder how much longer until that was the case.

A month?

Two?

Sylver chuckled beside me, and I shifted my gaze to him in time to see that he was now showing us where we were to sleep for the night. He spoke, "We have a couple of spare cots set up over here in case anyone gets lost, or in case anyone just needs some good rest after days of sleeping out in the dunes." He used his arm to indicate those were located opposite the hearth to our left.

I was right in my assumption that the worn keep was no more than a large room.

Kieran was the first to stalk over to the two cots and dumped our supplies on them. He didn't look over his shoulder as he responded with a gruff, "Thanks again," and continued unpacking our things.

Sylver elbowed me in the shoulder and asked, "Do you want anything to eat or something?" His gray eyes were stark against his skin, which now appeared paler than it had when the glow of the lights made it appear golden like Kieran's—striking, even so.

"Well, first I'd like to know why you keep staring at me." I didn't falter as I glared him down and stepped out of his reach. A nice-looking visage shouldn't absolve him from ignoring common decency. No, no, no. It was off-putting. His sheer confidence—*no*—arrogance rubbed me the wrong way.

Sylver stiffened at the tone and drawled, "I wasn't staring."

I crossed my arms and arched a brow. "Actually, you were staring—"

"Would you like some water?" Sylver interrupted. I scoffed. The fucking nerve. I opened my mouth to say just that, but my throat betrayed me. Aching and dry, it felt as if the desert had claimed both my mouth and my throat for itself. Whatever.

"Some water would be great. We've lost most of what we had out there." A pointed coughing fit erupted from where Kieran still unpacked our supplies, and I rolled my eyes. So dramatic.

I didn't care if Sylver had said that he hadn't been staring at me—I caught him analyzing my face yet again when I turned away from the cots back to him. Fine. If he wasn't going to relent, then two could play that game. Instead of turning away from his piercing gaze, I too took some time to scrutinize his features. Ashen eyes locked onto mine, and I slowly let my own shift to first his strong jawline, then to his high nasal bridge, before finally gazing at his thin, handsome lips. My eyes snagged on his hair—sleek and reflecting back the warm glow from the hearth. I yearned to run my fingers through the silky, fine locks. I shook my head as I dropped my gaze to the now filthy dress I was still wearing.

A foolish thought. Kieran and I would be leaving soon, and he was just another distraction that would try to keep me from going back to my home…

He would try to convince me to stay, and he wasn't enough—

"Sure thing." I could have sworn I heard Sylver's smile as he continued, "What's your name?"

"She never seems to tell anyone that willingly" Kieran's voice was closer to me than I'd expected, and frankly, his calm stealth made me a tad uneasy. He continued, seemingly ignoring our exchange, "Her name is *Moira*." He intoned my name, omitting the sensuality of before.

The fucking prick.

I closed my eyes waiting for the recognition—the sure acknowledgement of my otherworldly capabilities from Sylver and sighed. Kieran just had to make my life difficult. Just because *he* didn't have any clue who I was didn't necessarily mean that everyone else on this side of the Aspitha was just as ignorant to my name and what it meant.

"Moira, such a unique name. Nice to meet you." My jaw slackened. Sylver grinned, and said, "I take it you already know my name, but just in case you didn't hear Waha over there, it's Sylver." He was still grinning at me as he said, "Get comfortable. I'll bring you both some water and whatever else I can scrounge up." I watched him pivot and stroll a few steps to the makeshift kitchen and I figured that instead of staring at him like an idiot, I'd better head over to the cot before he returned with water for both Kieran and me.

As I sat down, I briefly glanced to Kieran and saw he was still tense from the encounter with Sylver. His eyes lingered on Sylver's movements, watching him prepare the meal from afar, surely to make sure he wasn't poisoning us, or at least him. Although, with the way Sylver had been staring at me, I couldn't help but wonder if I should be worried too.

My flicker practically balked at the thought and lashed me with a whip of flame as it scolded, *Since when do you care?*

Whatever.

Sylver returned, handing Kieran a glass of water first, before he said, "I don't think I caught your name. Let me guess, Moira will have to tell me that little secret herself?" He gave me wicked grin and I couldn't help but laugh near-silently to myself. Despise was too shallow a word for what I felt regarding these *ridiculous* warring emotions.

Kieran hesitantly took a sip of water, then breathed, "Kieran. My name is Kieran."

Alarm flashed across Sylver's features as he walked towards me, eyes widening with what I could only assume was fear or shock—maybe a bit of both. He exhaled and questioned offhandedly, "Kieran…as in the guy that took over Sin's Forum a few years ago over in Neosordess?"

It was an effort to contain my shock.

Sylver had heard of *Kieran*—a random, albeit pretty man from Neosordess who had killed a couple to steal power for himself—yet he didn't know who *the Moira* was?

I blinked, completely beside myself.

When Sylver went to pass me the glass, he let our hands graze ever so slightly. Rough calluses greeted my own unblemished hands, and I opened my mouth to ask him what exactly he did, but—

"Yes, that's *exactly* who I am." Kieran took a deeper sip of his water then continued, "To be frank, I didn't think my reputation would reach this far out here." Him and I both. He was trying to joke about it, but no humour shone as he spoke.

Sylver didn't turn to face Kieran. He instead remained staring at me; confusion and dread soiling his happy features. I merely took a mouthful of water and swallowed. I seriously couldn't care what Kieran's past alluded to.

He was most likely my salvation.

"We'll be leaving first thing in the morning, so if my presence *offends* you, it should please you that we'll only be here temporarily. Unless you want us both to leave now?" Kieran pushed past Sylver to reach the small prep area and returned his glass before coming to the cot across from me to lie down.

Sylver exhaled through his teeth then replied, "It's fine. I'll bring you guys some food after I help Waha to bed." He went to Waha who was still sitting in front of the hearth, sleeping by the look of it, and bent over him momentarily so he could heft him up into his arms and carry him to the large bed adorning the space to the hearth's left.

With Sylver out of earshot of both Kieran and me, I whispered into the space between the two cots, "I think I know why my flicker led us here."

"Besides it trying to keep us alive?"

"Yes."

Kieran shifted so he leaned towards me then asked, "What then?"

I glanced across the room to where Sylver was helping Waha to bed, then nodded, "Him."

"Sylver? Why would the flicker want him?" Kieran huffed on a quiet laugh, "Or did you just want to drag him along for the ride? You don't have to make excuses—I get it. I wouldn't blame you if that's the case…"

"Why don't you ask him yourself what he's doing here with Waha, and maybe you'll figure that out on your own, because you're *wrong*." Even as I interrupted him, I couldn't help but sneak yet another glance Sylver's way. I muttered, "He has calluses, so he isn't just…" I let my voice trail off as I studied the stranger, taking another swig from the glass.

The man truly was a marvel to look at. His pale attire clung to his muscled frame, accentuating his…I tore my eyes away from his toned buttocks as he began his trek to the kitchen and back to the quilts adorning the cots Kieran and I sat upon. Torn and faded burgundy and mustard fabric was strewn about, and it was an effort to not act disgusted as I examined them, but it was still better than staring at the gorgeous man not thirty feet away.

"I don't want to talk to him. I can tell he already has a not-so-good opinion of me, so I think you'd probably get more information from him than I would." Kieran groaned. "Just let me know what's going on. The sooner I can get where I want to be, the better."

I nodded my agreement, not really hearing what he'd said, before murmuring, "I'll do what needs to be done." From the corner of my eye, I noticed that Sylver had finished grabbing us whatever he had prepared for us to eat, so I breathed, "We'll discuss this later."

Kieran only gave me a terse nod before flipping back the other way towards the wall.

"I made this for the two of us earlier today." Sylver approached, food-in-hand. "It's not much, only some of the food I could scrounge up out there." He indicated the desert with his head, then continued, "We weren't expecting company, so I hope this works for you two."

He leaned in towards me, passing me a plate of what looked to be beans and some other green stuff I couldn't quite make out. Then, after giving me yet another extravagant smile, he quickly placed a plate on the ground beside Kieran's cot. Damn—he must have *really* disliked Kieran.

"Thank you for…" I paused, incapable of stopping myself as I bit into the beans. I savoured the feeling of a real meal in my mouth. All the time I'd spent travelling meant I couldn't exactly enjoy a good homecooked meal.

Sylver chuckled, watching me eat. "Is it really that good?"

I moaned as I bit into what I assumed to be squash. "You have *no* idea."

"If you want," He hesitated as I moaned again, biting into yet another appetizer on the plate, "we can go to the kitchen, so you don't disturb Kieran while he's trying to sleep."

I glanced up for a moment to Sylver, then nodded as I noticed him staring at the plate that was already more than halfway done on my lap.

I didn't bother finishing what remained before standing up. Only too late did I notice that Sylver was too close to my cot for there to be enough room for both of us to stand—hemmed in place, my chest brushed against his and my plate nearly toppled over. He placed his hands on my shoulders, and effortlessly, as if dancing, spun me around so that both the food wouldn't spill and so that I'd be able to leave the space first. His hands swallowed my shoulders entirely and I gulped.

"Ladies first," he said from behind me.

That was the second time he'd said that to me.

Little did he know that I wasn't a "lady" at all—a *disgrace*, would be a lot more accurate.

Keeping all of my surprise secret was still a necessity. Even though I wasn't in agreement with the title, *lady*, I couldn't have him treating me like some of the other men I'd met if instead they were in his shoes. I'd somehow managed to find myself situated with the sole exceptions of this bullshit society. I kept my head high as I walked into the little preparation area with Sylver before inquiring, "So, how exactly did you end up with Waha?"

Sylver didn't resemble the man in the least, instead looking rather out place in the desert setting, while Waha seemed to live and breathe the tranquillity of the landscape. He was gifted with the darker skin of the locals, preventing him (mostly) from being burnt by the sun.

"Well," He reached into a basket of sorts that contained what looked to be dry goods, then continued, "several years back, Waha saved me after I spent just over two days in the desert without water." He chuckled, and his laugh…it almost sounded familiar. I couldn't place where it resonated in my memory, but I swore on my existence that I'd heard it somewhere before.

I was either losing my mind or I was *severely* dehydrated.

Pinching the skin on my hand, I watched as it held its form even after I'd removed my thumb and pointer finger. I exhaled slowly.

Dehydration then—it had to be that.

"Why did you decide to stay with Waha?" I asked.

Sylver twisted to look at me after putting some more food on my plate, appearing confused with my question.

I elaborated. "I mean, he's not a relative and you're not ethically forced to—"

"Let me stop you there." He interrupted me. "I didn't take you to be a heartless one there, Moira." He handed me the plate, then leaned back against the prep area with one arm, muscles taut with the movement. "I stayed with him because he *saved* my life, and I was grateful." Grateful? I couldn't relate—Salvador, despite saving my life, did *nothing* to earn my thanks…hell, after he'd kept me captive for just over three months once he'd caught those men with me—I still couldn't decide who I hated more. Admittedly, sometimes I wish that he'd never found me. "Plus, I could see how lonely he was out here with no one to help him out." Sylver pushed himself off the ledge, and stared into my eyes as he whispered, "No one ever wants to be completely alone."

I nodded at his words before I swallowed, "Were you alone too? Out in the desert, I mean?"

How could he be lonely? If he was lonely, it could only be by choice. With his rugged face and gray eyes that resembled not only the gleaming of coins I'd noticed at first glance, but also a pool of still water at twilight…anyone would desire him.

Except me.

"I tried to be with someone once. Long ago." Sylver shook his head at the memory, causing hair to fall into his face again. "It was short-lived, but I wouldn't take a second of it back." His response startled me.

"What happened?" Why wasn't he be able to obtain what he wanted? It wasn't like he had anything holding him back. My stomach twisted—what chance did I really have?

Sylver blew out a long breath before asking, "Do you want to go outside so we can sit and talk without waking anyone?" He glanced behind me back to both Kieran and Waha who were seemingly passed out in their designated locations.

My flicker let a whisper of fire caress my neck, and I understood what it wanted from me—never *mind* the fact that I had no idea who this stranger was in the middle of the *fucking* desert…

It couldn't care if it was directly responsible for my death.

Gift indeed.

Blatantly ignoring any self-preservation instinct I possessed, I dipped my chin and gave Sylver a quiet smile. I couldn't quite bring myself to care that I hadn't eaten any of the food he'd just prepared for me. *Although,* there was a part of me that was half-tempted to carry the plate outside…I decided against it. His smouldering eyes left me bare, stealing away my appetite and any qualms I could have against him.

What the fuck was wrong with me? My little dancer twirled, thrilled to finally be in his midst, free of prying eyes, and I felt the coiling of its flames around my core. A comforting warmth settled within me, and I couldn't help but ease into it. I'd never felt like this for anyone before.

My flicker silently mouthed an oeuvre of beautiful thoughts and imaginings over my lower abdomen, and I shuddered as I watched Sylver bridge the space between us, returning my plate. I noted the flutter of his eyelashes and the part of his lips, and I had to turn away.

For the first time in five years, despite leading so many men to their desires, I could almost understand why so many yearned for lust or even love. I could understand lust as I peeked and watched Sylver's muscled form hover over the sink. But even so, love had always been a foolish desire to me. I'd always thought others weak for it.

My experience had demonstrated love to be a fickle, imaginary entity that never lasted. But despite that, people still chose to fight for it. People still chose to unite together and to war with each other over the mere concept of love. People still chose to desire "love" despite never possessing any material evidence of its existence.

I couldn't ever desire something so…fleeting.

But I supposed that that thought alone was one typical of my immortality.

Sylver led the way out of the keep, tiptoeing through the space so both Kieran and Waha could remain peacefully asleep. We exited, the moonlight greeting us as we rounded its other side.

Palm trees were scattered all around, breaking through the monotony of the endless sand, framing what looked to be a pond where one could cool off during a hot desert day. The lights from within the keep just touched the surface of the calm water, making it glisten and twinkle as the water rippled with the occasional breeze. It seemed like it was plucked from a dream.

Sylver smiled at what I was sure was awe stretched across my features.

I smiled back.

My little dancer now dawdled on my skin, casually waltzing, probably enjoying the serenity of it all for once, instead of trying to burn me alive to prove a point.

Sylver held out a hand, an offering for me to hold it as he led me to a bench not too far away overlooking the pond, under another couple of palm fronds.

I took it.

It was the first time I'd ever held someone's hand to just *hold* it.

Granted, I'd held the hands of men before; however, as his warm, calloused hand interlaced and engulfed my own, I wanted *more*.

So different from Salvador's as he yanked me free from the cage he'd delightfully imprisoned me in...or those from the beasts of men that had chosen to maul me when I'd first arrived here.

What was *wrong* with me? I never wanted something more than to go back home. *Was* there something wrong with me? I casually brought my free hand up to wipe my forehead. I didn't seem to be dying...

Or was this simply how life was like when you didn't spend every waking hour trying and *failing* to go back to something you couldn't even remember?

Everything I'd loved had been stolen from me, and I wasn't even capable of remembering anything that I'd lost. Memories were shrouded, hidden from my mind's eye. I was only an empty vessel, void of the pleasure I'd once been able to wield so freely, yearning to return to those feelings. Perhaps those intangible, fading memories of feeling *something* were as close as I'd ever get to my home now.

It didn't matter. Nothing else mattered right at this moment.

It seemed my flicker was *finally* giving me a gift; allowing me to reach my own conclusions about what I actually wanted without the added pressure of always hunting for someone else's desires. Maybe it truly believed there was a chance I would never find someone whose true desire aligned with my own deepest wish…pitying my fruitless attempts.

With a blink, I shut out the intrusive thoughts.

Maybe I *could* want this instead.

Maybe I could allow myself to want this; something that so many people had come to me desiring so badly.

Maybe I could finally be happy—satisfied—for the first time in at least five years.

I gazed up at Sylver while we were walking, and noticed he was shyly smiling down at me.

Could it really be this easy?

I'd spent five years in search of a ghost—my home—and I could have…and I could have had Sylver, or someone like him all along. After all, if I had been okay chasing a home—a paradise—no one in their right mind would actually believe existed…

Was love so different?

Was it so different for so many others to desire something that, to me, didn't really exist?

Maybe I wouldn't have had to suffer so long if I'd noted the parallel earlier.

No, *no*. But I would have. Mourning the loss of my home would have brought forth the worst kind of suffering. And my home *did* exist…just maybe not here.

I had to turn my head away to blink back the tears limning my eyes.

"What are you thinking about?" Sylver's voice lulled my thoughts, and I laughed half-heartedly, brushing away a stray tear.

"How nice this is," I said. I released his grasp to indicate the wonderful scene unfolding around me, before continuing, "and how nice you are." I omitted the other more depressing ideas as I sat down on the bench and looked to the pond now ahead of us.

I heard Sylver as he approached the bench and sat down beside me. He didn't speak right away, so I glanced up at him from the corner of my eye and noticed that he, like me, was looking at the water as it peacefully rippled, reflecting the light from both the keep and the moon above us.

His hair glistened in the moonlight, casting his face in shadow as it hung just to the collar of his blanched robe. He chuckled after a minute, then said, "It is beautiful." Sylver turned to me and whispered, "But this," He gestured to the palms and the pond and the moon high above us, "none of it will ever compare to how special you are."

My little dancer fawned at the compliment, and it forced a blush to my cheeks, a grin to my mouth…before I remembered haphazardly what I'd told Kieran—I still had questions to ask of Sylver. I wiped the fool's smile off my face entirely before asking, "So, what do you do here exactly? You say that Waha took you in, right?"

"Well, the only reason why Waha even found me in the first place is because he's a desert guide. He decided to be my mentor the day when I told him that I'd wanted to help him out around the keep."

A guide. *That* was why my flicker wanted him with us.

So Sylver wasn't just a gift for my own sake…if he could even be considered that.

"I also help out in the shop. Waha's a merchant too." Sylver chortled. "He takes advantage of the fact that people are usually really desperate when they're this far out in the desert and makes a living off of it."

"So basically," I chuckled, "he takes advantage of people like us, who are stupid enough to wander off into the desert without any background in how to survive it."

"Yep."

Sounded about right.

I slapped his leg in jest, "Maybe I should go back inside. You don't seem like such a "nice" guy after all."

He smirked. "I can't blame you for the mistake. We've only known each other now for..." He paused, acting as if he was in deep thought before beginning to count using his fingers. "Maybe an hour or two?"

I laughed again and watched the stars gazing down at us from the sky. It was hard to believe I had been with Qasir not even a week ago, when happiness was such a foreign thought. The slur he had used to shame me in his final minute rattled through me: *oath breaker*.

I didn't care; I still deserved joy in my miserable life. Breaking one damned oath five years ago shouldn't have been enough to condemn me to a life of suffering. It hadn't even been my choice to leave Laspiar.

I'd returned my gaze to the rippling water sparkling before me when Sylver whispered, "How long have the two of you been travelling together for?" He waited, and before I could respond asked, "You two aren't together, are you? I mean..." He huffed, frustrated, then quit trying to clarify himself.

I laughed quietly. "Kieran and I have been travelling together for just over two days. Myself on the other hand, I've been travelling for just over four weeks straight now. So, no. We aren't together."

Sylver practically bowed over with relief. "You have no idea how happy I am to hear you say that." I looked up to see that he was still grinning at me.

No one had ever...no one had ever been interested in me before. They had only ever been interested in what I could offer them or in how I could serve them. I didn't quite realize just how pathetic I'd let myself become over the years out of sheer desperation.

He began laughing as he continued, "For a second, I was worried I'd have to face him in the morning." His laughter subsided after a few seconds, and his tone changed to something curious, something wonderful. "If you've been travelling for just over four weeks as you said, why aren't you burnt to a crisp?"

I shrugged. "Sylver, you're assuming that it never gets cloudy. But in earnest, I never seem to burn. I never seem to tan either for that matter." I rolled my eyes. "Everyone always asks me that, but I don't see why it matters."

"You..." He paused, and a bemused gleam suffused his eyes. "You look like you've never seen the sun in your life. To be honest, I thought you were a mole or something."

I snapped, "I could say the same about you. You literally live in the desert, and yet you're just as pale as I am. What does that say about you?"

I expected him to argue the point; however, he just resigned quickly, mumbling, "I guess we're both strange then."

I nodded, then faced the water after a minute. My flicker hadn't quite dissipated from my skin, and its prickling heat was beginning to grate on my nerves. "Can we go in?"

"What?" Sylver sounded shocked at my request. "Are you sure that you want to go in the water right now?"

"Don't you?" I retorted. I stood up from the bench, then glanced over my shoulder back at him. My flickering dancer banked its intensity, but my mind was set. The idea of entering the pond made me shiver, but after two days of nothing but the desert's disgusting heat and my dancer's invisible flames, plus the apparent case of dehydration I was suffering through, I needed to remember the soothing nature of cold water on my body.

I began shrugging off the dress Kieran had given me back in Neosordess and Sylver balked. "What do you plan on wearing in there?" I could have sworn his eyes kindled with their own fire as they trailed my hands with each inch that my flowing gown slid from my shoulders.

It was time for me to pursue some *semblance* of happiness. I owed myself that much after five years of nothing but despair. Lust, love...whatever. I needed to do this. I needed to experience him—*this*. I needed to stop holding myself back as a punishment for something that wasn't even my fault. I couldn't help but let some of my own desire flood my eyes as I mouthed, "Nothing."

His stare followed as I first decided to shuck off the cropped top.

I did it slowly, accentuating each movement, and finally grabbed the elastic beneath my breasts and hoisted it over my head in one smooth maneuver.

Sylver's eyes seemed to smolder; it was as if the ash I'd seen earlier were actually cinders, now yawning awake. He strained against the already tight confines of his pants.

He desired me.

I felt that truth in my little dancer as it sensed his intense need and urged me towards him, searing me when I looked down towards the water for a brief second. It didn't matter that this would be my first time *choosing* to be with someone else. It didn't matter that it would only ever *be* this. I wanted it to be him. I'd been unable to pleasure myself while travelling with Qasir nor with Kieran, and the thought of having him inside me…

His desire was so strong, and it was directed exclusively towards me. It was a heady feeling, but it only made me yearn to strip for him faster. I wanted him.

My breasts hardened, and my inner thighs ached.

I fought against the impulse to launch myself at him, and instead grabbed the hem of my skirt, caressing my hind end, as I asked, "Aren't you coming in with me?" My voice was not my own. It was seductive and coy, and about an octave lower than usual.

Clearly, my body needed the release more than I'd realized.

Sylver swallowed, then rose from the bench before chuckling, "Well, I would be foolish to say no…" He made to take off his flowing white pants, but halted himself, deciding to remove his kaftan instead, revealing his beautiful figure. Sylver's frame wasn't bulky like some of the men I'd seen, but lithe—predatory. I could see that his chest was well-muscled and that those very muscles trailed beneath the fold of his pants.

My mouth went dry, and I could feel a wetness gathering at the apex of my thighs. I dragged my hands down my rear, then brought them up only to pull my skirt off entirely.

He took one stride to reach me from where he was standing before the bench, then cupped my ass with one calloused hand as he brought my face towards his with the other and licked the seam of my mouth in one smooth manoeuvre.

I could feel his hardness pressing against me and I nearly climaxed at the light touch. Opening my mouth fully for him, I sighed as I tasted him for the first time. I brought my hands up from where they had been at my sides and forced his mouth to mine. I let my hands tangle in his hair, scraping my nails over his scalp, and opened my eyes to notice that his hair acted as a veil to shroud us both from the desert around us.

He was smoke, and his scent of burning wood coupled with his taste, was the most enticing thing I'd ever felt. It was more than I could ever do for myself.

Sylver didn't pull away from our kiss as he reached for the pants still preventing us from fusing together as one, when common-sense screamed at me that I didn't even know who he was. I knew his name, but...he was still a *stranger* despite what we *both* wanted.

But I deserved happiness.

I broke from the depth of our kiss to gaze at Sylver under heavy lids, and breathed, "Just sex."

I couldn't have, nor did I *want* a relationship with this man.

Love was still a waste of time.

I just wanted—*craved* the release that was sure to come if we continued down this path.

Sylver paused his hands on his pants and stood straight, stepping out of my embrace. His eyes, which only seconds ago were alive with flame, extinguished entirely.

No.

I needed this.

I threw my arms around the back of Sylver's neck and forced my lips to meet his once more...but he didn't kiss me back. I tried bucking my hips against his, and where I could previously feel him yearning for us to join, there was nothing.

No.

I took a step back, then rubbed my hands through my hair.

Why could I never get what I wanted?

He gave me a half-suppressed grin. "It's getting pretty late. We should probably head to bed if you're to take off again tomorrow." Sylver's voice was upbeat, unnaturally so, and he stalked back to the keep, leaving me naked and alone under the palm fronds.

I watched as his muscled silhouette disappeared around the corner of the keep, and only then did I notice how chilly the desert could become at night. The heat of my own desire and the taste of warmth, his scent an amalgamation of burning wood and smoke, must have been what was responsible for staving off the freezing temperature. A desert wind ruffled my now a strewn hair.

A ghostly ice swept over me, replacing the dancing flame I'd grown accustomed to, and it became clear just how much of a fool I'd made of myself. *Fucking pathetic.*

Shivering, I quickly donned my dress before trudging after Sylver, savoring the idea of the keep's hearth after being left so…cold.

I knew that he'd wanted me, but he'd rejected what I'd so willingly offered him.

Fucking *archaic*.

So be it. I was destined to always be alone.

Chapter 9

Moira

I DIDN'T SPEAK TO SYLVER once after that.

It was morning now—the sun had just crested over the dunes east of the keep, and despite its beauty, I couldn't enjoy it. I'd even taken it upon myself to eat some of the food Sylver had told us we could eat in order to perhaps lift my spirits, but it only tasted of ash in my mouth.

Kieran gestured to both me and Sylver with the fork. "Did something happen between you two last night?" He whispered this to me near-silently as Sylver helped Waha get dressed for the day at the other side of the keep.

I snapped, "What does it matter to *you*?"

"So," he murmured, "something did." Kieran bit into his food, then mumbled, "Interesting."

I ignored him.

It was none of his business if I'd tried and subsequently failed to have sex with Sylver last night. I already knew I was stupid. More than ready to throw away so much just because of a teensy bit of lust—I didn't need a man like Kieran rubbing it in. A man who was soon to get everything he wanted, leaving me alone and hopeless once again.

I stabbed into the green pile of shit on my plate without looking up and took another bite.

"Did you at least get anything useful out of him?" Kieran used his fork yet again to casually point in Sylver's direction as he finished swallowing whatever had been on there prior.

Perfect, caring Sylver, who thought having a one-night stand was below him.

Whatever.

I sighed. "I guess I did." Speaking was hard; I wanted to forget about Sylver altogether and just move on from the utter embarrassment of last night. My flicker scorched my spine in response to that particular thought, so…fine. That wasn't an option. Not yet anyway.

Kieran flicked my hand with a finger to catch my attention and dipped his chin almost as if to say, *Continue please.*

For fuck's sake, I didn't want to do that. Besides, whenever I tried speaking, I swore I could still taste the remnants of Sylver's smoke and fire in my mouth. But I diligently forced myself to swallow past his lingering aftertaste as I spoke, "He's a desert guide. I guess he'll keep us from dying out there." I glanced up from my plate to watch Sylver, who was just finishing up whatever he was doing with Waha.

"So, he *is* useful," Kieran mused. "I should really give 'burning desire' some more credit." He chuckled to himself, then wiped at his mouth with a napkin. "Don't worry, you won't have to talk to him."

Whatever.

Even if Kieran was doing me a small favor, it didn't mean I had to acknowledge it. I didn't have to acknowledge shit if I didn't want to. I was doing him perhaps the greatest favor anyone could ask for: finding him what it was he desired most at my expense.

I rolled my eyes as he stood up from his cot in a fluid movement and crossed the space to Sylver. Kieran nodded to the old man, who still held a vacant smile on his face, then decreed just as any ruler would, "When we leave today, you're coming with us."

I could see Sylver sneer as he said, "Waha? He can't go."

"You're right." Kieran's grin was nothing short of grotesque. "Waha won't be coming with us. *You* will be." There was no room in his tone for insincerity.

"Yeah, sure I am." Sylver glanced to me quickly, then returned his gaze to Kieran. "You may have held some power back in Neosordess, but out here in the desert, you're just like every other man."

Kieran's voice turned quiet as he spoke. "But I'm not like *every other man*, and I never will be."

I stared down at the food on my lap for only a second, before shoving the plate aside onto the quilts folded on the cot beside me. I didn't have the appetite to finish what was left.

But at least I was fed.

Another second passed, and I heard Sylver exhort, "You can't do this."

"Oh, but I can."

I glanced up to find Kieran with a blade drawn on Waha's throat.

I hadn't even heard him *move*.

His grace last night had made me uneasy for a reason...apparently.

My legs moved of their own accord as I rose from my cot. "You've crossed a line." I glared across the space to Kieran, who only cocked his head to the side and responded,

"Moira." He paused, then continued, "I'm not quite the person you thought me to be, am I?" He still kept his eyes fastened on me even though he spoke to Sylver. "All you have to do to prevent Waha's demise, is come with us as we continue our journey through the desert. That's it. Then you can venture right back here and live your life as it was."

Sylver spit. "You aren't exactly known for being a man of your word, so how can I trust you?"

"A man of my word? Well Sylver, one of two things will happen whether you trust me or not. Trust me and help us out there," He nodded to the door, "or you can be a fool and have me kill Waha before knocking you unconscious and having you help us out there anyways."

Sylver's face became lined with hatred as he said, "But, I can't leave him." He shifted his gaze to me, and his eyes locked on mine, pleading for me to help.

I started, "Kieran, how will Waha care for himself—"

"I can look after myself just fine!" Waha interrupted. He poked a finger out towards Sylver. "Just because I've let you help me out for the past five years doesn't mean I'm useless." The fragility lacing each of his words, fearless as they were, was not very reassuring.

I could see tears begin to well up in Sylver's eyes. "I can't just leave you." Resignation. I fought the urge to roll my eyes. Considering the words he'd uttered the night before regarding how grateful he was to Waha for saving his life…I expected more of a fight from him.

Kieran's blade was still outstretched towards Waha, but his eyes lacked the pride one would come to expect in a man content with his actions. Somewhere in his heart, somewhere beneath his callous and cruel front, perhaps there was a slim chance he realized that this was wrong.

"You can't do this Kieran." I stared daggers into his eyes as they gradually shifted back to me. Sylver kneeled down in front of Waha and began whispering to him while I continued. "I can see that you don't want to do this. You're—"

"Listen now Moira. *You* have no idea who I am nor what I want." Kieran's hiss was venomous as he spoke. His eyes no longer showed any sign of remorse.

Maybe I was wrong.

Maybe my flicker was *wrong* for helping out such a heartless man. But if it meant I was able to return…

Sylver asked, "How long do I have?"

Again, Kieran didn't tear his gaze from me as he stated, "Moira and I should be ready to head out in about an hour. Pack what we'll need to bring for at least a week." He must've figured that he would forever be the ruler he'd been back in Neosordess; giving out orders as if he knew better.

"Actually, it could be closer to two or three weeks, so pack expecting the worst." I gave Sylver a small, trivial smile, then rubbed at my face.

It was probably going to be a matter of weeks to our location one way if Kieran's guess was any indication…and it would be at least double that before Sylver could possibly see Waha again.

The old man would most likely be dead by then.

Sylver bent down to talk to Waha again, and I could only glare at Kieran. I knew it was *my* flicker that insisted we bring him, but it didn't have to be done like this.

Kieran still stood with the blade within striking distance of Waha's throat, but he lowered it as Sylver said, "Yes. I'll do it. Just don't harm him." Tears were freely streaming down Sylver's face as he let go of Waha's hand.

I didn't realize he'd even been holding it. I had to turn away from the whole image. Back home I would have never dealt with shit like this. When I thought of my home, only the feelings of peace and longing seemed to burble up inside of me.

But *this* feeling was more akin to dread—*guilt*.

Guilt had often haunted me these past years. Men speaking tongues I couldn't comprehend sniggering as they spread my legs—

"Do you have a problem with the way I do business, Moira?" Kieran's voice echoed through the space, now home to an air of bleak, hopeless, silence, and I heard his footsteps approach my left side.

I punched him in the jaw.

Or at least I would have if he didn't have his freakishly fast reflexes. My fist was on track to hit him directly on the dimple of his chin—a sure way to make him go unconscious—but miraculously Kieran sidestepped it and did a manoeuvre that somehow led to me landing chest-first on the sandstone floor.

"Moira—"

"Don't be so dramatic. She's fine." Kieran said while pressing me into the rock beneath with a knee.

Breathing became difficult.

I choked, "I am…fine." It was my own ridiculous impulses that had brought me to this low point anyways. Besides, there was no need in making the situation any worse for Sylver. Better that he just focussed on Waha and his needs—

Then, just like that, I was free.

Obviously, Kieran had believed he'd proven his point and released me of his own volition. I rose onto my elbows, coughing, then turned my gaze upwards.

Fuck me.

Sylver had thrown Kieran off me and was currently sparring with him on the ground not a few feet away. Did he seriously think it was worth it to risk Waha for me?

He didn't even *know* me.

If he'd only known the truth about me; about everything I'd done and everyone I'd failed. He would regret this. I was a pathetic waste of breath, just as Qasir had said. It would be an overstatement to describe myself as a shell of the entity I once was. *Oath breaker*. Even last night. I'd practically broken an oath that I'd made to myself after Salvador found me: to never lose sight of my only goal…and yet, human hormones nearly wrecked that one too.

Waha and I could only watch the chaos unfold. Both men were close to a head taller than me, and Waha was just too broken as it was to stand a fighting chance even if he tried to act exclusively as a mediator.

Sylver threw a wild swing into Kieran's torso, forcing Kieran to bow forward with the impact. He went to deal him another blow to knock him down, but Kieran feinted away, dodging the punch, and dropped to the ground before sweeping a foot at one of Sylver's ankles, causing Sylver to fall flat on his ass. Kieran then continued the sweep in a fluid spinning motion and landed on his feet before drawing his blade and pointing it at Sylver, who was still in the midst trying to stand up.

I had no idea how Kieran could be so *good*.

Panic lit Sylver's ashen eyes. He'd already shattered his promise to Kieran.

Relatable.

Kieran sneered, a lupine smile blossoming on his full mouth. "Looks like *I'm* not the one who can't be trusted..."

"Please...don't." I begged. I couldn't let Kieran do this.

"Moira, I'm not going to punish Sylver for being a decent guy. It wasn't as if he tried to attack me unprovoked like the last guy you were with." Kieran sheathed his blade, then cast a kinder smile at me. "There might still be hope for you two after all."

Sylver, still on the ground, just lay there as Kieran turned on his heel back to the cot.

I took a step to where Sylver lay sprawled on the ground.

"Thank you, Moira," he breathed. "I-I—"

"I should be thanking *you*." I faltered. "You came to my rescue. Not many people would do that for me."

"I could be saying the same to you." Sylver pushed himself off the floor, then rose to his feet.

In the light, I glimpsed a now bloody lip from the brawl, and an eyebrow that was already beginning to swell. I didn't even realize he'd been hit. "You should put some ice on that," I said, inclining my head to let him know I meant his face, and he gave me a grim smile in return.

"We're in the middle of the desert, Moira."

Right.

I had to be the biggest idiot.

Sylver continued, "But besides that little fact, I think it would be best to spend my remaining time packing and getting Waha ready for the next little bit." Sylver went to walk away, but he stopped himself before saying, "I really mean it though; thank you for trying to prevent this...*kidnapping*."

He had no clue that I was the one behind it.

I was practically a honey trap.

I gave a terse bob of the head, then went back to the cot so I could try to forget just how horrid a person I was. I plopped down on the cot beside Kieran's and put my hands over my eyes. Perhaps my flicker would be generous and do me a favor and scorch away the cacophony of my thoughts. Burning alive would be better than this. I missed being numb to everything.

I whispered, "You already know what to do, just make it quick."

"Is "burning desire" needing a target again?" I could hear Kieran chuckle as he sat on his cot across from me. "Just let me know when you're ready." How could he be so cheery after he just condemned Waha to death?

Perhaps he was only being considerate because I was a means to an end for him. That was all I'd ever seemed to be. I grumbled, "Now. Do it."

The pain in my spine radiated forward into my chest and I sighed as the pain brought me to the edge of darkness. My little dancer numbed my senses, and I silently thanked it as I opened my eyes. I sat back up on the cot and looked first north towards the oasis with no luck; sharp pain leaked through, fracturing its soothing, dulling façade. I then shifted counterclockwise until I faced west, where the pain subsided into nothing but a caress.

I inclined my head to the wall. "We continue our path westward until I'm told to do otherwise." I closed my eyes again and eased myself into the quilts. I was a horrible person; I was just as responsible for Waha's inevitable death as was Kieran.

Whatever. I would be home soon enough if my little flicker was to be believed, and there...there I would no longer have to worry about the mistakes I'd made these last five years—just the one I'd made upon leaving. Involuntarily or no.

"Sounds good to me. Don't fall asleep for too long, we're going to be leaving sooner than you might think." I heard the creak as Kieran rose from his cot, then the sound of his footsteps as he went somewhere else in the keep.

I didn't want to think about anything; I just wanted to forget about *everything*.

It will all be worth it once we're back home, I thought to myself.

I repeated this prayer over and over in my head until I became settled enough to finally fall asleep yet again.

Chapter 10

Moira

THE THREE OF US HAD BEEN WALKING westward for what seemed to be forever, but only now was the sky beginning to shift to its nighttime equivalent. Kieran's voice was the first to crack through the very heavy silence that began upon abandoning Waha at the keep. "We should camp here for the night."

The dune we were perched upon wasn't anything special, but it would do until morning.

Sylver didn't bother agreeing, he only dropped the heavy backpack he'd been wearing since we left and went to the side of the hill to relieve himself.

I hadn't watched Sylver much while we were walking; I was too afraid I'd see him crying as he had when he'd told Waha that he loved him, probably for the last time. Tears made his feathered hair cling to his face, and he didn't even bother wiping them away.

I hated it here.

"Why do you seem so depressed?" Kieran asked as he shucked off his bag and began preparing the sleeping bags for all of us. "It isn't like—"

"You just left him to die."

"And why do you care all of a sudden? Funny, I didn't take you for one to actually be considerate of others besides yourself." He barked a cruel laugh. "You're selfish. Isn't that why one of the first things you told me about your gift is that *you* don't actually benefit from it?" He paused. "Someone that actually gave a shit would have been content with helping others."

The fucking nerve. "You're one to talk!" I was yelling now. "You're just a fucking hypocrite. Do as you say, but not as you do?! I might be selfish, but you," I cast him a withering glare, "you're a tyrant. How can you expect me to be okay with what you did back there?!"

"I don't expect you to be *okay* with it, but you know that it had to be done." He hesitated. "And how exactly am I a hypocrite, Moira? I never told you to do anything. In fact, you offered your services to me if I remember correctly. If you're going to insult me, at least do a good job."

Sylver came back over the dune and demanded of us both, "What the fuck is going on now?"

"Oh," Kieran sneered, "just getting into it with the sanctimonious cunt over there."

He jerked his chin at me, before Sylver growled, "How dare you—"

Kieran laughed again, cutting off whatever Sylver was about to say. "Did you finally grow a pair of balls over there Sylver while you were taking a piss? You wouldn't even bother fighting me when you knew that Waha would be dead either way. You only bothered when you thought that she," Another nod my way, "was going to get hurt. You're just as selfish as your girlfriend over there, and a coward. But thankfully, you serve a purpose, otherwise I'd have killed both you and the old man already."

Cinders came alight once more as Sylver snarled, "I've never been a coward." He pointed his finger at Kieran. "You're the coward; needing to abuse women in order to feel tough." His face contorted with revulsion. "That's *real* manly of you."

"You don't know anything." Kieran spat this at Sylver before stripping off his weapons belt, slinging it into the sand before him. "About Moira, myself, or our little arrangement." Kieran spun and grabbed a swig of water from one of the leather-skins we'd brought with us upon our departure.

That was when Sylver moved.

He didn't announce the attack. Bolting on soundless feet to where Kieran had thrown his blade, Sylver seized it, then swung downward on Kieran, who was still bent over, now returning the flask to where it had been in his backpack.

One second, Kieran was bowed over.

The next, a banshee's cursed baying clawed its way out of Kieran's throat and his back...

It was home to the most horrid injury I'd ever beheld. The blade had sliced clean through Kieran's trench coat, carving him at his right shoulder before transecting his back down to his left hip. I could see the off-white shade of his ribs poking out through the torn fabric.

Kieran wobbled, shifting to us as if he'd fight the traitor who'd maimed him, but fell promptly and landed face first on the sac he'd been carrying the entirety of the day.

I screamed, nauseated as I watched Kieran's bones rise and fall with each breath. *"WHAT THE FUCK ARE YOU DOING?!"* I was going to vomit.

Sylver twisted towards me and dropped Kieran's blade.

The quicksilver of the sword had become marred by the blood that now dripped from its edge into the sand, and I gagged as it stained the once golden earth. I ripped my eyes away from the weapon and saw Sylver sprint the last few feet to me.

"Let's leave. Now." Sylver made to clasp my skirt, but I jumped back before he could touch me.

I hissed, "Why do you think I would ever follow you now?"

"Because," Sylver breathed, the coal in his eyes aflame with victory, "I was saving us. Now you're safe and I can go back home and return to Waha, and you can stay with us." His voice was bright and cheery with the hope of returning to his home.

If my flicker was doing me a service for once, Kieran was probably my first, my last, and my only chance of ever returning to *my* home. Or at *least* that was the desire I pleaded to any and every deity I could ever think of. Kieran had to be different—I wasn't sure how much longer I could fight otherwise.

"I can't." I rushed past Sylver and leaned down beside Kieran.

If I didn't help him soon, he'd lose too much blood—it was already seeping through his jacket, gleaming in the moonlight.

"What do you mean, you can't?" Sylver tried to pull me away from Kieran's limp body, but I fought against his touch. Kieran's body still rose and fell, but it was becoming more strained. He needed me to help him, *now*.

"Because Kieran might be my only way back home." I could feel Sylver take a step back, so I continued, trying to staunch the blood flow with a palm. "It wasn't him who wanted you to come with us…it was me." I gazed over my shoulder to see shock stiffen Sylver, replacing the hope that had been on his face only seconds before. I whispered into the gap widening between us, "I'm the reason Waha was sentenced to die, not Kieran."

Sylver started, "But—"

"Kieran was using me, like everyone else does, to get whatever it was he desired most." I sighed. "I'm the reason this has happened to you. I'm more of a monster than he is." The tang of his blood was overwhelming.

I returned to Kieran's injury and took a deep breath.

My hand alone wasn't enough to keep his death at bay, I'd have to remove his coat so I could get a grasp of how bad the injury was. I'd seen some ribs, but the back—anatomically, it was one of the best places he could have been struck.

Kieran's gaze flicked, dazed towards me and he groaned something unintelligible as I used all my strength to flip him onto his side. I couldn't bring myself to bother with niceties as I began unbuttoning his trench coat. My thighs pinned him still in that position, and I prayed it would be enough to keep him from falling over. Urgh. I growled. I didn't agree to deal with all of this unnecessary bullshit.

And I still didn't understand why he would wear such heavy, dark material in the middle of the desert. Whatever. It wasn't my call to tell him what he could wear, despite what I'd said to him a couple days ago.

I cast the thought away—a distraction on my behalf could very well lead to Kieran bleeding out. I was such an *idiot*. But so were both of the men that led to this fucking scenario. Typical that I was left to clean up their mess.

I tore at the buttons holding his sticky trench coat in place. He *needed* to survive. One button. Two buttons. Three buttons. About half-way down, I went to undo his belt, and it came to my attention that he was also wearing some sort of a white wrap underneath. Why did he have to wear even *more* unnecessary clothing?

That would have to come off too.

I stripped the coat from his torso, then carefully slid his arms out of the sleeves so that only his white undershirt was left.

I checked his back and peeled back the gauzy material which clung to his body as a result of the blood loss. I gagged. But he was still bleeding—and breathing. He was still *alive*. There was still hope for me.

My hands became red, blood dripping from them as I made to turn him back over so I could remove the remaining fabric. He had already lost *so* much blood. I fought back shaking as I took in his wound in its entirety. Sinew and bone and blood.

It didn't matter, Kieran *had* to survive. I would accept no other alternative.

Kieran was unconscious when I finally peeled the lingering fabric from his body.

I gasped, then jumped backwards at the sight.

"Don't tell me he's dead already," Sylver mumbled from where he stood beside his bag.

I couldn't believe my eyes.

How was that even possible?

"Kieran is…"

A violent shake rattled through me..

How could I be so fucking ignorant to miss something so obvious?

I exhaled deeply in an attempt to regain both control of my body and of my surroundings, before breathing, "Kieran is a *woman*."

Chapter 11

Alterra

HE HELD ME IN HIS ARMS *and inhaled the scent of my hair as we lay together under my favorite rowan tree. Orange and red berries hung from each of the tree's branches, which now bowed low—no doubt a result of their impressive weight this time of year.*

I dragged my hand through the moss just under my fingertips, gripping a red berry that had fallen there, and breathed, "I love you; more than you'll ever know." I twisted my head over a shoulder so I could look into his eyes.

Storm clouds. They always reminded me of storm clouds.

Those eyes sparked with amusement as he flicked my nose. "Are you so ready to doubt my intellect, Alterra darling?"

I laughed before facing him entirely and popped the berry into my mouth.

"Aren't those berries only good in jams?"

"Well, that depends..." I tore my gaze away from his incredulous eyes for a mere second to search for another berry that was to my liking. "This one here," I picked up a particularly red one from the moss, its equivalent the shade of only the deepest ruby, "might prove to be something great. Or perhaps it will prove itself to be a bit off. Dare to be adventurous for once and see for yourself what you're missing?"

He rolled his eyes, chuckling. "For once? Alterra, I am the very definition of adventure."

I sighed, "Of course you are." and rolled my eyes back for him to see. I waited, silently counting the seconds until he asked,

"May I please," He batted his eyelashes at me, "have the rowan berry now?"

"Sure." I didn't hesitate as I plopped the berry into his outstretched palm and he folded his calloused hand around mine, holding me there. "Don't dawdle." I slid my hand from his grasp and scooted a good two feet away from his warmth for good measure. "Just try it, and maybe you'll like it."

He threw the jewel-coloured berry into the air just above his mouth and let it land on his awaiting tongue before biting down. His face contorted and he began coughing, spitting out the seedy core.

"It can't be that bad," I mumbled.

He pretended to claw at his tongue to scrape off the rest of the berry that lingered, and I laughed, my mouth parting as I leaned in to kiss him, stealing away whatever taste remained.

It was disgusting, bitter, rancid. I made to break away from the horrid taste of his mouth, but he held me there, forcing me to endure the experience I'd unwittingly bestowed upon him. But still, I savoured the kiss.

He was my angel.

With hair and skin that glowed with an inner warmth, and his body...sculpted, smooth, agile. When I'd first caught sight of him, he'd reminded me of a lone statue I'd seen years ago of one of our old gods. And his voice. Silky, with the slightest accent that only made him more...perfect.

I spoke around the kiss. "So maybe," I swallowed, "there's a slim chance that that was a bad one."

He only chuckled as he continued to torture me with the over-ripe flavour of the berry that coated his tongue.

Only after minutes had passed did we finally decide to break from the kiss. And only seconds after that, did I yearn to kiss him again, rancid berry taste or no.

"What's that beautiful head of yours thinking about now?" He kissed the top of my head, then lay back in the moss, berries squishing and squelching beneath his weight. His arms flexed as he brought them behind his head, and he grinned. "You don't want me to eat another one, do you?" His eyes were joking, teasing; grey and blue and violet.

"No." I smacked his arm in jest. "It's just..." I stammered. "How are you going to tell your parents that we're a thing now?" I'd delayed this conversation for too long as it was.

His eyebrows rose in surprise. "Well, first I'd start with a hello..."

I punched him in the arm a bit harder this time, and he began sniggering.

"But seriously, Alterra." His eyes raked over me, studying me, noticing how the question made me stiffen and slump over ever so slightly. "I'll be frank with them about it." He exhaled, then rose from where he lay in a fluid movement—air incarnate. "What we have, it's different than anything else I've ever even heard of, let alone seen."

I gazed into his loving, beautiful eyes, and sighed. "Your family..." I paused. "Your family isn't known for being accepting. No one seems to be very tolerant around here." I gestured to the space around us in a very exaggerated arm movement that sent him laughing again.

"Yes, because the little rabbits and fireflies out over the bog are such critics." He mocked me, but I couldn't help but laugh with him. The rowan tree was just far enough from the bog to prevent the moss from being soggy, but it was still close enough that at night, the lights of fireflies could often be seen flickering contentedly over the stagnant pools.

"Thyello, I just...I don't want to ever lose this." I placed my hand on his muscled chest and brought my mouth to his neck. I whispered, grazing his neck with my lips. "I would fight, you know. If anyone ever tried to rip us apart, I'd kill them."

I kissed his neck, then continued a trail downwards to his navel.

He moaned before he flipped himself over on top of me and began kissing a trail of his own.

I scowled at the too-tight dress that halted his mouth from grazing my breasts, and I bared my neck to his lips. I felt him smile as his weight pressed against me, but it wasn't enough. It would never be enough. He let his teeth scrape the spot just above my collarbone as he spoke, "As would I my dear." His breath then tickled the shell of my ear. "You are my life. You're worth more to me than the earth I walk on."

"And you're worth more to me than the air I breathe."

It was one of the most beautiful moments of my life.

Fuck.

Why did my back feel like someone had ripped it apart, then tried piecing it back together again? It must have been one hell of a rough night at the Forum for me to be left in *this* bad of shape.

I respired slowly, then opened my eyes so I could try to gauge what exactly had happened the night before, but instead of gazing at my dilapidated room in the Forum, I was looking at a dimly lit desert sky.

What the fuck happened last night?

"I am so glad you're done dreaming." That voice... Moira. She was perched to my right.

"Don't move." And *that* was Sylver. He was on my left.

Who was he to think he could order me around? I scowled and made to move anyways, then shrieked against the pain that came from my back. A tear slipped past my guard onto my cheek. I glared at the two of them. Neither had stopped staring at me since I noticed them in the first place. I snapped, "What are you two looking at?"

Instead of responding, they only looked to my torso, so automatically I followed their gaze, deciding to take a look for myself at what seemed to have them at a loss for words.

Oh no.

Oh fucking no.

Where was my trench coat?

I was essentially bare, the only thing I could see that I was wearing was…was that *my* dress?

I made to rise from where I was lying yet again, then sobbed against the ache radiating from my damned back and shut my eyes. The light always showed too much. "What happened?" I didn't care as more tears slid free from my eyes. I didn't care how pathetic I looked to them. I was in too much pain to *care*.

"Sylver, in his attempt to save both me and Waha, quite literally struck you with your own blade from behind."

I ground my teeth and snarled. "So I *was* right about you being a coward." There were too many cowardly fucks in this place.

Moira continued. "And in order for me to save your life, I had to expose the wound, and so—"

"You know I'm a *woman*." I didn't bother disguising the disgust in my tone.

"We didn't want to leave you to die." Moira sounded unsure, like she was trying her best at sounding somewhat altruistic but wasn't exactly sure if her act was convincing anyone. And Sylver. He still didn't bother speaking or *apologizing* for his attempt on my life.

I opened my eyes and stared daggers at him, lips twitching upward as I noted that one of his eyes had now swollen shut. "Too busy pitying yourself to apologize? I know you would have left me to die." I paused, taking a shuddering breath before hissing, "You would have left me for dead if—" Lancing pain halted the words on my tongue. *Certainly*, they would have left me for dead if Moira didn't need me for some fucking reason. That part was now obvious—it wasn't as if I'd treated her kindly. She very well could have been free of her bond to me if only she would have let me bleed out. Moira had an agenda.

"Listen, if you weren't being such a twat, and if you had some better communication skills, I wouldn't have done what I did to you." Sylver splayed his hands wide as he crouched and continued. "I am sorry that I struck you, but you weren't exactly giving me much of a choice." A hiss of breath. "It was a mistake, and if you can't forgive me for that, then…" He only shook his head.

Moira's voice was cool, callous even, as she pressed onward. "I made a promise to you—an *oath*. I didn't leave you; I chose to stay because…" She shook her head. "I chose to stay and that is what matters." Moira had a secret agenda *I* wasn't privy to. Fuck.

My eyes shuttered. I was so tired.

I cleared my throat, then spoke again to them both, struggling against the urge to close my eyes once more. "Fine. I get it. How long exactly have I been out for?" I cherished my voice as it carried clearly towards them, undisguised and feminine for the first time in three years.

"I stitched up your back with a needle and some pig's skin I'd brought in my bag, then used some alcohol on it to disinfect it so infection wouldn't set in." Sylver said, glancing to Moira who was still perched across from him on my right. "You've been out for almost a full twenty-four hours."

Moira nodded curtly before adding, "We didn't want to move you while your wound was still so fresh. Plus, when you slipped into that dream of yours about five hours ago, I wouldn't have been able to move you even if I wanted to." She cast me a saccharine smile. "Thanks a lot for that by the way."

What a nasty bitch.

I shook my head, clearing it of the vile insults that were ready to fall out of my mouth, then wondered, if I'd already been out for over a day, then how much longer would I need before I could even move, let alone travel for days on end?

Hysteria crept over me and I closed my eyes once more. I could not, *would* not allow myself to become hopeless. A faraway berceuse ambled through my panic, soothing my too-fast, too-shallow breathing. *Everything will be okay in the end.*

I sighed after a moment, then opened my eyes once again. "I'm sorry that I've treated you both so terribly. I'm not usually that way," I tittered. "Surely now you guys realize that there's more to the situation than you initially thought."

That was the understatement of the century.

I let my eyes close, avoiding the questions I was sure lingered in their heavy gazes, then swallowed. I hadn't realized just how badly I needed water; it felt as if my tongue had been replaced by sandpaper; gritty, uncomfortable. I smacked my lips together before asking, "Where can I find myself some water?" I didn't actually want to know where the water was, but I didn't exactly feel like ordering them around to fetch some for me.

I remembered now; tyrant. As if.

"How did we forget *that*?" Moira's sardonic voice rattled through the space.

I heard the brush of her dress on the sand, then Sylver as he told me to drink. I felt a calloused hand at the back of my head, tilting it forward, and nearly sobbed at the memory.

Thyello.

My Thyello.

"Please, whatever or whoever it is you're thinking of, stop." I could hear the strain in Moira's voice as she spoke.

Fuck. I'd already forgotten about that too. I opened my eyes to noiselessly mouth the word, *Sorry*, to her before sipping from the flask Sylver brought to my mouth.

I fought against the urge to gulp it all down in one go, and instead took small sips from the flask. I didn't want to be responsible for wasting any of the water we had—*Moira* had already done a good enough job of that as it was—nor did I feel like getting sick. I felt like shit enough as it was.

"So, who exactly are you, if you're not Kieran?" Sylver's voice was hesitant, cautious.

I remembered sounding just the same when I wanted Moira to talk a couple of days back. But still, I must have played my role awfully well for him if he was still so fearful of me, afraid of my wrath, even though he was now the one holding my head up after incapacitating me so thoroughly. Like I was still some threat. *Pfft.*

I weighed my options. How much did I actually want them to know about me? They already knew I was a woman. That was fine. I'd just have to deal with the idea that I would no longer be able to hide that little fact from them anymore, but I would never be able to go so far as to tell them the whole truth. But my first name on the other hand...that would be harmless.

No one here truly knew who I was.

Sylver began lowering my head slowly down onto the sand and Moira stepped in to place a pillow of sorts beneath my head. At least I wouldn't have to worry about cleaning the sand from my hair when they finally deemed me ready to move again. "Thank you," I murmured.

It was always this same damned fine line with people. I'd always been forced to keep a low-profile around others, never exposing the truth about myself, my beliefs, my values, or my desires. There was only ever one—besides my mother—who did not use me against me. I took a deep breath, "My name is Alterra." I took another deep breath and shut my eyes against the sunlight now falling lower over the ridge of the dunes. "You can call me by Kieran though if the name change is too weird for you." I chuckled, but only to shield myself from the hurt I'd feel if they still chose to call me by my other name. It would be as if I wasn't good enough for either of them. Not like people ever thought I was good enough for them at any other time.

Moira was the first to respond. "I like the name Alterra."

"Yeah. It's great for nicknames: Al, Ally, Terry, Terra..." Sylver said, then laughed. "I think I'll stick with Al or Terra for short though; the other ones just don't suit a woman who can knock me on my ass in a fight."

I cracked an eye open against the sunlight sinking beneath the horizon and smiled in earnest at the two of them before replying, "So how much longer do you think until we can get back on track?"

Moira and Sylver seemed dependable enough—Moira's secrets and all—but even so, I would always have to lie to them. As I'd once told my mother at the wise age of four, *Sometimes you have to lie.* The truth…sometimes my truth even seemed crazy to me. And because of that, any relationship I would come to have with either of them would be limited; superficial at best, non-existent at worst.

I had to remain focused.

Their friendship wasn't what I desired; Thyello was my only goal.

I doubted that Moira was lying to me about her exceptional gift, so hypothetically she'd be capable of reuniting us after the five years we'd spent apart, and then it would be worth it. Every horrible thing I'd done during that time so I could return to him again…

It would all be worth it.

Moira's eyes flashed with annoyance. "Not any time soon." I made a sound of contempt, so she continued, "Maybe a week or so before you can walk?"

"If you're lucky," Sylver went on, a bit baffled. "You do realize that your bone was showing, so it might take a bit longer, depending on the damage done."

Thanks to him. I glowered. "No, I didn't realize that." I heaved a sigh before shaking my head, my back screaming with the movement. "It's fine. Obviously, you didn't hit anything too important, otherwise I'd be dead."

"Yeah, about that…" Shame sluiced across Sylver's features. "Al, Moira and I might need to leave."

"What?"

"Don't look at me like that. I know what you're thinking, but we need to get some more supplies so—"

I sneered. "Leave me behind in the desert while you two get all cozy back at the keep?" Sylver's face appeared appalled with my accusation, but I trudged onward, seething. "Oh, I know you were saying that you were going off to get supplies, but you have to admit that it is awfully convenient that you're leaving *together* while I am fucking out of commission." A breath, "Well, fine. Broken or not, I've been alone most of my life anyways, so I guess even if you two did decide to abandon me out here, I'd be able to cope."

"No need to be so defensive, Alterra. We don't have enough of anything to last for another two weeks after you heal." Moira's brows furrowed. "Unless you want all of us to die out here?"

It was a fine excuse to abandon me. I let out a harsh laugh. I was done. Done with them, done with being injured. I'd opened up to them, and they were rejecting me, abandoning me. Like so many others had already done in my life.

I shut my eyes. I was being defensive—overly so. The heat always brought on these *fucking* mood swings with me. Stupid, *stupid*—I brought the heels of my palms up, careful not to reopen my gash. I had to calm my breathing. *Everything will be okay in the end…*

Everything will be okay in the end…

As I massaged, the heavy ache that had crept into the space just behind my eyes began to ease off ever so slightly, clearing my head.

Everything will be okay in the end…

"It should only take us about a day to get back to the keep and back here. You'll still be immobile, so it really shouldn't change anything, except where we stand in a few weeks time when it comes to how much supplies we have left." I understood Moira's logic, but hell; so many things could go wrong in the meantime.

I wouldn't even be able to defend myself if—if somehow the disciples tracked me down…

I cast the thought out of my mind.

Everything will be okay in the end.

I'd been through much worse.

I kept my hands where they were against my eyes, massaging them, then whispered into the desert, "I'm tired."

"We were actually planning on leaving now."

Great.

Sylver continued, "Rest, heal, and by the time day breaks tomorrow, we should be back with new supplies...*Alterra.*"

I didn't have the energy to continue arguing with them, and even though there were so many flaws in their makeshift plan, I ultimately conceded to it because it was the only option that didn't require me to think too hard—

I grumbled against my own judgement. "Sure thing."

I was so exhausted. And it was *such* a mistake to have revealed so much of myself to them. *Seriously*—regret ate away any and all of the energy which had somehow managed to linger in my decrepit body. I shouldn't have been so bloody cocky. I knew that I'd pushed Sylver too far. Messiah above, I'd pushed them both too far, but I just kept pushing and pushing because...because I wanted him to rally his anger and fight me. I wanted him to have some sort of justice. I wanted him to fight the monster that I'd had to become these last few years.

Hell, even *I* wanted to fight the monster I'd become.

I hated myself.

Leaving Waha alone at his keep was a death sentence to him, and it wasn't like I was blind to Sylver's love for the man. What Waha meant to him...

I would have never willingly left my own mother—

I was fighting to return to her too.

I ground my teeth and inhaled through my nose.

My own guilt.

I'd done this to myself.

"Here." Sylver's voice fought against the raging thoughts bedeviling my head. "Just in case we're late coming back, I'll put this right here." I heard the sound of a tarp rustling around above my head, then the sound of something metal being shoved deep into the sand. I didn't realize Sylver was so prepared. "Also, take these—one contains water, and the other alcohol." Two thuds were audible from the sand to the left of me. "That should be it. We'll be quick, so this will be more than enough."

I decided to peel my hands from my eyes so I could see what sort of precautions Sylver had put in place to keep me docile while they were gone. A makeshift lean-to now hung above me, using two poles Sylver had been carrying with him. To my left there were two flasks.

I closed my eyes again, then breathed, "Don't get into too much trouble. The desert's a dangerous place."

Sylver laughed, albeit a bit breathlessly. "I'm a guide, remember?"

I heard the two of them rustling about some more, supposedly getting the last of the stuff prepared for the trip they were to have ahead of them, when Moira came to my side and said, "I would have told Sylver to stay back with you if I thought I was capable of returning there on my own." I could hear her inhale deeply before continuing, "But, I can't say that I am, and I'm not a fool willing to risk my life over an ego, so…" She vacillated. "You're tough. Knowing you're a woman doesn't change that."

She didn't bother saying goodbye before trotting off after Sylver who only yelled to me from afar, "We'll be back before you know it, Al!"

I mumbled sarcastically, only the desert wind for an ear. "Messiah save them."

CHAPTER 12

Alterra

I HAD A HORRIBLE DAY—*worse than what I'd usually have to suffer through.*

My mother had always said to me that the others were just jealous and that, with time, things would improve for me. But I didn't see how that was even possible.

I had no friends. I never did.

I never would.

I'd been crying in one of my favorite hiding places; a craggy little grotto I'd found when I was just a little girl, overlooking a patch of cranberry shrubs near the bog. It always made me feel safe there, even when the rest of the world made me feel angry or afraid.

It was turning dusk by the time I decided it'd be too dangerous to remain and that it'd be best for me to return home. I may have felt safe in my little spot near the mire; however, there were always threats to watch out for. Mother had told me tales of the many dangers of the bog; great beasts lurked there, each eager to flay me navel to sternum. I shivered as the thought crossed my mind and hurried my pace. The moss cushioned each of my footfalls, and my eyes adjusted to the inevitable darkness of night. Cautiously, I meandered through the forest, avoiding any fallen branches that could alert potential predators of my whereabouts and dodged the silvered trunks of trees.

Golden light from our little cabin held the terrors of the world at bay and gave me the courage to sprint the final stretch. Twigs and branches snapped beneath me. I couldn't let them catch me. Visible knots in the wood of our cabin told me to move even faster.

Just a few more strides.

Somehow, as if knowing I'd be arriving at that very moment, my mother swung open the oak door. The moment I saw the love and affection in her sea-green eyes, my own eyes flooded with tears yet again. But I couldn't cry; I was strong.

"Alterra, what's wrong my baby girl?" My mother's concern. She embraced me, held me in her arms, and stroked my back gently, soothingly. She was the only one who would ever love me.

I couldn't fight the sobs that ravaged me any longer. Tears spilled over my cheeks and felt endless. I said, "All I wanted was to play with them. That's all I wanted." I clasped my hands behind her back. "But they said I'd never be good enough to; that I would always be a wretched, worthless, waste of breath. That my father..." I sobbed harder, choking on my sorrow. "That he was right to abandon us both."

I felt my mother tense as I spoke about him, but she only continued stroking my back before whispering, "Honey, they will never be good enough to play with you. You will never be a waste of breath." She paused, then pulled back to look into my eyes. "Your father, he...he's the one they should be calling a waste of breath." Only candor shone in her viridescent eyes as she brought me in for another hug and began her soothing strokes again.

I let my mother's hand relieve me, ground me.

I laid my head on her shoulder as she continued, "Don't let them win Ally. They win when you lose your will—your will to keep fighting, your will to keep being, your will to keep succeeding, your will to keep breathing." My mother released me at last, then repeated the words I'd heard hundreds of times before. *"Your will is what guides your path in life, and with it, anything you dream of can be made possible."*

My tears had finally ceased when I brought myself to ask, "Why can't they just accept me for me? Why do they have to..."

I didn't know what I was going to say.

My mother gave me a knowing smile, then knelt down so she was almost eye-level with me and kissed my forehead. She murmured, "You're special Alterra. Most aren't even gifted, nonetheless as gifted as you are. They become envious when they realize they simply can't compare." She wiped at a tear that was beginning its descent down my cheek. "They lash out."

"But...but don't they realize that when they do that..." My words faded as I drifted into thought once more. Maybe if I was the best, they wouldn't want to put me down anymore. Maybe they'd finally respect me and recognize me for everything I'd done. Maybe they wouldn't betray or hurt or hate me any longer. Maybe—

"Honey, this life isn't for the weak. Sometimes it doesn't matter if you do everything right in life." She grasped my hands firmly, engulfing them with her own. "If they don't want to like you for whatever reason, even if it's just because of who you're related to or who you are, they will find anything they can to use against you so that you won't succeed or bypass them later in life."

I'd always wondered how she could know exactly what was going on through my mind, even without me ever speaking a word aloud. It was always such an effort to speak anyways, especially when every word I'd ever articulated had been used against me time and again.

I wiped at my eyes before realizing just how cold I'd become while in my hiding place. A tremor rattled through me. I removed my leather boots, along with the matching leather jacket my mother had sewn for me a while back, before heading to the singular bed the two of us shared in the main room.

We only had the one bed in the household because my mother had wanted to protect me; one bed in the main room meant that if anyone or anything bad were to ever force their way in while we were sleeping, she'd have an easier time shielding me. I'd be at her side instead of her needing to scramble elsewhere in the room to save me.

I yawned as I approached the bed, then threw myself upon it face-first. I was too tired to care about throwing on my nightgown. My mother laughed from behind me, and I heard her light the hearth and continue to the old rocking chair placed beside our bed for her comfort. She'd always sing songs or read books to me come bedtime, and when she didn't want to fall asleep beside me in the bed just yet, she'd use sitting in the chair as her incentive to stay awake for a while longer.

Then, as she'd done a million times before, she began humming my melody to me. It wasn't a complex tune by any means; the same few notes were repeated over and over, but no one could deny the love that nevertheless flowed merrily through it.

Ahhh, aha, aha, ahuh.
Ahhh, aha, aha, ahuh.
Ahhh, aha, aha, ahuh.
And then, like always, she sang my lullaby for me.
"I'm so sorry little one...
I wish I could salve the pain that you're feeling,
But pain is a fact in this life and needs healing.
I know you may feel helpless, and weak,
But you're strong like the earth beneath your feet.
Only your heart and your will are your limit,
And my little girl, some trouble'll come with it.
And trust me my dear, in time when you're older,
All will make sense and you will grow bolder.
Believe me when I say that my dear Alterra,
Everything will be okay in the end.
Everything will be okay in the end."

Chapter 13

Moira

I HAD NO IDEA WHY SYLVER and I had decided to take off from the campsite at dusk.

It would have been a lot more reasonable if we had only waited until dawn, but I didn't want to wait; my impatience was a living thing that had begun gnawing away at my sanity as soon as Sylver had slowed us down upon nearly killing Alterra.

I was still in disbelief of the night before—a heated argument one minute, then the next…

When I'd removed the fabric from her chest and discovered Kieran was in fact, female, I'd gone blank. Every thought had eddied away from me and I was just left gaping at her naked, supine body.

Even in the dark I'd noticed the pallor of her midriff when compared to her golden face, and the pair of full breasts that were peaked against the frigid desert air. Her listless face and parted mouth made her appear youthful, as if she was merely dreaming, and not staving off the death that loomed above her.

My flicker urged me to her, and I made to take a step forward, but I couldn't. I couldn't bring myself to move towards that beautiful woman. Blood began pooling in the sand beneath where she lay, and still, I watched unmoving, frozen as the air drifted past us.

Sylver only gawked at my inaction. "What happened to saving him—her—whatever?" I'd heard him approach from where he'd been beside his backpack. "I thought you said that he was your only chance of going back to your home?" Sylver splayed his arms as he rounded to face me. "Does Kieran suddenly being a woman change that?"

"I can't deal with this right now; I have too much to think about as it is." My flicker seared me, and I hissed shakily, "Save Kieran, Sylver. Do whatever needs to be done, but just save her." Even though I'd been in shock, I wasn't stupid enough to let her die.

She could be my only chance of returning to the life I used to have, and I wouldn't lose her. Possibly—as long as I was interpreting my little dancer's rendition of conversation correctly.

"Fine. At least this way I won't have to apologize to her when she wakes." I'd watched as Sylver took up a crouch in front of Kieran's body and reached into the bag, and said over a shoulder, "You know, Kieran being a woman might actually be a *good* thing—we know now that *clearly* there is some other shit going on here that we simply weren't privy to…" He chuckled, more to himself than me, as he grabbed some more of the white gauzy stuff she had packed away. "*Maybe*, she's actually a nice person."

I'd rolled my eyes, and just watched him silently for an eternity as he stitched her up—I was more than grateful to Sylver for what he had done. Grateful that he'd actually known something about medicine. Grateful that he'd still bothered helping me by helping Alterra, despite the fact that he knew I was just as responsible as Kieran for the whole Waha situation. But I didn't say as much.

I was still pissed with him. If it wasn't for his idiotic behaviour, we could—*I* could—be one day closer to the home I'd desired to return to for five fucking years. But no. Because of him and his bullshit, I was delayed for at least a week. Another week of endless bullshit to trudge through.

We now walked together through the desert back to Waha's keep in a stilted silence; moonlight cast shadows off dunes and the occasional tumbleweed, breaking up the otherwise repetitive trek. I'd always enjoyed the silence—the peace that came with a starlit sky, although interruptions marred its perfection.

My thoughts were addled and confused, preventing me from enjoying the desert's nighttime serenity. One moment I was there walking with Sylver admiring the blue and silver hues of the dunes in the lambent moonlight, and then the next, questions. Thousands of questions seemed to amble through me all at once.

How did Alterra become Kieran? How did I not realize that he was, in fact, a female? Did Derrik know that Kieran was actually a woman? Why would she choose to become Kieran in the first place? How long had she been Kieran? What other secrets did she keep?

Then others.

Did Sylver find Alterra attractive? Did Alterra find Sylver attractive? Was Sylver's old flame like Alterra? Did Sylver—

I didn't want to acknowledge *any* of those questions. I silently quarrelled against the raging thoughts afflicting my mind, my sanity, and vented my internal annoyance with a snarl.

Sylver whipped his head to me, alarmed, before asking, a hint of a smile gracing his mouth, "Do I even want to know what's going on over there?"

I chided, "How am I supposed to know what you want." My little dancer sent itself into a quickstep on my spine at the words and I straightened.

Right.

"Are you still pissed with me?" Yes. He sighed. "Or is it something else?"

"Why can't it be both?" I halted my steps. I was pissed with him *and* I was simultaneously facing a seemingly endless torrent of questions.

"Tell me what's on your mind Moira." He took a step, bridging the gap between us and it became difficult to breathe. Even my flicker leapt with joy at his approach. Predictable little thing.

"I just…" I scrupled. "What happened last night was too much. I had no idea about Kieran, and I…I feel like there are so many questions and I am overwhelmed because I don't want to deal with any of them." I heaved a sigh as I continued, "I have too many things to think about and I feel like last night…it just made my situation more complicated."

He chuckled. "Yeah, last night was definitely complicated." Sylver angled his head. "Moira, I'm not going to claim to know what you're dealing with, so I'm not going to say with certainty that I can help you out, but, maybe?" He sucked on his teeth. "How about we play a game to take your mind off things?"

I furrowed my brow. "What kind of a game?"

"Just the worst kind." He threw me a devilish grin and I couldn't stop the laugh that erupted out of my throat. "Twenty questions."

"Twenty questions? I don't even know how to play that."

A look of reproach crept over his features, and he quipped, placing a hand on his chest, "Have you ever heard of "fun" before?"

Fun. Like I had the time to have fun. I rolled my eyes and began walking through the sand once more. "Humor me."

He easily kept pace as he said, "In order to play the game, one of us has to ask the other twenty questions, and the other person has to answer them." A pause. "*Truthfully.*"

"That's not fun!" I protested. "Didn't you hear me when I told you that I had enough questions going through my head, overwhelming me?"

Sylver laughed. "It's fun when you're the one asking questions. But, fine. If you want, you can go first to start the game off."

I slowed my pace and peered sideways at him, a tress slipping forward blocking him from sight as I asked, "I can ask you *anything?*"

"Anything." His words were laced with arrogance—cocksure and lazy like the desert wind whispering past us.

I brushed my hair away with a hand and surveyed him for another moment before I faced the dunes once more. Maybe this game would be fun. I smiled. If I could ask him anything and he had to answer the questions honestly...

Perhaps I would be able to quell some of the thoughts that fought to destroy me.

A deep breath. "What were your thoughts last night when you saw for yourself that Kieran was a woman?"

He released a harsh laugh. "Well, I don't think I had a thought, per se. I think it was just more of a shock to me. If I would have killed him—her..." Sylver shook his head, and his hair, darker than the navy sky above us, shifted with the gesture. "I don't know if I would have ever forgiven myself if she died. I feel guilty about it as it is. I didn't know *anything*. But how was I supposed to know? It wasn't as if he was going to willingly divulge that information." He shrugged. "That was one, ask me another."

"Do you think she's pretty?"

"Yeah. I'm not blind Moira."

I grumbled, and Sylver's lips twitched towards a smile as he began walking forward yet again.

"Another."

I stalked after him. "What do you like the most about her?"

He drawled, "Ah...so, you're jealous of her." A smirk. "I guess I like her spirit, her will. It's hard to explain. But, somehow, she clawed her way to the top of Sin's Forum of all places in this misogynistic place. I'd be lying if I said that wasn't impressive."

I snorted, "I thought you couldn't stand those same things about *Kieran?*"

"That's true. But the difference is, Kieran's actions painted him as just another violent, power-hungry individual, eager to climb to the top of the ladder by any means necessary. Alterra's actions prove her to be calculated. Moira, Neosordess would *never* have let a woman make it. I don't think you realize that she has—against all odds—remained hidden from the disciples *and* the Messiah for crying out loud, for *years*. That's fucking impressive."

"Double standard much? Stop drooling Sylver."

"I'm not drooling. I'm answering your question. Besides, she's pretty Moira, but she's not my type."

Huh.

My face slackened. What had he seen in *me*, if someone as perfect as Alterra wasn't good enough for him? I mulled over asking him just that, when he continued, "In case you didn't realize this Moira, the game twenty questions is supposed to let us get to know each other better, so…" He smirked like a cat. "I dare you to ask me something that doesn't involve Alterra *or* Kieran this time."

That wasn't fair, but whatever. "What were your thoughts when you first saw me?"

He raised his eyebrows and halted his steps as we reached the highpoint of a particularly steep dune before responding. "I thought a great many things when I saw you, Moira." He glanced to me, and I could have sworn that the embers of a fire flared awake. "I felt sorry for you. I thought that you were his…" A huff of laughter. "Or at least I thought that until you whipped your head to him like he was a thief. And then…" Sylver brought his hand up to rub his chin before letting it fall. "You made me *very* curious."

"About what? What were you so curious about?"

"That's seven."

"I know."

He grinned. "I wondered why you were with Kieran. Why you were with him, but also if you two were, you know…a thing. I wondered where you were from and where you two had to go so badly." Sylver paused, a blush staining his cheeks darker in the moonlight, as he simpered. "I wondered how it was possible for someone's eyes to be so *enchanting*."

I rolled my eyes even as I felt a blush of my own creep over my features, then launched myself down the dune to avoid him noticing how he made my damned body react. I stumbled on Alterra's dress and fell forward, sand and rock surging to meet my face—

A pair of familiar hands clasped one of the arms I'd thrown behind me, pinwheeling to remain upright, and I staggered back into his warmth. "Thank you," I gasped.

"My pleasure." I heard the smile in Sylver's words as he released his grip, and I stepped forward, eager to remove myself from his scent which still threatened to undo me, so I could ask him another question.

I swallowed. "Why did you shut down on me the other night?" The question ripped its way out of my mouth before I could reprimand it, and I winced. It wasn't hard to remember the feeling of his warmth leeching from my very soul when he'd pretended to be tired after our…incident. How was it possible that *that* was only a couple of nights ago? It felt like it had already been weeks.

"I don't know, Moira."

"You promised me honesty, Sylver. Was I not good enough? Did I offend you in some way?" I spun around so I could face him and splayed my arms. "Or was it just because I said I only wanted sex?" I huffed on a laugh. "Because that's awfully archaic if that's the—"

"Maybe I don't just want to be a fuck, Moira." He loosed a breath, and I could have sworn that the fire of his eyes banked as he continued, "Maybe I want something more than just sex."

I rolled my eyes and murmured, "Whatever," before twisting away from his agonized face. He was already weaker for lust—the possibility of love…like so many others.

Stupid game.

I took a step forward, and each step away from him reminded me of my one and only goal: home. Even if I could barely remember it anymore. Only that would ever bring me happiness.

Another step.

Only there would I ever be free.

Another step.

Only then would I be able to be me.

Sylver and I didn't bother speaking to each other after that.

The sun had just begun its ascent over the dunes as we finally approached Waha's keep. Gilding the sand in orange and gold and red, the sun wiped away the smear of deafening silence that had fallen over both Sylver and me after I'd stormed off away from him.

He deserved it.

He was the one who'd suggested playing that game in the first place, and it wasn't my fault that the game had gone south. If it wasn't for him daring me to ask questions that weren't concerned with Alterra, the game could have probably lasted a bit longer. But no. I wouldn't apologize to him for demanding a few answers to the questions that had haunted me since that night.

Maybe I don't just want to be a fuck, Moira. I couldn't stop myself from mulling over his words. What did it even matter to him; it was just skin. It wasn't even like the act meant anything here anyway.

Movement caught my eye from the northern side of the keep and I halted my steps. Sylver rushed forward, and I found myself staring after him as he barrelled toward the palms and the pond and the oh-so-fun memories.

"*WAHA!!!*" Sylver yelled as he ran, and a slow, hunched figure hobbled forward to meet him from the shadow of the keep.

"Sylver?" A cough. "What are you doing here?"

The recognizable sound of Waha's fragile, off-kilter voice sent my feet moving again. I watched as they embraced and as smiles bloomed over their features. Their happiness hit me like a physical blow. I scowled.

I didn't care that no one ever looked at me with that amount of...joy.

None of it mattered.

"It's a long story." Sylver raked a hand through his midnight hair and asked hoarsely, "Why are you out here this early?"

"You're always worrying about me." Waha gestured to where I now stood with an arthritic finger. "What's she doing all the way over there?"

"That's also a long story..." Sylver pivoted to me and gave me the slightest of nods.

Like I would listen to the subtle command.

Like I would do anything for him.

I firmly planted my heels into the sand and gave him a smirk. If he was going to make *my* life miserable with his bullshit morals, I would help to return the favour to him. A piercing flame rippled outward from my spine at the thought, and I reeled.

Whatever.

I approached the old man and forced a smile to my face. He didn't have to know why I couldn't stand to even look at his apprentice—or whatever Sylver was to him. From the corner of my eye, I noted that Sylver was casting me a merciful glance. Obviously, he thought that I moved towards them of my own volition.

Waha only beamed at me. I had half the nerve to roll my eyes but (incredibly) decided against the reflex. I doubted that Sylver would appreciate me taking out my bad mood on the practically ancient fool instead of him. Not like his opinion mattered but...

My little dancer let a transient warmth sink into my bones as if to say, *That's better*, and I had to reign in the urge to roll my eyes again.

"Hey Waha, how are you doing?" I hated small talk. It would always be a pointless waste of time, but it would keep me busy enough to stop me from following through on my callous impulses.

"Moira, there's no need to be so formal around me. Sylver's just a busybody that assumes that I'm incapable of fending for myself, despite fending for myself my entire life. Alas, until I stumbled across him out there." Waha pointed eastward towards the rising sun. "Five years ago."

I furrowed my brow. *Five* years ago? That was when *I'd* lost everything; my home, my purpose, myself...what had Sylver been doing out there?

Sylver chuckled and placed a careful arm on the old man's shoulder. "Just because you were alone for all of that time Waha, doesn't mean that your life wouldn't have been a bit easier if you'd have only had someone to help you out earlier on."

No one ever wants to be completely alone. Sylver didn't have to reiterate the words he'd said to me only a few nights ago—they hadn't even applied to me (really) anyway. No one in this place would ever elicit that particular effect on me. Never would I let my emotions nor those *other* feelings to go awry.

I was a fool to have almost listened when he'd first spoken those words to me. Desperate, pathetic, lost.

The last few hours had strengthened my resolve.

I had to believe that Alterra's desire would lead me back to my home, back to everything I once was. There, loneliness would soon be a foreign concept.

There, all of my feelings would vanish.

However.

I let my face relax into the smile that had been plastered on moments before for Waha, and threw Sylver a heavy-lidded, lustful gaze before biting my lip. Let him believe that his words had reminded me of some of the words we'd spoken only a few nights ago when things weren't so...strained. Let him think that I forgave him for whatever he thought he needed my forgiveness for.

He knew that I would soon be long gone, but he didn't know that any possible guilt from my current actions would also disappear with me. I toyed with the thought: if I played my hand exactly right, I could lead Sylver to believe that I'd fallen for him— enough so that he'd think I desired more than "just sex" from him. What would it matter anyway if I never saw him again? He'd never know the difference. I could lie to him, manipulate him, and sleep with him; experience the fire lurking deep within him, and then I could leave to return back home—alone—where he would dissipate into no more than a memory, like ashes in a gust of wind. I smiled as "immorality" dawned upon me.

I wouldn't even have to make him feel as awful as he did me. I was fated to be alone, but I didn't necessarily have to suffer.

My little dancer used a flame-licked hand to pound its way over my back, branding me with its disapproval, but I couldn't care; it was too flawless a plan to abandon.

Sylver gave me a weary smile in return.

Perfect.

I stifled my wince as my flicker whipped me with invisible flames and turned to face the garden Waha had been bent over moments earlier. Succulents and beans and peas and some type of grain became golden in the sun's rays as it rose higher and higher in the distance. Waha and Sylver must have traded with those who were foolish enough to wind up out here for the other foods that couldn't be grown.

Waha and Sylver began talking once again, but I didn't listen; not as the flicker lashed at me over and over and over. I kept a bland smile on my face while gazing at the lonely garden beside the keep. My plan was the embodiment of iniquity. But as far as I was concerned, Sylver had rejected me twice.

I deserved to get what I desired for once—all of it. The human part of me yearned to live, to experience everything this life had to offer. The flame…the flame didn't want anything. But I wanted *for* it. I wanted to return to my former glory. The memories of home were practically intangible, but I could vaguely remember how it had felt. The soft caress of a breeze and the near-silent whispers of flames…

Who was Sylver to deny me my only human desire?

I barely noticed as Waha and Sylver departed the garden to go within the keep, and my legs were foreign entities as I took a step to follow them. The wicked fire in my spine did not cease as it continued to attack me, and my legs became numb.

It didn't matter how my little dancer hurt or maimed me; I'd made my decision. I'd chosen myself for once, and I would allow myself this piece of happiness. Even if it meant Sylver would be denied his own.

Chapter 14

Aterra

DESPITE BEING AWAKE, I KEPT MY EYES CLOSED.

 I didn't want to disturb the peace that dream had blessed me with. It had been so long since I'd dreamed of my mother at all; so long since I had seen her face or heard her voice. Even though the lullaby—*my lullaby*—couldn't be deemed cheery by any means, it always managed to soothe me.

 I remembered that day. I was eight or nine years old at the time. I'd tried to play with some of the other children my age out in the meadow, but they had just insulted me. I could only watch as they laughed and sang and had the time of their lives with one another. I could only watch as they pretended to be kings and monsters and knights and princesses. I could only watch as both young love and lifelong camaraderie bloomed in the meadows. I was abandoned—cursed to watch them from the sidelines. I used to climb the limbs of nearby trees so I wouldn't be put-down for wanting to be a part of it.

A part of them.

I had too many memories like that.

I wiped the thought from my mind, then slowly cracked open my eyes.

The sky wasn't yet bright from the sun, but I could see that ahead of me the sky was becoming tinted with its yellow-orange glow. It was dawn.

I glanced upwards to the makeshift tarp-thing that Sylver had placed over my head to keep off the sun and noticed that it was now falling over; one of the poles was leaning awry and the tarp, still attached, dragged the other pole with it, so it hung just over my practically exposed head—reckless desert winds must have knocked it askew in the middle of the night. *Shit*. If I still wanted to stay at least somewhat comfortable while both Sylver and Moira were away, I needed to figure out how to keep the sun off my face. I wouldn't allow myself to become more dehydrated. I was already dehydrated enough as it was.

I groaned.

In order to do that, I'd have to *move* somehow.

I dragged my eyes down from the tarp to assess my body, its aches, its pains. It was strange. I'd grown so used to wearing the extra material under my clothes to keep my breasts hidden from everyone, that I now almost felt bare without it—like I'd shed a second skin. Sometimes, on rare occasions, I'd accidently wrap it too tight around my chest and I'd find myself suffocating at various times throughout the day. I was just happy that that was something I'd no longer have to deal with.

I didn't dawdle as I began slowly rotating my ankles over and over. They were stiff, and a bit sore from the exertion of walking for hours without end, but really, they didn't hurt as bad as they could have. I copied the movement with my wrists—practically pain-free.

Finally, some good news.

I wondered; was it possible for me to avoid hurting myself more if I succeeded and moved without someone else present to spot me? Probably not, but what would be worse? I'd already learned to tolerate excessive amounts of pain in my life, so tugging on some stitches wouldn't be the worst thing I'd ever felt. But the idea of the desert sun beating down on my face and of having no way of escaping its rays, baking, and burning…it would be worth it to fix the lean-to, if only to stop that horrible fate, even if the pain from doing so exceeded anything I'd ever felt.

I brought my right leg over my left and tried using my bodyweight to flip myself over onto my side. I figured that because the slice was from my right shoulder down to my left hip, that that would be the best way to get started. I could feel the stitches in my back tug a bit, but even so, I had to resume. The sun had risen higher overhead and now its outline hovered clearly over the dunes. I couldn't wait any longer for Sylver and Moira to return.

I brought my arms to my chest and used my right leg to further roll onto my left side so that I'd be able to eventually rise onto my knees. I fought a wince as the pressure of my body's weight pulled on Sylver's stitches, but still persevered through the slight twinge of pain. It was nothing. I was almost thankful that my mother had taught me to be inured to the sensation.

Fully on my left side, the stitches in my right shoulder strained as I tried rising. It became very clear that the only way I would get even *remotely* close to a kneeling position would be to continue rolling until I was fully on my chest, then to push up from there.

I could do it.

Mind over matter.

I pushed myself to use my right leg to roll over further, then removed both hands from my chest, placing my right hand on the ground ahead of me, thereby preventing myself from having it trapped beneath. My stitches were recalcitrant as I silently pleaded for them to hold.

Why did I have to feel so *weak*?

I let my hand slide into the sand from the mat I rested on, and I shifted so as to get my left hand out from underneath.

A guffaw fell out of my mouth as I felt the skin tear at my right shoulder. The sharpness in tandem with the cool sensation of blood as it dribbled from the wound I'd unintentionally created, genuinely tickled. I was so fucked—

I finished rolling over and forced my left arm out from under me, letting it rest at my side.

I was already so tired, and the idea of doing a push-up...

Without hesitation, I pushed up with all of the strength I could muster and secured a position on my knees.

Laughter wrangled with my desire to throw up as I felt my stitches rip apart—as I felt my skin peel from where it had been mending. But I had to fix the lean-to thing.

Sweat dripped into my eyes as I crawled back onto my mat to the tarp leaning awkwardly to the side, and hemmed it on the poles Sylver had provided, stabbing through the thin material with the small spikes to be sure. Exertion made my breathing laboured, and my arms buckled, causing me to fall face first onto the mat. But the job was done.

I giggled again. This was nothing. The blood dripping into the sand beside me was nothing. *Nothing.* I'd succeeded all on my own; however, I wasn't reckless enough to believe I was *safe* yet. *Please, hurry up. Please, please, please.* But I knew hope wouldn't bring Sylver and Moira back any faster. I needed a miracle. I already felt so weak.

Was *this* even worth it?

"Come on guys, work with me here."

Everything will be okay in the end.

Everything will be okay—

I closed my eyes. Maybe—*maybe*, it was possible for me to send a message to Moira...

I didn't stop myself as I let my mind wander to him, to the only person who had ever offered me any sense of camaraderie. To the only man I'd ever loved. Thyello.

My Thyello.

Chapter 15

Moira

"ARE THE TWO OF YOU SURE that you don't want to stay here a while longer?" Waha's trembling voice echoed through the keep after we'd spent the last thirty minutes filling him in on the barest of details whilst simultaneously collecting more supplies for the weeks ahead: three more full water bladders, flasks full of both alcohol and more water, more gauze for Alterra's back, five more loaves of a hearty whole-grain bread, more legumes...

"Waha, you know that I'd love to stay, but Kieran—*Alterra*—needs for us to return." Sylver ran a hand through his charcoal hair as he continued, "You're certain that you'll be okay out here?"

"Sylver, I'm an old man, and you're still young. Don't stop living your life for me." A sad smile graced Waha's features as he shook the hand Sylver held limp at his side. "I'll be fine, and you will be too."

Sylver only nodded.

I nearly rolled my eyes as I exhaled. "It's only going to be several weeks, guys. It's not going to be forever." Sylver would be allowed to go wherever the hell he wanted after I lead Alterra to her desire.

After I reach my own.

He could crawl right back to this one-room keep in the middle of the dunes and spend the rest of his life caring for the old man…that was his prerogative. Perhaps it would help him cope with the fact that he would never keep me.

That I would only ever be willing to sleep with him.

It could never be anything more. Because that was all I could—*would*—ever want from him.

Only a few more words I couldn't bother hearing were uttered between the two of them before Sylver and I swiftly left the keep. The sun was now well overhead, and it would only be a matter of time before Sylver's lean-to collapsed, leaving Alterra exposed. Maybe she'd be lucky. Maybe she'd choose to sleep and wouldn't notice as her skin began burning…

"Okay, so I know that the last game we played together could have gone a *bit* better," Sylver hedged, interrupting my inner monologue, "but would you like to play another one just until we get back?"

I sighed "Sylver, the last game was an absolute failure."

"This one doesn't have to be." His brows raised with the challenge.

I took a second to think.

If I wanted Sylver to fuck me, I'd have to play the part. And if that meant playing another *stupid* game—

"Fine."

His face contorted with shock—he must have assumed I'd put up more of a fight.

I continued, shrugging off his reaction. "But we are not playing twenty questions again. Ever." I couldn't afford to be honest with him, not as long as he was of use to me.

A deep, wholehearted laugh rumbled its way out of his mouth, and he inclined his head. "Wouldn't want things to get *boring*. There are many other games for us to play." Sylver's voice dropped an octave, and my toes curled.

Why did this damned body of mine have to yield so easily to him? These reactions made me weak, vulnerable—at his fucking mercy. Sylver was just another costly distraction that I'd have to deal with, and if I wasn't careful, he could very well have me at his whim, and everything I worked for these past years… I had to stick to the plan, even if every human instinct told me to launch myself at him and to devour him whole. Even if every human instinct told me to extend our time together for as long as possible—

Enough.

He wanted more than just sex and I just had to play the part.

I almost laughed—even if *I* wanted more from him, even if I wanted him to return home with me, Dima would never let it happen.

"What game do you want to play, Sylver?"

"I wasn't expecting you to actually agree." He strode ahead of me as we began ascending yet another dune, and I noted his kaftan which had been cinched at the waist, accentuating his broad shoulders and narrow—

Focus Moira.

Sylver began humming an ancient, living melody that stopped me short as my little dancer began twirling and floating and twining with the beautiful music. My heart leapt at the sound.

A memory.

A figurative veil of smoke effectively blocked me from seeing where I'd been, but it was a *memory*. Fleeting as it was, it was still a piece of *me*. A wisp of thought, a flurry of feeling. An intrinsic piece of self recognized the friendly harmonies. *You are not alone*, it seemed to whisper. My flicker and my very bones knew the flowing notes somehow, but I couldn't remember.

I'd forgotten most of my time during the first few months here.

Perhaps Salvador had hummed the same tune to me while I was in the cage...healing. I mean, that was likely. Salvador had always been a nicer man than his brother Qasir was.

Sylver twisted towards where I still stood gaping up at his muscled form and furrowed a confused brow. "Is there a reason you stopped?"

I didn't respond, but I did make sure to move my feet.

His lips twitched upwards. "How about we play a game of word association?"

I nodded, not really paying attention, as I too crested the dune and forced myself to gaze at our surroundings. The desert was as desolate as it had been the first time we'd walked through it, with only the occasional breeze tossing the barren sand, letting it drift free of the restraints this world forced upon it—as I'd once been.

My little dancer grappled to find that faraway memory, burning through each unimportant, trivial thought that found its way inside my consciousness.

A quiet, serene male voice eventually trickled through the shroud—Salvador? I could almost see his mouth quirk to the side as he noticed my attention...but how did Sylver know of it?

Sylver continued. "The game is easy. All you have to do, is say the first word that comes into your mind after I say a word. It's as simple as it can get."

I nodded again. No. That couldn't be it. Salvador had never done *anything* serene in his life that I was aware of. Internally, I replayed Sylver's brief music, and barely held in a gasp as a different vision greeted me.

The memory was hazy, but I could just begin to see the reflection of the moon and of the stars. Yes...maybe it came from another client to the north of here or—

"Distracted." Sylver cast me a sidelong glance.

"What?"

He chuckled. "Were you even paying attention Moira?"

"Yes." No, not really. I shook my head, clearing it of the fog, and asked, "I just say the first word that comes to mind. That's it, right?"

"Ah, so you were *almost* paying attention…yes." He smiled before he began descending the dune and declared the first word. "Night."

"Day." I took up a casual stroll and let the steepness of the dune propel me downwards behind him. The sun was now casting its light on this side of the dune.

"Sunshine."

"Moonlight."

"Darkness."

"Fear."

"Ignorance."

"Truth."

"Lies."

"Reasons."

"Excuses."

"Focused."

"Determined."

Each word posed both a question and answer. I made to respond, opening my mouth to say, *Foolish*, when my little dancer twinged.

"Fire."

I couldn't think around the scalding pain radiating from my spine, and I arched against it, grinding my teeth.

"Well that's a little off the mark…"

The flames were vicious as they ripped and tore through every nerve on my body, and I collapsed into the sand. My breathing became difficult, and once again I was suffocating. I clawed at the tightness in my chest and the closed throat that was still refusing my ability to breathe, and I screamed.

The fire writhed and sought to consume every fiber of my being and I was drowning in it.

Something was wrong.

Sylver's callused hands reached for me, and I let my eyes flutter closed.

"Alterra," I sobbed, clenching my teeth as another searing flame enveloped me. "She needs us right now."

"Moira, what's going on?" I felt one of Sylver's hands brace me upright, whilst the other went to my forehead.

I continued, "Alterra's in trouble."

Then, nothing.

Chapter 16

Alterra

I MISSED IT HERE.

It'd been a while since I'd last tried to contact Thyello. Each time I'd tried to see him, the more it became clear to me that he could no longer access his staircase, and *that* thought scared me more than I cared to admit.

I paced in our dreamscape of clouds and lightning…

It never changed here.

Clouds still floated around at my feet, on the walls, and on the ceiling above me, and the lightning flickered my innermost emotions and memories upon the walls.

My own staircase was behind me.

Flowers, moss, vines, roots, branches of trees...they'd each grown into something more. In becoming one, they'd become a staircase forged from our very world to lead me to him.

"Thyello!" I called out, but only my voice echoed back to me.

Lightning flashed and the walls reflected back my hopelessness. My pain. My fear.

The cracking boom of thunder erupted around me in response. Some unconscious part of me must have still been hoping that something, anything, had changed in the last year, and that Thyello would finally be reunited with me here. But there was nothing. There had been no trace of him here since that fateful day five years ago. A lifetime ago.

I felt tears begin to well up in my eyes, and I shook them away. I didn't come here out of my own self-pity; I was here to send a message to Moira. I was still bleeding out.

My desperate panic flashed on the clouds before me, and I could only watch the wisps of life at my feet as even more blood seemed to drench the gauze at my back, now pooling around my listless body, lying prone, face down on one of the three mats in the midst of the desert sand.

I was losing too much blood.

Another boom of thunder shook the dreamscape. Perhaps the clouds were now sensing my foreseeable death in that faraway realm. I didn't even know if I'd be able to stay here within our intertwined souls if I died somewhere else.

I didn't want to find out either.

I closed my eyes, then whispered into the swirling tempest now engulfing the space surrounding me, "You're mine, Thyello, and there is nothing that I won't do to see you or to hear your voice again." I opened my eyes, then dragged my hand through the clouds gathering at my legs. "You're worth more to me than the air I breathe." I took a ragged breath. "More than life itself."

Chain lightning set the clouds aflame, shifting them into exhilarating shades of blue, grey, purple, pink. The dreamscape was trying to comfort me. The clouds became his eyes. I smiled, and thunder exploded around me once more. I was safe here. I would always be safe with Thyello.

"ALTERRA!!!" A voice, a bang as loud as the thunder booming around me, screamed at my limp body. I stared at the clouds immersing my feet and watched as a figure wrapped in white fabric approached.

It encroached upon where I lay, and it continued screaming my name. I watched as the figure came closer and closer, and observed that it wasn't merely a figure, but two. The one screaming my name was carrying another.

Sylver carried Moira over a shoulder as he ran to the lean-to I'd fixed.

How long had I been here?

He eased Moira down onto the mat beside mine along with the various sacs he'd brought with them and rushed to me. Grabbing a hold of my wrist, Sylver's brow furrowed as he mouthed something inaudible that I couldn't read, before turning to Moira, who still seemed too exhausted to even stand. He breathed into the desert, "She's still alive. Her pulse is weak, but she's still in there."

Little did he know that I was actually somewhere else entirely; high above them both, in a dreamscape forged of hope, of love, of life, of air, of Thyello...

Our intertwined souls had merged and had breathed life into a new world only we could ever access or experience.

Sylver removed the gauze that had been wrapped around me to keep the stitches in place, then sprinted to his bag not a body's length away, grabbing what looked to be his needle and the pig's gut he'd told me he'd used to fix me earlier.

He didn't bother being gentle as he pierced through my skin with the needle over and over and over. Once satisfied, he knelt down to the sand beside me, grabbed one of the two flasks they'd left for me while they were gone, and spilled some of the liquid onto my back, on top of the sutures he'd just made.

The piece of me that still held residency in the body now so far away could almost smell the alcohol's aroma as it worked to disinfect the ravaged skin of my back.

Sylver grimaced over his shoulder at where Moira kneeled, already tearing the fabric of her—my—skirt, before turning back to me and asking, "What did you think you were doing?"

I scoffed at him from where I stood above him in the clouds. It was his own shoddy craftsmanship that led me up here. Thunder cracked in confirmation of my thoughts around me, and I smirked.

Moira practically crawled to Sylver's side and passed him the fabric. It was too bad that she'd ripped it—again; it had been one of my favorite outfits. I sighed to myself. This wasn't exactly the time to be worrying about clothing choices.

Sylver made to wrap the fabric over my sutures again, but Moira stopped him with a hand and asked, "How long do you think until she wakes up?"

"Not too long; we're going to have to wake her." Sylver ran a hand through his dishevelled hair, murmuring, "If she doesn't drink something soon, she'll wind up with the same fate as if we didn't find her to begin with."

Sylver was right; I'd have to leave this last piece of Thyello. I couldn't let everything I'd done be for naught. Everything I'd done to return to Thyello these past years would have been for naught if I didn't muster up the courage to descend my staircase.

I breathed in Thyello's lingering scent of cedar and sage and mist one last time before beginning my descent.

I clenched my hands around my railing of roots and blossoms, stepping down onto the silvery limb of my favourite rowan tree, and gazed ahead into the complete darkness that could only exist between realms.

His clouds were still thin wisps around me; caressing me as he had once done.

I would miss them too, more than the air I breathed. More than my own life. Just like I did him.

I stared behind into the clouds still resting peacefully on our balcony of storms and watched as Sylver finished wrapping me in the almost clean material Moira had pilfered from the skirt I'd lent her. I tore my gaze away from Sylver's crouched form, and willed *myself to take another step forward down my staircase as he bellowed, "Alterra, Alterra—"*

I opened my eyes to the harsh light of the desert, before seeing both Sylver and Moira waiting above me.

To my surprise, they *both* looked relieved to see me awake. Sylver brought the other flask to my lips, and I drank heartily before he took it away. I was going to live. And I was going to see my Thyello again. No matter what.

Moira flinched, then gave me a disapproving look. "Was that really necessary?" She paused, then said, "You could have just waited for us to return before doing whatever it was you decided to do."

My voice was weak as I replied. "The sun…the lean-to had practically fallen over in the night. And when I woke up…" I took another sip of water from Sylver, then continued, "I was afraid that I was going to bake alive."

"And you thought about your desire as a way to signal me," Moira mused. "Smart, but risky. You're lucky that I'm beginning to build up a tolerance to the flesh searing off my back, or else I would have just passed out and we both would have wound up unconscious for nothing."

Sylver's lips twitched upwards, and he interrupted me, placing the flask to my mouth again and cogitated of his own accord. "I'm just amazed you were able to move this early on without any help from one of us."

He took the flask from my mouth yet again, so I glanced to Moira before saying, "I knew it was a risk, but it had to be done. I have never been able to handle being overheated." I then looked to Sylver who was still perched above me. "And yeah, I've been trained to cope with all types of pain. When faced with the feeling of my back being torn apart and everything else that came with that,

I decided I could deal with it—*all of it*—as long as it meant I wouldn't burn."

"I'm still not sure how you could do it."

"I'm just a fast healer I guess."

Sylver gave me a look that suggested he thought something else was afoot, and I could see he was going to press me for a better answer, but I went on, cutting him off, "Moira, did you guys at least succeed in getting more supplies for the trip ahead?"

Moira perked her head up, then grabbed the bag at her feet. "We were able to get an extra two week's worth of rations, plus Sylver also managed to carry enough water to last us approximately the same amount of time as the rations, so I'd say we were pretty successful." She rolled her eyes. "It would have amounted to more, but because of that stint you pulled, we lost a good quarter of what we were carrying initially."

Sylver crooned, "Moira, you weren't actually carrying *that* much." He smiled as he glanced to me. "Don't let her trick you. After she told me that you needed us, she actually *did* pass out from the pain by the way, and because I felt the need to save her too, I did leave behind one water bladder so that I could carry her."

I nodded, still exhausted from blood loss, the extent of which was still visible on both the mat and sand adjacent to where I was now positioned. I asked, "Did Waha seem to be doing well?"

Sylver peered at me. "He's better than I thought he'd be." His tone was clipped—harsh—before he twisted to face Moira. "At one point he even tried to kick us out. Told the two of us that he could take care of himself and that we should just have some fun and not worry so much about him." He grinned, and I couldn't help but give Moira a knowing look; however, she didn't seem to be paying any heed to our conversation. Sylver continued unphased. "Apparently the old man wasn't kidding when he said he could handle his own out there; he seemed livelier than ever." Sylver paused in what seemed to be contemplation, then continued, "It was nice to see that he wasn't lying to us before."

I couldn't hide my relief as I sighed, "I'm glad he's okay."

"Well, I'm glad to see that you suddenly care about his well-being."

I shut my eyes.

"Sylver, it was *never* my intention to—"

"Your intentions don't really matter Alterra. What's done is done, and he's doing well. Let's keep it at that."

I reigned in my retort. I felt guilty enough for everything I'd already put him through, and I didn't want to argue. We'd left Waha alone for less than a week…it would still be a miracle if he kept his heart beating until Sylver returned. And Sylver wasn't stupid as far as I could tell. He'd too probably already guessed that Waha's survival was still a long shot.

Sylver, seemingly happy with the amount of water I'd drank, then shifted to Moira's side and gave her a rather sultry expression that I had to look away from.

In time, Alterra. In time you'll be able to give that same look to Thyello.

"Seriously, Al?" Moira glared over Sylver's shoulder at me, and I could only shrug in return.

Everything will be okay in the end.

"I'm tired guys, so I think I am going to nap until I feel a bit better." I lied. I just didn't want to be awake to envy the so-obvious spark between Moira and Sylver. Perhaps they'd already managed to work through some of their differences. Although, I doubted that Moira would admit to it.

Sylver cast me a cursory glance from where he sat in front of Moira and said, "Okay, rest well. We'll be here when you get up, so you don't need to worry about that happening again." Sylver's smile feigned reassurance before he again turned to Moira, who was now beaming.

Maybe "beaming" was a strong word. Her mouth curved into an easy smile as she'd glanced Sylver's way, but her eyes were disinterested, tired. Perhaps her incessant travelling was finally starting to wear down on her, but I really doubted that. It was more likely that she was simply growing bored of Sylver, or maybe…

I shook my head and tore my own gaze away. I was nitpicking again, desperate to find a fault in their burgeoning relationship so that I wouldn't have to feel so bad about my own unremitting loneliness.

Clearly, I couldn't bring myself to look at their happiness.

I was happy for them, but I couldn't help but have my mind drift...

Ground your thoughts, Ally.

There was no need to put Moira through any more unnecessary pain than I had already.

I closed my eyes, soothing myself. I had to remember that I'd just been blessed with a gift—how beautiful and perfect it was to escape into a thunderstorm in the midst of a desert.

My mother's lullaby further comforted me, easing both my thoughts and my pain so that their sharp edges would no longer slice my soul to shreds little by little.

Everything will be okay in the end.

Maybe she really was right about that after all.

Chapter 17

Moira

"I DON'T THINK YOU EVER quite explained to me how you wound up here…" Sylver positioned himself beside me after Alterra had told us that she was wanting some sleep.

Understandable. It was a pain in the ass that she'd have to take even longer to heal up and that it would take me even longer to reach Laspiar again, but at least Alterra was still breathing. It was a miracle she'd even survived what she did. Blood still drenched the sand at her side, and her face held a sickly pallor to it. So unlike the golden tan that had only grown darker on our voyage to her fate.

"What do you want to know?" I trawled my hand through the infinite granules at my fingertips, finding nothing but more sand beneath. I suspired.

I really did hate the desert.

"What were you doing before you met her?" He tilted his head to where Alterra was sprawled, sleeping beneath the lean-to, and continued, "You'd told me that she was using you. What did you mean by that? Also, how did you know that she needed help earlier?"

I breathed, "That's a lot of questions."

"Are you going to answer them?" Sylver's eyes kindled with their inner fire once more, and I rolled my eyes. If I ever wanted to trick the oaf into bed, I'd have to show that I trusted him—somewhat.

I started, "Before I met Alterra, I was working in the circus."

Sylver barked a laugh. "The *circus?*"

"*Yes*, the circus," I bristled. "And if you're not going to let me finish the story, you'll only hear my silence for the rest of the day." He chuckled and lifted his hands in surrender, so I continued. "My stage name was *the Moira*." I waited a moment, half-expecting some glimmer of acknowledgement from him, then continued. "I was working there because I have a gift." At Sylver's raised brows, I elaborated, "I can sense where the desires of others lie."

"That's why she's using you?"

"Sylver, this is your final warning."

"Fair enough." He sighed, then shifted so as to lie on his side. The muscles limning his arms and core contorted with the movement, and I felt the need to tear my gaze away from his figure before he could notice where my attention lingered. Only when he faced me once more, the epitome of innocence, did I begin my storytelling yet again.

"Over the past so many years, I've had many men pay for my services. All of them desiring money, women, power. The last man that I'd been forced to help, by the name of Qasir, wanted just that. But I didn't know what he wanted when we'd initially crossed paths north of Neosordess." I omitted Salvador's involvement in the arrangement. "It was only a while into the trip that I finally got an idea of just how much of a prick he was."

Pictures of the village flashed across my mind, and I combed a hand through my hair, to clear the memory. "It took us around four weeks to reach Neosordess, and less than a day after that, I was able to lead him to his desire before he wound-up dead because he wouldn't listen to me, at Alterra's hand." I plowed ahead, envisioning that night, letting the memories consume me. "I didn't know where he'd find his desire in Sin's Forum—I didn't even know what Sin's Forum was at the time, but whatever. The point is that he thought he was going to assassinate Kieran the same way that Kieran had assassinated the Forum's previous ruler. He tried to stab him in the back with a dagger, but Kieran somehow managed to survive, and then Qasir tried to pin his failed coup on me." I sighed. "I was fully expecting to be killed that night, but by a miracle, Kieran saw through Qasir and his attempts to smooth over his earlier actions and punished him for it. Kieran slit his throat on the mezzanine for everyone below to watch.

"But Kieran didn't let me leave after this. Instead, he kept me as his guest in the cells above the forum and attempted to have me divulge my secrets. I think he—*she*—thought I was a spy or something, but when I wouldn't speak, I think Kieran began meditating or something and then my gift—my *flicker*—nearly killed me. It was very similar to what happened when you had to carry me a little while ago. But *that* never happened to me before, so I didn't know what was going on. My flicker usually just burns me a little bit around my spine when it's trying to lead me to someone's desires." I began braiding my hair into a plait while Sylver watched, mesmerized. "Alterra's desire is so strong that my flicker nearly kills me whenever she thinks of it. I am still not exactly sure why that is."

I took another breath. "When it finally occurred to me that the reason why my flicker decided to scald me alive was because Kieran *desired* something, I offered my services to him free of charge, so that I'd be free of the cells and be free of that horrid city." My lips twitched upward when I finally finished the plait and returned my gaze to Sylver's before whispering, "Then I met you."

I almost cringed as the words toppled free of my mouth—

"And then you met me..." Sylver shook his head slowly, seemingly not quite believing what I'd said. He asked, "Do you know what Al wants?"

"I have no idea. It could be anything."

"But you'd said before that she could be the way back to your home."

"Well, that's only a fool's hope." I'd told him too much already. I sounded like a loon as it was.

Maybe I'd already lost it.

Besides, he'd never touch me if I bothered speaking *that* teensy truth to him: the fact that I couldn't even guarantee that I was interpreting my flicker's signals correctly...

Tendrils of flame curled around my heart, and I wanted to believe the comforting, somnolent touch of my little dancer. But even still, a growing part of me recognized the subjectivity that came with communing with the invisible entity. If I'd been *wrong*—I staunched that train of thought. I hadn't been wrong once during these past years, and I wasn't suddenly wrong now.

Nevertheless, Sylver would never learn of my home because it wasn't here. Laspiar was practically a mythical entity—I could barely envisage the place I'd spent most of my existence. I'd spent nearly half of a decade searching for my home, and during that time, only one thing had become clear: Laspiar wasn't a part of this world.

"Where is your home, Moira?"

I stiffened at the concern marking Sylver's words. "It doesn't matter."

A nod. "If that's what you want me to believe..."

"It's the truth." It didn't matter to him. It never would.

Another nod. "Sure thing." He then rose onto his feet, taking a few steps to where our supplies still rested, before he returned, rations and water for us both in-hand. "Figured you're probably hungry."

My stomach let out an affirming growl and Sylver laughed, dropping both a chunk of dried, hearty bread and a flask into my lap before taking up his spot to the left of me once more. The last time I'd had anything to eat was while we were at Waha's.

I nibbled on the loaf and swigged occasionally from the flask to quench my thirst, Sylver and I watching Alterra sleep in companionable silence while doing so.

Her face was still dotted in what looked to be stubble, and her chest rose and fell in an even rhythm; it was hard to believe she was the monster so many feared.

Sylver's humming rumbled through the silence, and I glanced to where he now sprawled. "Where did you learn that?" My little flicker began the same dance to the tune as before upon my spine—floating and merging with the comfort of a faraway memory I couldn't yet place.

He ceased his humming for only a second to murmur, "Learn what?"

"That music." I swayed as some part of me remembered how the tune would climb towards a looming precipice first, before subsequently tumbling down, eventually easing into a soothing echo of its former glory. I whispered, "It reminds me of before…" I closed my eyes, content to just drift away with the melody, and shifted my body closer to him.

He halted his beautiful music once more. "Before what, Moira?"

"I don't remember…" I breathed, sighing as I reached the warmth of his side, inhaling his scent of burning wood and smoke. "Please, don't stop." I didn't care that I couldn't remember why his melody calmed me, and I certainly didn't care that I hadn't finished the food he'd given me.

I felt his quiet laughter reverberate against my head as I rested it on his chest, before he crooned, cocooning me into him, "Whatever you desire, Moira."

When I fell asleep, I was no longer in the midst of a desert.

Sylver, with his wonderful voice, had carried me back to a place I could call home.

Chapter 18

Alterra

TODAY WAS GOING TO BE DIFFICULT.

The Messiah was planning on visiting the Forum.

I knew what He wanted—always the same three girls every time He came. I wasn't certain what He did to them exactly, but they never seemed too upset to see Him leave.

I washed up in my personal chambers and applied the same cosmetics as I did everyday to my face; with a brush, I applied a brown cream of sorts so as to grant me the appearance of having both a five o' clock shadow and of having thickened, darker eyebrows. Occasionally, I also added it to the sides of my face to make it look like my sideburns had grown in. But today I couldn't be bothered. I'd have to tell Derrik that I'd shaved them off last night. I couldn't bother styling my hair either. I kept it messy and unkempt and short. Nor could I ever wear any of the form fitting clothing I liked.

I could never let them glimpse the hourglass silhouette I still made sure to keep underneath my manly exterior.

I grabbed the drab white fabric and began to wrap my chest extra-tight for the next few hours. It was a miracle that no one had ever gleaned I didn't belong here.

It was a miracle that I'd actually managed to learn the language enough in the first few months after I'd arrived here to be able to spend the rest of my time perfecting the accent of the city bustling around me.

If the Messiah ever found out a that woman was running things around here...

I shook my head at the thought.

Suffocating myself was a worthy sacrifice if it meant I wouldn't have to face the consequences of being caught today.

I donned my black leather trench coat, then looked in the mirror. I guessed that I looked manly enough, but only my mannerisms would work to keep the façade authentic. I watched as I willed my face to shift into one that translated into either, I mean business, or Mess with me and your throat will be slit. I changed my posture into the same cocky thing Thyello used when talking to people he didn't particularly like; people who were supposed to respect him, nonetheless. He always appeared confident, powerful...untouchable.

I took a deep breath before leaving my room.

Derrik stood guard, waiting for me as usual, so I cooed in my deeper, subdued voice, "His room is ready, and the girls know that He will be "gracing" them with his presence?"

Derrik rolled his eyes before starting to the staircase. "Oh yeah. How could I forget about the high prick himself?"

I chuckled. "Don't let His disciples catch wind of you saying that." I blew out a breath. "But seriously, we have to keep things tight and precise. If word got out about the truth of that man, Neosordess would fall in a matter of days, and I don't really want to be here to pick up the pieces."

Derrik was a hard man, but I could trust him to look after the Forum upon my departure; he never mistreated the girls. He respected them, a rare quality in these parts.

"Oh, I'm aware Kieran. I just don't like how the girls act when He leaves."

"What exactly do you mean?"

"They're just quiet." He breathed, "I tried asking Lyn what had happened, and she refused to tell me."

I rolled my neck and shoulders at the lip of the staircase.

If the girls didn't want out of their predicament with Him, then I wasn't going to do anything about it. That would draw His attention, and I still had to play this role. It was my only shot at returning to Thyello. Only the people who held power ever achieved their desires in this city—or at least, that was the only impression I'd drawn since I'd found myself here.

I scratched the top of my head. The Messiah would be arriving shortly but disguised (of course), so He could still remain His holy self in the eyes of His sheep.

A step behind Derrik, I plastered a cool smile onto my face as I entered the darkness of the stairwell. His disciples would be here already, guns in-hand.

They always arrived before He did to guarantee His safety.

It wasn't like anyone in this city—besides me—was even capable of taking on one of the disciples without a gun. But then again, that, along with the fact that He could hold complete control over them, was exactly why He'd stolen the guns from the people when He came into power to begin with. Or at least that was what I'd imagined took place. I never actually learned the complete history of Neosordess; it only came to me in bits and pieces, and those bits and pieces rarely came from those who were actually from the city...

A few had told me briefly of a war, and a few others told stories of how the Messiah had saved the city by warning the people of the betrayal of another.

Some even told me that Neosordess had never been a "city", but instead a district that was governed by some overhead body far to the north of here. According to those same people, there were many districts—three of which relied upon the Aspitha as a water source: Neosordess, Aktearean, and Meriyaet.

Although, my favourite tales were always those that claimed He could control the storms; droughts would be ended and floods would dry up, all at His oh-so-powerful hands. I smiled to myself at the thought. No mere man would ever be capable of ruling over the skies.

Ever since I'd met the Messiah, I'd spent many hours contemplating his downfall. The only way I could see someone ever taking down the empire the Messiah had built for himself would be to hire help from outside Neosordess; perhaps Aktearean, a place rumored to still have citizens with autonomy, situated to the northwest on Masyron's coast.

I was sure the Messiah was well aware of this too. That was why He tortured the people of Neosordess endlessly—sleep deprivation via the lights He mandated were to stay on at all times. He'd claimed the lights were a means to wash away man's sinful nature and to protect His people from harm, but I knew better.

The captain in me had to give it to Him; He knew what He was doing. He was sadistic and immoral, but efficient.

"Kieran, He should be here by now."

I nodded.

Derrik was the first to descend to my balcony, and I followed, alert, ready for anyone or anything to catch me off-guard. Every breath, every word, every move of mine had to be calculated; a slip on my behalf would mean death with possible torture beforehand.

I'd always hated being tortured.

Derrik had ensured that the balcony would remain in near-complete darkness ahead. He'd always believed that the latter protocol was done out of concern for the Messiah's anonymity. He never guessed that the dark also worked to keep my secrets safe too.

A hooded man stood before my makeshift throne, and I stiffened.

"Kieran." The Messiah's voice was cold and cruel, spiked with the ignorance that only years of lying to oneself could accomplish. He turned to face me.

I fought the urge to unsheathe the sword at my side and gave him a smile. "Your Holiness."

A whisper of laughter. "You don't have to be so formal. This isn't our first-time meeting here." He hesitated before continuing, "Call me Donovir."

I quelled the urge to laugh at the "honor" He bestowed me and kept my face aloof. It was just so...expected, that a man with His ego thought that I'd legitimately care about His title.

"As you wish, Donovir." I gestured with an arm to a hidden passage behind some of the curtains dangling in the space. "The girls are within there as always. Enjoy."

He'd ventured here enough to know how the business worked. One of His disciples discreetly handed me an envelope—money for both the girls and the supplies He no doubt had difficulty attaining on His own.

The Messiah took no time before strutting in the direction of the passage, and I exhaled.

He didn't notice me.

I twisted away from the now swaying curtains and made myself cross the space to where the speakers thrummed with life. I cranked the volume to its highest limit; I didn't need any excess noise travelling down below to the other paying patrons. The force of the bass from the speakers shook the mezzanine and I cast a wicked grin to the disciples, their faces now contorting with fear. Good; I wanted them to fear me. Their fear would keep me from prying eyes.

My trench coat flared on an invisible wind as I strutted to the railing not a few steps away. It was the only location in the building capable of granting me access to every corner of the Forum below, and I grimaced in the spotlights as I watched women and men alike writhe and twist to the wild bass booming behind me.

I'd never thought my life would become this.

After everything I'd survived and fought and suffered through, I'd never imagined I'd be stripped of everything I'd worked so hard to achieve. But it didn't surprise me. Life was unjust.

Damn, I was really starting to screw up my nights and days.

I woke up and I could just make out the full moon in the distance from where I was still lying, casting the dunes in its silvery-gray light. My legs and arms were aching, longing to be moved, but I fought against the impulse. I had to heal, and that wouldn't happen if I kept retearing my stitches.

Moira and Sylver appeared to be sleeping now; she'd let her head rest on his chest.

Thy—

I had to stop allowing intrusive thoughts about *him* to slip by my defenses. My jealousy would do no one any good. Moira needed her sleep. It was still hard to believe she'd been travelling for practically a month straight now—if not longer—on foot. She was obviously a more determined person than what she chose to let others see. Maybe she too had something that she desired above all else. Did she lose something too?

Or someone?

I glanced to Sylver, sprawled out below Moira on his sleeping mat, and couldn't help but wonder the same thing. But unlike Moira, he seemed perfectly content to stay where he was back at Waha's keep. As far as I could tell, he didn't seem to yearn for anything else like the two of us clearly did; or at least he didn't do so before Moira wandered into his life.

The gurgling of my stomach snapped me back into reality. I was hungry. Actually, to be more honest with myself, I was *starving*. I dragged my eyes over to the space to the left of the mat. There, someone, probably Sylver, had left me both a flask and a piece of dry bread.

Scowling, I used my left arm to reach towards them both, and I visibly sighed in relief as the stitches holding me together didn't stretch or strain with the movement.

I devoured the bread as quickly as I could grab it, and the water didn't take long to follow suit.

I dropped the empty flask at my side.

My hunger and thirst had subsided, and I was thankful to whoever it was who had enough foresight to think about my comfort.

Sylver then.

I watched Sylver and Moira for a moment longer, then glanced to the sky above us, now flecked with stars.

It had been so long since I'd seen stars like this.

In Neosordess, with the omnipresent lighting, it was impossible to make out anything in the beautiful universe poised before us; one of the *many* downfalls of the city.

I shut my eyes, savoring the feeling of the wind embracing me under the starlit sky above. I could almost pretend—*no*. I'd promised myself that I wouldn't think of...

At least if all else were to fail, I could say that I was finally allowed to enjoy a couple of little pieces of home...even if the night's sky did not resemble my own. If Moira was to fail, I'd have to write this excursion off as a long-awaited vacation. In the three years I'd worked my ass off in the Forum, I'd yet to take any kind of a break.

I wondered how Derrik now handled all the responsibility I'd placed on his shoulders, left alone to deal with the Messiah and the others. Would the Messiah care of my sudden departure? Would Derrik finally uncover what the Messiah was doing to the girls when He paid for them?

Nausea churned low in my gut, and I scowled again. I shouldn't have ignored their suffering at His hand. Derrik had told me of Lyn's silence perhaps six months ago, and I'd waved it off. But her silence was indication enough.

I'd let such horrible things go unpunished while I'd ruled the Forum, *all* under the guise of returning to Thyello.

My eyes shot to Moira who was still passed out.

I was a monster.

I *was* the monster all those children had seen in me and feared when they rejected me.

Time and time again.

Tears streamed down my face as I let my thoughts wander some more.

They would never accept me.

Everything will be okay in the end.

I scoffed as my mother's words echoed through my mind, and I winced as I hefted my arms to my eyes to soothe myself.

Would Thyello come to accept the person I'd become to reach him again? He'd told me that he loved me unconditionally—I implored that he was telling me the truth.

I did everything for him.

For us.

Taking deep breaths, in and out, I pressed my palms firmly to my tear-streaked eyes and calmed my racing heartbeat. In and out. In and out. In and out. Minutes passed, and only after the sound of my breathing mirrored the desert winds, did I let myself finally fall asleep once more.

Chapter 19

Alterra

FOUR DAYS HAD PASSED since Sylver had redone my sutures.

Aside from when I felt the need to relieve myself, I'd only been moved twice in the meantime; both times I was moved in order to have some more alcohol poured onto the wound so I could heal with no complications.

I'd suggested only once that they should drag me back to Waha's keep; however, both Moira and Sylver insisted I remain here, half-buried in the dunes, to prevent any further harm from occurring.

I didn't argue.

Each time I was moved, Sylver held me in place while Moira either disinfected the slice or helped me in other, more hygienic ways; helping where possible when I had to piss or shit myself. I hated it.

I hated needing to rely on her—on *them*. I really fucking regretted egging Sylver on…despite feeling guilty for abandoning Waha or not.

I could tell Moira also didn't particularly enjoy nursing me back to health, but she endured it. I didn't complain either; frankly, I was still grateful to be on the receiving end of any help from either of them. Although, Sylver seemed to believe that today would be the last that their tender love and care would be necessary.

I was skeptical.

The feeling of my skin peeling from my ribcage still haunted me, sleeping and awake. I couldn't say I was *nervous* about testing out the integrity of Sylver's handiwork, but the idea of not being well enough to continue moving after the check-up, made me unsure. I didn't want to place too much hope in an idea only to have it fall flat.

I'd done *that* enough as it was already.

Plus, the idea of reliving that beautiful sensation was not one I yearned for.

Sylver was propping me up yet again to examine the sutures when he marvelled at my back. "I need to remove them."

"Are you sure?" I'd healed that much already? I twisted my head over a shoulder to Sylver. "I thought you said that you'd sliced me down to the bone?" No one ever healed *that* quickly. At least not here.

Moira rushed to Sylver's side and gawked. "It was—I was sure…" She was apparently at a loss for words. "I'll grab the bag with your supplies in it." She scurried away to Sylver's bag, which was at the other side of the campsite, then returned, bag-in-hand.

"Okay, so we'll need either a small blade, or scissors, and maybe tweezers to pull them free." Sylver still held me while Moira dug around in his satchel in search of the things he'd asked for. She finally placed some scissors and a pair of tweezers on the sand beside us.

Of course, she'd placed them in the gritty, good-for-nothing sand. I fought back a grimace, as I imagined the small stones finding their way into the wound, or merely scraping against the barely healed skin...

Sylver directed his attention to me and asked, "Do you think you can hold yourself up for a second?"

"I can." I shrugged away from his hand.

"Wait." He held out an arm, then indicated to the ground with a curt nod. "Get onto your stomach—it will make the procedure a lot easier for the both of us."

"Sure." Feeling a bit bruised, I moved so that I was lying facedown on the mat. I felt more than saw Sylver as he hovered over me from behind and I couldn't help but watch Moira while she kept stock of his each and every movement.

I was quickly taken aback when I noted her eyes. Sure, I'd known they were stunning, azure... But, fixated on Sylver and analytical, I watched as her eyes flicked to me, to Sylver...and it was as if the bluest, innermost part of a candle's flame watched us.

I closed my eyes.

I felt some pressure and tugging on my skin—admittedly, it was almost soothing—but after a matter of a couple of minutes, Sylver's voice rang out, startling my eyes open once more. "Done! Honestly, I'm surprised it wasn't as bad as it was."

"Will there be a scar?" I kept my voice neutral—my mother would be *furious* if I returned home with evidence that anything had maimed my body...and I really loathed the idea of conflict, even though I had to face the throes of it almost every day of my life.

"There *should* be a scar, but at the rate you're healing, who knows?" *Great.* Sylver backed away from where he'd been perched before saying, "You should be okay to stand as is, but we'll wait to get back on the road until tomorrow."

Without delay, I rolled over onto my side to get into a kneeling position. No pain. Yes, yes, yes, yes, yes. I got my feet underneath me and made to stand in one fluid movement.

"Impressive." Sylver's voice was quiet—awestruck.

I was standing.

"So tomorrow we can get back on track." Moira shook her head before adding. "I'm just happy we won't be held up by any of Sylver's mistakes anymore."

Sylver playfully bumped her shoulder, then asked me, "How do you feel?"

I felt relieved. I hated feeling useless; helpless.

"Better." It was all I could bring myself to say.

I stretched my arms out in front of me and felt some pulling where the scar tissue now was, but the sensation was a hell of a lot better than anything I'd hoped for in such a short period of time. It'd been years since I'd last been seriously injured, and I was pleased to see that I'd retained something from my youth.

"You're sure that we can't head out today?" My anxiety sought to get the three of us back on track as there was no *real* reason to reside where we were currently situated in the sand.

Moira seemed inclined to agree with me.

Sylver's exasperation was comical. "Al, I get that you want to leave, but we still have to pack everything up, and it's already midday. First thing in the morning we can head out."

Stupid, *sensible* logic.

It was an effort to distract myself. "Moira, do we need to home in on our destination again?" I craved the thought of Thyello; he was always a welcome diversion.

"You've thought about your desire enough." She glared at me, and again, I could have sworn that her eyes flickered with an inner blue fire just a bit. "We're still to head northwest."

"Northwest?" Sylver's voice was alarmed.

"Yes, that's where my flicker wants us to go. What's your problem?"

"The Dunes of Almalto lie out that way." He shuddered. "I've only heard rumors of the danger those dunes bring—or any place west of here in general."

I stiffened. "Rumors don't mean anything." There were more than enough rumors about both me and my mother, and they were rarely ever true.

"You don't understand." Sylver's insolent gaze raked over me, and I returned his sentiment. "They're only rumors because no one has ever gone out that way and survived to tell the tale for themselves."

"It really can't be *that* bad Sylver." I smirked as an image of the Forum crept into my mind, along with the daily shenanigans I'd dealt with from its many patrons. "I'm sure that I've been through worse."

Sylver sighed. "I really doubt it Alterra."

Moira interjected, "What's supposed to be so bad about those dunes anyway?"

"It storms there. It never rains, but lightning creates shards of glass that can easily slice someone in half during a sandstorm. I remember too, some man also told Waha and I that when he approached the dunes, he heard clicking."

I scoffed. "*Clicking*? You would think that he would be more concerned about the shards of glass being whipped at his body."

"The man said it sounded like something large dwelled under the sand, and that it scared him enough to get the hell out of there before he knew where or what it was coming from."

Moira cocked her head. "What would be capable of making that sound in the desert?" She tapped a finger on her chin for a moment, then mused aloud. "Maybe an insect of sorts or a snake?"

I shrugged. "Well, I have to have faith in Moira; her flicker led both of us to shelter after…after we ran out of water. Her flicker allowed me to let you guys know that I was dying. Not to mention, her flicker—" I paused, not wanting to mention that the flicker also let Moira and I know that Sylver was an asset we needed desperately for the journey. "I doubt that its goal is to kill the three of us. I mean, if that's its goal, I would personally feel a bit ripped off; she told me she would lead me to my greatest desire, and trust me, my desire isn't to go to an early grave."

Sylver bowed his head, resigned. "If we die, I'm blaming you Alterra and that foolish desire of yours."

I reigned in my retort and smiled at him instead. "Great. So, we leave at dawn."

Sylver and Moira packed the majority of our supplies a while later after we'd finished eating. They'd remembered to leave the sleeping bags out—a blessing, because I was not even close to ready to sleep in the sand for a night.

After days of sleeping out in the desert, I still hadn't become habituated to the environment; I was still on-guard for snakes and other animals that could cause us problems in the night. Even though we had yet to see one snake or animal throughout the entire time we'd been travelling.

Sylver and Moira didn't seem to have a problem settling down for the night, but for some reason my mind wouldn't wind down enough for me to join them. I remained awake, watching both them and the sky.

Needless to say, I was exhausted when they woke at dawn.

We began our journey shortly after we all ate, and despite only being healed enough to stand the day before, I was more than able to keep up with both Sylver and Moira today.

My body was just happy. Happy that I no longer had to wear such a heavy, tight, restrictive trench coat anymore while travelling through the desert. Happy that I could move my aching muscles again…

Moira and Sylver kept each other company while I trailed behind them.

I was grateful that I no longer had to carry any of our supplies because of my back "still needing time to heal." I smiled to myself. So, there *was* an upside to nearly being sliced in half over Sylver's unexpected, expected outburst.

Despite the hours I spent trudging along behind them, I didn't pay Sylver nor Moira much heed. I only now noticed that Moira had donned one of the other dresses I'd lent her; this one a light blush pink, while she used the skirt of the flowing sand-coloured one as a headdress.

I only bothered slipping on my own headdress when the sun was high overhead. The water we still had was a finite resource, and I wasn't foolish enough to let myself become dehydrated. I absolutely despised anything on my head, especially when it only made it more difficult to discern our surroundings. But the headdress made my body only *marginally* less happy.

For the majority of the trek, I watched the dunes.

The utter lack of life unnerved me—no green things, no water, no animals…there was nothing in our line of sight besides the endless sprawl of sand around us.

I'd been startled more than once when Sylver or Moira or both of them broke out into laughter out of seemingly nowhere. At those moments, it was instinct to think of Thyello and his diabolical, angelic grin, but I didn't allow myself to dwell on my own loneliness. I was as close to happy as I'd been in…

Since before I'd lost him.

A few more days of walking had passed when Sylver announced, "We'll hit the Dunes of Almalto within a day."

How could he be so certain if he'd never been there before?

Moira paused her walking, and seemed to be wondering the same thing when she asked, "How exactly can you tell? It all looks the same to me."

I caught up to the two of them before quickly observing our surroundings; I couldn't actually see a marked difference in the sand, but I could feel it.

Sylver hedged. "The air—can't you two feel the difference from what we've experienced the last two weeks?"

"I can feel it." My skin tingled and it reminded me of… I mumbled, "Electricity. The air feels charged, not stagnant like I'd come to expect with the storms I'm used to, but *something* must be up ahead."

Sylver's face pleaded to Moira. "Are you certain that we're still to continue this way?"

There was no hesitation before she responded, "I always am."

Just as Sylver had guessed, a day later we saw them: the Dunes of Almalto.

At first from afar, we could only make out that the sky was a much darker, purple grey to the northwest. But as the day progressed, we could begin to make out the blinding white flashes of lightning striking the sand. And then we heard it.

The clicking.

It was barely noticeable at first; faint clicks, like little pebbles dropping onto one another. It was nothing outrageous—I didn't think anything of the quiet click, click, click, as we continued. Or at least that had been the case until the clicking became an insistent and forceful popping.

How could they not hear it?

Beneath our feet, the sand sounded like boiling grease in a skillet, and I shouted, "Stop moving!"

Surprisingly, they both halted and Sylver demanded, "What's wrong?"

"Listen."

The desert had gone eerily silent. Silent even for a desert void of sound in the first place. There wasn't even a gust of wind.

But then a very distinct clicking began again beneath the sand.

I could hear it moving; beginning in the dunes themselves, then outwards towards where we stood frozen, then back again before stopping altogether.

Sylver whispered, panic igniting his features. "See? I had a feeling this was a bad idea."

Moira shook her head. "My flicker is still telling me to go forward—*us* to go forward, I mean." She added, "We don't know what that sound is. For all we know, it's harmless." She tapped a finger on an arm. "My gift has never done wrong by me...*really*. I trust it with my life."

I glanced forward to the Dunes of Almalto again; the sky was dark violet in areas, navy in others, and every few seconds chain lightning ripped across the sky, striking the dunes over and over without visible rhyme or reason. "What do you think is causing the storm?"

Sylver chuckled a bit breathlessly and said, "Hopefully not the same thing that seems to be scurrying beneath us."

Right. The incessant clicking.

"Well, there's no point to just standing here." Advancing forward again, Moira didn't check to observe if Sylver or I followed. She was such a ray of sunshine—it was no wonder why Sylver pined after her day in, and day out.

I smirked at Sylver as I strode by him and caught up to Moira before asking, "How much longer until we're actually in the dunes?"

She shrugged. "I wouldn't know."

I heard some thuds on the sand behind us as Sylver approached. Was he *stomping*?

"I don't think we should be making so much noise Sylver. Who knows what will set those things clicking beneath us off."

Moira was very clearly thinking the same thing as she glared over a shoulder at Sylver.

I only heard a quick huff from him behind me as his steps quieted to near silence.

On noiseless feet, we started towards the Dunes of Almalto once again, even though the clicking became more and more conspicuous with each step forward. The sky also seemed to shift to an even more violent state than it had minutes earlier; lightning flashed every couple of seconds, but without the sound of thunder that accompanied the storms I yearned for.

Within twenty minutes, we'd made it to the dunes.

The sand didn't appear any different, so *that* didn't act to mark their beginning. But the charge from the air we'd all felt earlier shifted into static. I could feel my hair begin to stand on end.

Sylver shouted, alarmed, "What the *fuck* was that?"

My head whipped to his arm, which he was now shaking profusely, and then I felt it.

The air was shocking us. *Electrocuting* us.

"Sylver, Moira. Run."

They didn't dither as they ran through the sand as fast as they both could. Moira dropped the satchel she'd diligently held, and I wordlessly pleaded with any deity that would listen that we wouldn't be needing those supplies.

Everything will be okay in the end.

The shocks didn't worsen the further we rushed into the dunes. With each stride we took, shocks could be felt; first zapping our arms, then our legs. I could hear the two of them shouting profanities when they too were hit. I only locked my jaw and kept running. Shouting profanities wouldn't get rid of the pain—it would only help me to run out of breath sooner.

I watched as "lightning" struck the places their feet touched, chasing their heels. I'd seen lightning strike the ground before, hundreds of times—but this…phenomenon, wasn't lightning. The lightning I'd known for forever and loved for even longer, was larger than life and would have easily claimed the lives of both Moira and Sylver in one foul swoop.

They had to run faster. *We* had to run faster.

I set the example. Increasing my pace as much as physically possible, the adrenaline meritoriously wiped away the memory of the dull ache I could still feel across my back.

I passed them in a heartbeat.

I'd trained for situations like this, and much worse in my life.

I heard the snap each strike assaulted us with, and I let my fear of imminent electrocution drive my pace to be even faster. Moira and Sylver's footfalls quickened behind me, but I didn't dare look back again. We couldn't slow down.

As my feet pelted the sand with each stride, I could feel it as the ground beneath gradually transformed into a landscape littered in what looked to be off-white rocks and splinters.

My foot smashed into one of those grey-white boulders, and I yelped, instinctively tearing my gaze away from the path ahead of me to where my foot now throbbed. Shards of glass jutted out of the ground along with...bones. The Dunes of Almalto were littered in the bones of those who had died here before us. Sylver hadn't been exaggerating. Undiluted fear pummelled into me, and I no longer felt the pain radiating from my foot, nor the rasping burn of my lungs as I ran.

And I ran.

And I ran.

"*STOP!!!*" Moira's voice echoed across the dunes.

It was an effort to slow my pace, to force myself to pivot towards her, to not continue running from the horrors of the dunes.

Sylver stood, panting beside her, and merely glowered at me.

"Why'd you tell us to stop?"

"The shocks. They've stopped." Moira nodded behind her and gasped before adding, "I had to stop. I'm not made for running long distances. I want...I want to drop."

Her face was beat red and sweat forcibly clung loose strands of hair to her face. I'd forgotten the struggles of having long hair.

My voice was hoarse from exertion, "I'm so sorry. I wasn't thinking." I splayed my arms and looked to Sylver, and saw he was in a similar condition to Moira.

"We'll make it," she snapped, before gracing me with a look that suggested she believed me to be a complete asshole. I couldn't help but agree with her. I felt like one too.

Moira gave Sylver a small smile and made to sit down in the sand, but I halted her. "We should walk around a bit first. Lower our pulses a bit."

"And now you're so caring?" Sylver scoffed. "You couldn't have cared less if you'd left us both!" He threw his backpack into the sand.

"That's not true! I do care." I wrung my hands in front of me, then brought them up to my eyes. They weren't understanding. I needed to breathe. I paced, needing to calm myself down a bit. I'd always hated my tendency to say things I regretted if I didn't allow myself the small courtesy.

"You can't hide from this Alterra!" Sylver bellowed. "Maybe you weren't just acting earlier when you played Kieran, eh?"

"Don't bring that into this." I was shaking with restraint as I hissed, "You don't know anything about me." I slowly removed my palms from my eyes before running them through my hair, and breathed, "I didn't want to leave you. But in all honesty, I just freaked out when I saw how the quote-unquote, lightning aimed for each of our steps and then I freaked out *again* when I kicked a *fucking* human bone." Another deep breath. "I'm sorry. I didn't mean to do that."

Moira took a step towards Sylver, who still seemed intent to rip me apart, before placing a hand on his chest. I saw her mumbling something to him before he began taking deep breaths, and my jaw practically dropped. Moira—*caring*? She mouthed, "Just breathe Sylver, you're fine. I'm fine." Moira turned from him and said with a chuckle, "Al, I'm not upset with you that you ran faster than us, I'm just pissed. We couldn't keep up, even if we wanted to. We could have *died*." Moira cocked her head to the side and asked, "How did you even manage to do that?"

I feigned nonchalance, feeling only slightly at ease with her words. "Years of practice Moira. It took me a long time to learn to pace myself properly."

Sylver mumbled, "Wish someone would have told us that beforehand."

Moira elbowed him in the side and jeered, "Don't whine Sylver; be a man."

His smirk…I had to look away. Soon I'd be with Thyello and then I wouldn't be so stupidly jealous of Sylver and—

"Ouch—wait!" Moira sprinted to my side and gestured to a large dune to the southwest. "We went too far north." There, where she pointed, just cresting the height of the dune, I could faintly make out a black smear.

"I thought it was mere legend." Sylver's awe was palpable.

"What *is* that?" Moira and I exchanged a worried look.

"Mount Poyanjen."

"Mount Poyanjen?" I twisted to where Sylver stood gaping at the darkness that lay ahead. "Isn't that just supposed to be a volcano?" It made sense that the black smear could be explained by falling ash.

"Yes. It's supposed to be a volcano." He shivered, then looked to me. "Why'd we have to be fated to go to the Mount? No one who ventures even close to it has ever made it back. And the bodies are never found."

I shrugged. "Well, it looks like we just found whole lot of them back there." A pause. "Perhaps *burning desire* gets a rise out of us when it puts us in danger." I smiled before looking to Moira. "Could that be true?"

"How am I supposed to know?" Moira flailed her arms, then brought one up to fix her hair. "My little flicker seems to enjoy tormenting me, so it wouldn't be unheard of for it to want your pain and suffering too."

"On the bright side," I glanced to face Sylver as he continued, "we've made it this far, and yes, the dunes were bad, and no one has ever made it back from here alive; however, maybe we'll be just fine." He halted, as if lost in thought, and picked up the supplies before adding, "Mount Poyanjen is also on the coast of the Masyron sea, so if you two get too hot at the foot of the volcano, you two can always cool off afterwards in the water."

I chuckled, rolling my eyes. "At least there's that."

"Well, enough chitchat." Moira's voice was a windchime as she plowed ahead. "There's no point in staying here forever, and besides, we might actually be able to make it to the Mount before nightfall if we leave now." Moira's face was impatient, and she merely turned on a heel without our approval before launching herself southwest.

Not like I'd disagreed with her plan, but considering she was the one who'd complained about needing to catch her breath not five minutes ago…

Sylver shrugged and gave me a look that suggested he was indifferent to the whole thing and trudged off behind her towards the dune and the dark stain ahead.

I sucked on a tooth as I glared at the dune blocking most of the Mount from sight, while I tried to shake out the aching pain that had gradually crept back into my foot. It was to no avail. I tore my gaze from the darkness to stare at the useless suede boot. Shards of glass had carved and sliced clean through its leather, exposing bare skin, and with it, bloodied nicks from shards that had painlessly ripped at the exposed skin while I'd ran. I curled my toes to assess the damage and winced at the sharp discomfort that accompanied the movement. How fucking wonderful. Climbing that dune was already going to be a bitch as it was, but with at least one broken toe?

I breathed deeply and whispered to myself, "Just a little bit longer, and soon, soon, you'll return home." I laughed, letting the steady throb in my foot ground me. "I've been through worse, even if no one else here seems to believe so."

I nodded and scanned behind me to the lightning flashing above the Dunes of Almalto, then began my climb to the dark smear. The pulsing ache oozing from my butchered foot didn't slow me as I followed them on the flicker's path to the Mount, and whatever sentence it would deal us upon our arrival.

Chapter 20

Alterra

THE SMEAR WE'D SEEN EARLIER had not been caused by ash as we'd assumed. Instead, it was Mount Poyanjen itself, smeared via its excessive radiating heat. It was terrifying.

We reached its base within half an hour of walking.

Standing at the foot of the volcano was like nothing I'd ever experienced. Glancing behind us, all that could be seen was the near endless sprawl of dunes and the violet clouds hovering over the Dunes of Almalto. But at the Mount's base, the sand was no longer golden as it had been throughout the entirety of our trek. It was now a charcoal that reached outwards, grasping at all of the honey-coloured sand it could reach, effectively converting it to its barren darkness. The volcano was an omnipresent figure, and we were nothing but specks of dust beneath its massive form.

The other side of the volcano was not visible from where we were perched at its base, but the calls of gulls were audible, suggesting that we were indeed close to the coast like Sylver had indicated earlier.

I crossed my arms over one another, then queried, "So Moira, where are we supposed to go now?"

Moira cocked her head at me before saying, "You know there's only one way to find out," she growled. "Might as well be quick about it."

I closed my eyes. "Sorry in advance."

Sun reflected off Thyello's golden curls in my memory, and he'd just opened his full mouth to whisper sweet nothings in my ear, when Moira muttered, almost in disbelief, "It can't be."

I opened my eyes to see her gaping at Mount Poyanjen.

"Are you serious?" I asked.

Typical of Moira to toy with my emotions... Mount Poyanjen was a *bloody* volcano—there would be no possible way for me to even survive whatever her "burning desire" intended, let alone to reach my Thyello again.

"My flicker has never lied to me before. Whatever you want, Alterra, it's within the Mount." She didn't *seem* to be joking. A skipping heartbeat kept track of the seconds as my brain sought to comprehend—*no*.

My jaw dropped and I implored, "But that's a death sentence." I threw a pleading glance Sylver's way and continued, "How am I supposed to do that?"

I'd hoped for so, *so* long that my sole desire wasn't hopeless, but that was *exactly* what it was—a fucking impossible task. I was never going to see Thyello again. Never again would I hold his hand, or dance with him under the moon, or read his loving, *perfect* letters, or hear his simply breathtaking voice, or watch him as his magnificent brain worked to solve any problem...at least, that wouldn't be possible in this lifetime. Tears streamed down my face. Apparently, I was depending on Moira's promise more than I'd initially planned. Apparently, my brain, (unbeknownst to me), had at some point reached the conclusion that she was my only, and *last* opportunity of ever…

I wailed against the misery pressing upon me. "No, no, *no!* You promised me Moira! You promised that you'd lead me to whatever I desired most!" I reached down, grabbed some of the blackened sand, and let it slip from my hand to the ground. "I don't desire death. If that's all I wanted, I could have come up with some much less convoluted way to do so without getting you involved."

I closed my eyes once more, then began doing some breathing exercises to calm myself.

"I'm sorry," Moira said quietly.

My hands closed into fists. "I don't care if you're sorry. Don't you understand that this was my only shot at getting my life back?"

They'd fucked me over. Nearly killed me.

"Alterra, Moira isn't to blame here."

I didn't want to deal with idealistic Sylver either. I wanted them to feel the sheer hopelessness and desperation I felt. The pure hate and madness and pain.

"Are you saying that *I* am to blame then?" I whipped my head to Sylver and hissed, "Because the way I see it, she was the one that told me that she could lead me to my desire. She didn't have to gift me with false promises. I've only desired one fucking thing, and now this."

Now I had nothing.

Sylver's voice resonated over my sobbing. "Are you sure, Moira, that it's inside?"

What did it even matter?

"Yes, I'm certain."

I felt Sylver's hand on my shoulder as he asked, "Can you give me any idea what it is you're after?"

"What does it matter?" I snapped.

It was impossible.

Even if I was capable of throwing myself into molten rock and surviving, he wasn't even here. I was certain that Thyello was still with the rowan trees of my home…he would never be caught in the middle of the scorching, *disgusting*, bleak piece of shit this desert was.

I shook as another sob shattered any semblance of hope I had left. What was the point? Was there even a point to everything I'd been forced to do to have a chance at finding him again?

"Don't write me off."

"Sylver, it's not an object if that's what you mean." I didn't even know how Moira's gift even found a way for me to get back to my home; back to him. So how was I supposed to know what to look out for?

But what did it matter?

Obviously, her flicker was trying to tell me that my quest to find him had been for naught so...

"Why don't we climb up to see what's actually going on instead of giving up, okay?" Sylver's attempt at reassuring me was pitiful. I could hear the falling sand and the thuds of his footsteps as he began his ascent up the Mount. I opened my eyes to see Moira following him up. It was useless.

Heat smeared the Mount's peak. It would be a feat in itself if we could even make it halfway up, and it wouldn't help that my suede boots no longer protected my feet from the scalding fire of the sand, but who was I to say that?

I started up after them.

The Mount's heat rose up mercilessly from the volcanic debris and my body, near-instantaneously became slick with sweat. Blisters formed on the pads of my toes as they accidentally touched the torched earth; however, the slope wasn't very steep, nor was the volcanic debris slippery, so I didn't have to get on my hands and knees to make it up the incline.

At least something was going right.

My breathing became laboured with every stride, as the temperature climbed alongside me to steal my breath. Sweat from my brow dripped onto the near-ebony sand, and I had to pause to wipe the salt away from my eyes.

Everything will be okay in the end.

Chapter 21

Moira

STEAM FROM CRACKS IN THE MOUNT billowed up around us as we stalked closer to its peak. Twenty or so minutes had already passed of this non-stop climbing, and I ground my teeth.

I still couldn't quite believe that my flicker had erupted into its frenzy when I'd gazed at the looming Mount itself. As urgent and unrelenting and overwhelming as it had been when we'd gotten close to Qasir's desire; however, this was an impossible task.

It had to know that.

Why would my flicker lie to me?

Why would my little dancer trick me into believing that if I just led Alterra to whatever it was she desired that I'd be led back to my home?

Why did she have to be yet another dead end?

Disappointment made every step onward difficult, but I fought against it; just as I'd fought against my disappointment for the last five years.

My little dancer still seemed to silently whisper, each flicker a symphony uttering the same words over and over, *Home Moira, take me home*, with its dance only becoming more fervent with each foot closer to the crater.

But I didn't let myself hope.

My flicker didn't seem to grasp that no human could survive venturing inside a volcano.

I blurted, "Sylver, why are you bothering with this?"

His steps were unfaltering as he continued ascending the Mount. He shrugged. "You said that you were certain that her desire could be found here." A pause as he hefted himself onto a small ledge of sorts. "I believe you. And I can't believe that this is the end of our journey together."

I cocked my head. "Why do you say that?"

"Do you believe in fate Moira?"

I rolled my eyes, refusing to say anything. Like fate was going to solve all my problems.

"We should probably wait here for a minute for Al to catch up..." Sylver gazed down behind where I still climbed to what I assumed was Alterra, taking her sweet time.

While she was wasting my time.

"She can keep up with us just fine," I grunted as I forced myself onto the rocky outcropping Sylver stood on, before my legs wobbled slightly. I was so bloody exhausted. Sylver helped to steady me with a hand, and I breathed, "After seeing her sprint through the Dunes of Almalto, I'd say she's just being slow."

Sylver gave me a look of reproach. "She can't handle the heat like we can Moira."

I dared a glance over my shoulder and found Alterra panting, sweat clinging to the fabric of the white T-shirt she'd taken back from the apparel she'd lent me, and I sighed. "I guess we can wait for her."

"How considerate of you." Sylver's lips twitched upwards, and the ashes of his eyes kindled awake.

Despite sleeping at his side for well over a week, his beauty never ceased to knock the breath of me—rugged, as if he'd been hewn from the very flames themselves. A familiar ache developed between my thighs, and I had to look away. He was still my one human desire. And with that one desire, it didn't matter if I was going back to my home or not.

Sylver mused, interrupting my train of thought, "I wonder what's up there."

"If we're lucky, it will be whatever Alterra desires."

And if *I* was lucky, we'd find the key back to the only place I'd ever truly belong.

Chapter 22

Alterra

AFTER ABOUT AN HOUR of climbing, we'd made it to a ledge where we could stand just a few feet below the main crater. The heat was suffocating, my skin was crawling, and I fought the impulse to remove the shirt I was wearing. Moira and Sylver didn't seem to be affected by the heat though…they never were.

"So, what was the point of doing this again?" I wanted to get my ass off this damned Mount so I could cool off. I couldn't *think* through the heat. I wanted to scream.

Actually, all I wanted to do was to hide away from everything and everyone and mourn, but the heat had already burnt away all my tears, leaving only the insufferable heavy ache behind my eyes, and there was no place I could even try escaping to in the desert wasteland before us.

It felt as if the Mount had become a monster, watching me, taunting me with my unattainable desire, and it was as if the blackened sand corrupting the golden halo of the desert surrounding it was its lair. But unlike the many monsters I'd already encountered in my life, I couldn't fight this one.

"Well, that depends." Sylver began climbing up further to the lip of the crater.

"What do you think you're doing? Are you *crazy*?" Asshole or not, I wasn't going to have him kill himself on my watch.

I made to reach towards him, to grab his leg, but he kicked my hand away and shucked off the satchel. "Trust me."

I derided, but I wasn't going to follow after him. I was too exhausted as it was and if that was his choice, so be it.

Sylver's hands reached into the near scalding earth at his feet, and I grimaced; we'd have to treat those burns upon our descent.

Then, he merely knelt at the lip of the volcano.

Moira warned, "Sylver, don't be an idiot."

"Well," He glanced into the heart of Mount Poyanjen. "There *is* magma way down in there." As if the heat wasn't indication enough. He chuckled. "I was sort of hoping it would be a dormant one." Impossible. That was what my desire was. Five years of hope. I'd let myself become a *monster*—

I could feel tears yearning to well up in my eyes yet again, but I already knew that there were none left to fall. Only their aching pressure remained, and *that* would only slowly go away upon their release. I'd sold my own soul to return to him; murdered people, so I could finally see his angelic face anywhere else than within a memory.

I'd expected Sylver to turn around to descend Mount Poyanjen, but he remained where he knelt, now biting his lip, throat bobbing.

"Get down from there Sylver." Moira's voice was firm, holding no room for debate.

"Moira, you said that you're certain that whatever Al desires lies inside?"

"I don't need to repeat myself." Moira heaved a shallow breath edged with nervousness. "Yes, but no one can survive it." She furrowed her brow when Sylver didn't move from where he stooped. "Are you deaf? Get away from there—you'll get yourself killed!"

"But I wouldn't be dying a selfish coward now, would I?" He gave me a pointed glare.

"No, but you'll die a fool." Moira held out her arm, "Come on, we'll regroup and think this through a bit more. There must be another way."

Sylver didn't grab it. Instead, he swung a leg over the ledge.

"Don't you dare." Moira's face was caught between something like shock and horror.

Sylver only gave Moira the most radiant of smiles before whispering something unintelligible into the desert wind, setting the silent embers in his eyes aflame.

I whipped my head to Moira to see if she'd understood what he'd said, and her face went slack.

I started, "What the hell is go—"

Sylver's smile didn't vanish as he pivoted to face the crater once more and threw his other leg over the lip of Mount Poyanjen.

Then he fell.

Chapter 23

Sylver

ONE CANNOT BURN A FLAME.

That's what I'd told Moira before I went over the edge. Her face slackened in understanding. And *that* was why I let myself fall into the pit of fire in the first place; she knew.

Alterra's scream travelled with me as my body plummeted towards the magma. The walls of the volcano tore at my loose clothing, and I threw out an arm to slow my descent, wincing as rocks pierced and stabbed my exposed skin.

My fingernails screamed as they latched onto a chunk of rock that bulged from the vent, and I fought back a gag as noxious fumes curled around me. The kaftan I'd worn ignited in the radiant heat, and I chuckled to myself. This was certainly a first.

The burbling of molten rock rumbled beneath where I held myself, naked, prostrate, sprawled against the wall of the volcanic vent, and I stared skyward.

I hadn't thought this through.

A glance over my shoulder into the angry gap told me it was a much tighter squeeze than I'd initially thought. In search of a foothold, I dragged a foot back and forth.

I couldn't let myself drop the twenty or so feet into the magma. That would be a death sentence; shattering bones and any possibility of ever proving myself to Moira for good.

My foot snagged on another extension from the vent, and I sighed. Slowly but surely, I would do this.

Minutes passed as I gradually lowered myself down the rocky overhang, halting only when my foot dangled high above the liquid blaze. I wasn't low enough. I scaled lower, muscles straining as I clenched onto the last bit of rock protruding before the open pit below. I tore my gaze from the sinister darkness emanating from the rocks at my cheek and noted that there was no possible way of descending further.

I had to let go.

🌲

My knees buckled as my feet hit the magma, and I collapsed forward. Magma swelled at my fingertips, and I marveled at its consistency. Gritty, heavy, but it didn't burn—nothing ever did. And I wasn't sinking either.

Digging was of no use—I would only manage to float back up to the magma's surface. I shoved my foot into the molten rock and hissed as it drifted back into my line of sight. Shit. How was I going to get into the lava, if I couldn't even sink into the damned stuff properly?

I *really* didn't think this through.

Lying amongst the burning debris, I wondered. Maybe Alterra's desire wasn't beneath, but instead in the exposed vent with me. I shook my head, watching as lava twined through my open hands. She said her desire was not an object, and she'd also be of the belief that I'd just killed myself, but Moira would have to convince her to stay nearby for a while longer. This had to work. I would get out of here. I would see them both again.

And I would get whatever the hell it was that Alterra desired so badly that it would lead her here of all places, causing Moira to react as if being branded every time Alterra thought of it. I couldn't imagine what her desire even was, but it was pretty obvious that it wasn't something she could attain on her own. And it was pretty obvious that she wasn't in search of a person.

It wasn't as if people miraculously grew on trees down here.

And if it wasn't an object...

The magma cradled me, soothed me.

I held my breath as I twisted to face the magma in an attempt to break its surface and forced my head underneath. A headache ensued, along with the distinctive feeling of it being crushed. Panic swept through me. I couldn't open my eyes. I couldn't breathe. I couldn't escape. The magma didn't hesitate as it shoved me out of its panic-inducing embrace, and I loosed a long breath as I gazed blearily towards the sky once more. Clearly, that wasn't going to work.

Rocks drifted by at my fingertips as I gazed around the vent yet again. Smoke billowed off the magma, curling itself through my hair, which mended into the shadowy fabric as if crafted from it.

Perhaps it was.

Perhaps both Moira and I had been crafted from the flames themselves; our hair an extension of the black smoke that would eddy from us both in another life...another world.

I'd known the truth about Moira after our first, and only, sexual encounter, but I'd been suspicious of her past after first gazing into her eyes. I'd seen eyes twinkle while here, but hers...they flickered. Some part of me knew what she was, but I couldn't be forthright.

I'd known she was like me, but she was oblivious. I'd known that we would have been able to have an actual relationship with one another—one of complete understanding that no one else in this realm could ever even grasp—but she'd written me off as just another fuck.

If only she'd known that instead, I was another castaway.

And *that* was why it had broken a piece of me when all she wanted was *sex*.

It only affirmed my suspicions when she told me that she didn't burn in the desert and again when she told me of her extraordinary gift.

She was like me, but she didn't *want* me. And when her face slackened when I finally spoke to her in the tongue of the flames, there was no denying the truth then. She was a flame. She was a spirifae. But how—and *why*? For years, I believed I had been the only one ripped away from our home of Laspiar. I thought I was the only one punished by Dima; but Moira was a spirifae like me, and she too came from the mire.

Dima must have anathematized us both to this realm, but little did she know that this place was a blessing. I was happy to be free from the bog…to be free of the title I'd possessed. In Laspiar, I was a social pariah—cursed, cast out, and forced to give up my Fae form so as to give all of myself over to the flame.

I hated being trapped. I was never meant to be a spirifae like the others. I never wanted that life. I never wanted to be cold, free of all feeling. I loved the heat and passion that came with emotion. I never wanted to return to my post as a flame when I could have a…fulfilling life as a Fae.

But Moira's eyes were blue; the colour of the spirifae who were still faithful. Did that mean that she actually *enjoyed* that existence? Why would Dima curse her to live out the rest of her life here, if she hadn't done anything to deserve this fate? I sucked on my teeth. Moira had been reticent about her past, but, surely, Dima must have smitten her here for a reason.

I let a foot plunge into the magma and recoiled as I felt a rock or something hit my ankle.

Maybe attaining Alterra's desire was an impossible task, but why would Moira's flicker set the three of us off on this wild goose chase if it couldn't be found? It had to be in here, whatever it was.

I forced my foot into the magma again; digging and sculpting a path deeper with my toes so that my leg could follow suit.

Another rock contacted my ankle, and I tried to shoo it away. I didn't let myself think about how it felt as if the rock had become tethered, wound even, around my leg. I was just imagining things. I wriggled my leg deeper, and yet another rock collided with the outstretched limb. I tried to shake it away, but still, it wouldn't budge. It was as if the magma was wrapping its invisible hands around my calf, holding me hostage under its prison of molten rock.

I took a breath and ran a hand through my hair. I was *definitely* imagining things.

I tried to withdraw my leg from where it was stuck, but it wouldn't move. Perhaps I'd drifted too close to the vent's wall and gotten it pinned. Twisting my foot this way and that, I made yet another attempt to pull my leg back, but with no success. I even let my leg and body go slack, before I tried pulling out again, but I still didn't move an inch.

I couldn't be stuck here.

I wouldn't be stuck here.

I thrashed myself, kicking with my free leg in a desperate attempt to flee from another one of my mistakes. I didn't care if I broke my foot or dislocated something or...I had too many things to live for now to care. Seconds turned to minutes, and I was practically breathless as I continued my futile struggle.

Waha's voice rattled in the frantic corner of my memory, *Sylver, fate has a way of guiding everyone down the exact path they are destined for in this life. Just be sure that you don't let her pass you by.* He'd murmured that to me the night Moira had crossed our Keep the first time with Alterra.

He'd always amazed me with his intuitive gift. But *clearly*, fate had a wicked sense of humor if it thought having me flail around in the middle of a volcanic vent was some sort of joke. I was pinned here and if I couldn't free myself...

Exhausted, I imagined the rocks enveloping my leg, wrapping themselves tighter so I would never be able to escape, and—

A yank from indiscernible hands pulled me beneath the magma's surface. I couldn't take a breath before the crushing warmth of the liquefied rocks squeezed every thought and reason out of my mind. I couldn't even open my eyes to see through the lava, and no random pockets of air were at my disposal to help me as I felt myself being dragged deeper into what I was sure the Messiah would describe only as hell.

Fuck.

My lungs began burning, begging for air, but I had to refuse them.

If I were to die down here, Alterra would always think me a fool. And maybe I was one. I'd only wanted to impress Moira by showing her the truth that I'd kept secret from her since we'd met, but *apparently*, I'd overlooked the likelihood of my survival in the meantime. Hard to believe I'd managed to survive a millennium as it was. *Stay awake, stay awake.* I couldn't let the invisible antagonist…win—I had to redeem myself.

I began choking on the air I couldn't exhale as I continued plunging deeper into the heart of Mount Poyanjen.

Think.

Think.

Think.

I wished that I could go back to her. Moira was everything I'd ever wanted—fiery tenacity and strength and stubbornness. I just wanted…there to be someone.

I shuddered as I exhaled and buckled in place as my lungs tried to refill but to no avail.

I had to fight.

I was not a "selfish" coward like Alterra thought.

I would always fight for Moira.

I just hoped she'd always fight for me too.

Chapter 24

Moira

IT WAS OFFICIAL. After five years of this never-ending bullshit, I'd finally lost my mind.

Sylver couldn't possibly be a flame; I would have known.

My flicker began a sock hop that trailed its way up my spine, and I closed my eyes. Sylver being a flame would definitely explain my little dancer's obsession with him. It would also explain why even the sound of his voice was enough to send me over the edge before I'd ever even laid eyes on him.

It had been about an hour since he'd thrown himself into the vent—and about forty-five minutes since I'd told Alterra that we would rest up closer to the sea for a few days before we decided to go anywhere else.

I wasn't going to elaborate to her about what Sylver had whispered to me before he'd fallen into what I knew she believed to be his death. He was an impulsive, fucking idiot. *One cannot burn a flame.* Those words had torn through the veil that hovered over my memories, and for the first time in five years, the tongue of the flames had allowed me to see my home again. I could remember the unkempt, overgrown bog I'd called home for centuries. It was alive there, with swimming ducks, skittering dunlins, and even the occasional deer that stumbled in from the meadows to the north. I could also see the dangers that lurked beneath; the ones I'd sworn to Dima to never let even touch the descendants of Raifaer Ave; the first of the four deities to have been crafted from the elements of Laspiar.

I wasn't the first of my kind that she'd made for that purpose, and I certainly wasn't one of the last she'd made either. Although, many of the others before me hadn't been quite right in her eyes; too closely imitating the Fae which the spirifae had been sculpted to only resemble, and as such, they'd all been punished.

The last of the first spirifae had been sentenced over a decade before I was forced to walk this other world in a foreign body. But I was still lost, incapable of recalling how that had even come to pass. I'd been drifting through the mire, contentedly waltzing through the earliest of dawn's rays, when suddenly my own inner fire banked—almost extinguished entirely—and then I'd woken up in the mountains without the only piece of myself that I'd ever cherished; the only piece of myself that ever had a fucking purpose. I'd been lucky enough that Salvador found me after those men…

He'd saved me—even though he only did so to add another slave to Pierserk's inventory. It was a mere fluke that I'd discovered that one of my sole gifts from back home had been brought here with me. It was also a fluke that Salvador had the sense to notice it. But that wasn't important.

I kicked at a piece of debris at my feet as Alterra made to set up two of the mats.

Sylver wouldn't be needing his for a while yet.

"So why is it that we have to stay here for a couple of days again?" I whipped my head to where she now stood with her arms hanging weakly at her sides. "We should just double back to Neosordess or something tomorrow. There's literally no possible way for me to reach what I want. It's hopeless."

"We should wait a while first, Al."

"Why are you suddenly so patient? What exactly is going on?"

I couldn't help but glance to the Mount as I murmured, "There's nothing going on. I just think we should take a day or two to count our blessings." An incredulous look swept into her gaze, and I forced myself to concoct an *almost* probable reason. "Okay, so I am not ready to give up on finding your desire just yet. My flicker has never let me down, so I'm not so ready to lose faith in its judgement."

She too gazed at the Mount looming behind me. "What else can we possibly do? It's in a *volcano,* Moira. The way back to Thy—" She halted herself, and I winced as fire shot down my legs. Alterra then whispered, shaking her head, "Why would Sylver do that? I mean, why would he kill himself for me? We don't even like each other."

I'd have been lying if I'd said that I hadn't been wondering the same thing. He'd risked his entire existence for her…

Unless he'd somehow had the opportunity to throw himself into a volcano before and knew for certain he would be able to survive the fall…

One cannot burn a flame.

I certainly hoped that to be the case.

I didn't bother responding as I trekked past Alterra to the sea, eager to feel the waves on my skin for the first time in what seemed to be weeks. If I couldn't go home, then this would be the closest thing to it. But Sylver *had* to succeed.

Five years.

I'd walked this barren land for five years, and I could hardly remember a thing about my past. I'd only known that there I felt safe, peaceful, serene even. And I'd walked for years alone, with only my little dancer for company—and Salvador. Maybe that was all my flicker could offer me, a chance to remember the life I used to have.

A chance to not feel.

Whatever.

The Masyron Sea was calm, and its waves lapped at the shoreline while I stared into its eternity. It was nothing like the mire. Gulls called overhead, and I reached downward to a sand dollar resting in the sand.

I would only ever be content to float just inches above the picture-perfect reflection of the sky. Ambience, the soft glow of the spirifae casting their own flawless light upon the still pools. I missed the fervour of dancing immortality away, of never needing worry of relationships or happiness. As a spirifae, I was whole.

But as I let the sweet caress of waves sweep past my ankles before silently retreating back to the sea, I could only feel *empty*. I hated the emptiness of being human—or whatever I could now be classified as. Mocking the beautiful water around me, thoughts too swept by.

Perhaps I had been wrong about Sylver. Obviously, he had known I was like him, but I still couldn't wrap my head around why he'd rejected my advances twice now. But then again, he still wanted me…

I threw the sand dollar into the too-blue sea and watched as its ripples came to pass me by. I tried to halt them from returning to the sea with a foot, but I couldn't stop the inevitable. They too were fated to return home to the sea as their brethren were, just as both Sylver and I were supposedly fated to return back home to Laspiar.

My plan was forfeit.

He wouldn't choose to stay here with an old man he'd only known for not even a decade, would he? No. That would be ridiculous. He would follow me back to the place he'd been created; to the place he'd existed with others like him for over a millennium.

Perhaps we would be able to exist there together…

Foolish. It was a foolish human desire, and it would soon pass.

As a flame, I wouldn't desire anything, and I would be happy. Memories of the heat and passion of this body would also pass, and I would be lucky if I could remember any part from this whole debacle in the next century.

Sylver would forget me too.

This time I threw a small rock at the water and exhaled as it found its course.

But if he was serious, and he truly desired me as my little dancer insisted, would he be able to forget me?

I hated it here, complicated, disappointing, demeaning...

Whatever.

It only mattered that Alterra stayed, and that her desire—whoever "Thy" was—was the path back to everything I'd been dreaming of for as long as I'd been here. My flicker sent radiant heat around my core, and I breathed deeply as it silently implored, *Trust me, Moira, and trust yourself.* I rolled my eyes. I'd already trusted it with my very existence, wasn't that enough as it was?

"It's pretty, isn't it?"

Alterra's voice cracked through the stupor of my thoughts as she approached my right side. I mumbled, "No. Not really. I don't like the sea." Waves kept crashing on the shoreline and gulls continued swooping down, stealing fish from the water with each pass.

It was practically impossible to compare the choppy sea to the calm, still pools of my home.

"I'm really sorry about Sylver, Moira. I know you two were close, and..." I turned to glance her way, a lock of hair falling into frame with the movement, as she continued, "And I just feel like if I didn't push so fucking hard; if I would have just accepted the impossibility of my sole desire, maybe he would still be here with you."

I didn't bother correcting her. "Thanks."

She splayed her arms. "That's it—*thanks*?"

"What did you want me to say? Thank you for the sentiment, now please leave me alone." I shook my head, glaring at her as I continued. "I can't deal with apologies or people or anything else at the moment." I was still trying to sort through my own bullshit. I didn't have the energy to help Alterra wade through hers.

"You didn't love him."

"What?" The statement caught me off-guard.

A sigh. "It all makes sense now. That's why you haven't shed a single fucking tear. Sylver's *dead,* Moira, and you don't even seem to care. You didn't truly love him."

"Oh, fuck off Alterra. You don't know anything."

She rolled her eyes and began trekking back to the bedrolls adjacent to the Mount. "At least he'll never know the truth, eh? You must be so happy now that you don't have to keep that a secret from him anymore. And believe it or not Moira, I do know *something.* I know what true love is."

The sound of her footfalls on the beach faded into near silence at last, and I groaned. She was right. I didn't love Sylver; I still barely knew him.

Hours passed, and I pointedly remained on the shore. The sky had finally begun darkening, and I could tell it would only be another hour or so before the sun's light disappeared for the day entirely.

How much longer was Sylver going to be?

I shook my head as Alterra's words crept into my mind, *Maybe he would still be here with you*. He wasn't dead. I wouldn't accept that. My flicker would have told me. It would have at least given me some sort of indication that we could finally leave the shadow of the decrepit Mount behind us. Unless it thought it was doing me some sort of service by keeping me in the dark.

I really did hate it here.

A chill wind whipped my hair into my face, and I growled. Scorching hot during the day and freezing cold at night. How fucking lovely.

I bundled myself in the headdress I'd donned earlier in the day and stalked towards the bedrolls Alterra had laid out. My teeth began chattering, and I cursed my little dancer for torturing me needlessly as I plopped myself onto the mat Alterra had placed beside her own. She faced the Mount itself, and emphatically ignored my presence.

That was when I heard it.

A low grumble came from the east, and my flicker began stabbing me with a searing poker stick.

"Do you hear that too?" Her voice was quiet, and she rose onto silent feet, gazing into the now open blackness of the desert.

"I do," I hissed, as my little dancer ground the invisible poker into my shoulder blade. I breathed, "It's not some innocent thunder, Al. Something's wrong."

She bent over, reaching down to hoist the bedroll into her arms, and hushed, "Moira, we have to get out of here."

"What is it?"

The sound came nearer, morphing into a snarling, rabid creature before she turned to me and whispered, "They're here."

Chapter 25

Sylver

"SISTER, WHAT CREATURE HAS VENTURED HERE *beneath the realms of man?"*

"He looks man, but somehow he defies his appearance."

"Saving him was only appropriate; curiosity got the better of me it seems."

Two voices, young and old.

I couldn't hear anything but their voices.

Although their voices travelled to other locations around me, I could hear no indicators of where they were at any given time. No footsteps.

"My dear sister, I do believe he is awake."

A voice carried on a phantom wind responded. *"Is he such a coward that he's trying to avoid the inevitability of our existence despite our presence mere feet from him?"*

I wasn't a coward.

The last thing I remembered was how it felt suffocating, unable to breathe, trapped underneath the lava of the crater because I couldn't open my eyes to find a way out. I couldn't find a way to escape the thing that tethered me to the Mount's core.

What the fuck was going on?

Shit. Was I hallucinating?

"Maybe a touch..."

My eyes snapped open, and the voice of shadow silenced, but I couldn't see anyone. I tried to get a grasp of my surroundings. I seemed to be within a hollow etched into Mount Poyanjen itself; a pillar of lava cascaded down a wall to my left, but it never passed into the cavern. Somehow, the cavity was a separate entity from the volcano.

Within it, but never touching.

It was beautiful and disturbing and if it was a hallucination— it was an awfully impressive one.

Where was I? And what did Alterra want that could lead us to come here?

I glanced upwards from where I still lay, sprawled on a blackened, hard, glass-like surface. There, glistening in the light emanating from the lava on the other side of the chamber, was a web. A web that absorbed all light from the volcano and radiated none to the wall on my right side; it still seemed to be encased in an impermeable darkness. I rose from my spot on the ground into a crouch and squinted into the shadows.

"Perhaps he isn't as cowardly as Alterra first imagined."

I whipped my head behind me to see who or what the voice belonged to, but no one was there. How did it know of Alterra?

I asked the darkness, "You know Alterra?"

"My sister and I know all, my dear. We know that you aren't what you've claimed to be these past five years." This time the

voice came from the web above me, but once again, I couldn't make out anyone or anything.

That knowledge would certainly make sense if it was a hallucination crafted by my own oxygen-deprived mind...

I stood swiftly, then gazed into the web. It was gilded in golden light and extended high above into the cavern. I reached to touch a golden thread—

"STOP!"

I whipped my head to my right and could just make out the faintest of shadows. "What are you?"

The shadow didn't vanish. Instead, another appeared out of the darkness.

"Sylver, some questions are not meant to be answered."

One of the twin shadows approached, slowly, hesitating beneath the web's light.

Then it merely materialized upon the web.

I could make out its eight legs, each encompassed with shadow; however, its other features were nothing more than an inky black stain upon the web's beautiful surface.

"Why can't you answer my simple question?" How could I ever get what I needed if I didn't even know what was going on?

"We know what you search for, but it will come at a price."

The second voice continued, *"Everything comes at a price."*

Laughter slithered by me, and I shivered.

"If you want to know the truth, you will have to tell us your truth as well."

I scoffed. Some hallucination. "But if you guys know everything already, why would it even be of interest to you to hear my side of the story?"

The floating disembodied voice whispered, *"The web doesn't tell us why things unfold."*

"It only shows us when things do." The other shadow finished the sentence, then began its approach closer to my side. *"Is it a deal?"*

"Is what a deal?" I couldn't handle all of their riddles; I just wanted to get back to—

"*Moira will be fine if you just listen to us.*"

My eyes widened.

The web above trembled and began a clicking, like we'd heard before the Dunes. Were they responsible for that? This whole scenario was really pretty creative if this were indeed a figure of— I choked. Never in my existence had I possessed an *imagination*.

I wasn't hallucinating at all.

They were real.

In an effort to maintain some semblance of dignity, I concealed the fear now gripping my chest. "If I tell you my truth, what will you do to me?"

"*We will do nothing* to *you my dear.*" The voice came closer, still closing in on me from the darkness to my right. "*A shadow cannot gutter the light of a flame.*"

"*We'll do what you please—*"

"*Consider it our gift to you—*"

"*Thanking you for disturbing the tedium of our existence.*"

The voices weaved between each other in an eery, dark harmony.

What other choice did I have?

"Fine." I exhaled and gazed into the web which had now stopped its rattling, as I felt more than saw the two beings gather around me.

"*Tell us of your curse, and what has happened since.*"

"*Your creation is of no secret nor importance to us.*"

"*Do begin soon; time is not on your side as you might have thought.*"

"What do you mean by that?"

The voices merely tittered, before one then caressed me with a leg encased in shadow.

I didn't jump.

"*Begin, my dear.*"

"*Or we won't remain so generous.*"

I clenched my hands into fists. "I was cursed a while ago by a powerful being by the name of Dima." I scratched at my jaw, and nearly winced as I rubbed Alterra's still-lingering bruise. "Because I was *selfish* and nearly exposed the spirifae to a Fae."

"*And this was a problem?*"

"Yes. It was a problem because spirifae are to remain a legend where I come from." Tension and stress forced me to exhale again before continuing, "I did so because...because I didn't enjoy my existence as a flame. I'd always preferred my Fae side because it allowed me to *feel* things. Allowed me to experience pain and happiness and I loved it."

No indication as to whether the shadows even cared for what I'd voiced. Another continued. "*What did you do to nearly expose your race, the spirifae?*"

"When I was at my post as a flame, I'd seen a young girl down at the edge of the bog one day and she was crying. I'd waited to see if someone would come for her, but she'd wept for minutes and no one came to her aid. I just couldn't stand for it. I'd shifted into my Fae self, so I could be there for her...at least for a bit. I was aware of the consequences to my actions, but like I said, I couldn't stand by and watch her while she was in pain."

"*But you were cursed for being selfish?*"

"Yes. My master—*Dima*—made us each swear an oath to protect the royal family, and by both ignoring my responsibility to protect them, and by possibly exposing us, I broke my oath." I kicked a loose stone at my feet before continuing. "Alterra had been right when she'd said that I was selfish." I hated that she was right. She barely knew me, yet it was as if she already knew of a truth I'd yet to voice to anyone else.

"*What was your curse?*"

"I was cursed to remain a flame forever." I shuddered against the memory. "The curse changed the colour of my flame to silver. I was never to feel again, never allowed to dance with the other flames...I was cursed to forever be known for the thing I hated about myself." I grit my teeth.

Selfish.

"*What happened five years ago?*"

"I don't know."

"*That's not an answer.*"

"But I *don't* know what happened five years ago. One moment I was floating through the bog, and the next I was here, human, and butt-naked in the middle of the desert with no food or water to survive with. After wandering aimlessly for a couple of days, lost, I curled into a ball and embraced my imminent doom."

"*Then Waha found you, yes?*"

"Yes. He took me in and taught me how to survive. He didn't know why or how I wound up in the middle of the desert with no food, clothes, or water, but he didn't ask questions." He never had to. "After living with him for a few weeks, I decided that in order to repay him—because he had no one—I would care for him. I wasn't going to abandon the man who had gone out of his way to save me, a complete stranger." I shook my head before continuing, "I grew to love him as a father figure and that's that."

I could sense the shadows contemplating the truth I'd just told, when one came even closer to murmur, "*So what do you know of Alterra and Moira?*"

"*Yes, what drove you to stay with them?*"

"*Wouldn't you have preferred to stay with Waha?*"

"Well," I mused, "I know that Alterra was disguised as Kieran for at least the last three years, and I know that Moira had no clue of Al's true identity at the time when they'd come to our Keep. Moira told me that she'd spent some time working in a circus beforehand because of her gift...a gift I've since concluded is a consequence of her being a faithful flame to our master."

Years ago, I too shared her power. I too was blessed with the ability to lead others to their desires, but no longer. I'd since been thrown out, made worthless by those I thought cared for me.

I continued, "But to answer your next question, Waha and I'd talked about what would be best for my future. He'd told me that he saw the blooming chemistry between Moira and I and believed that she was my future. My fate, so to speak. It would have broken his heart for me to limit my own happiness in life to look after him."

The memory of Waha's last words to me flashed into my mind.

"Sylver, you're the silver in the lining. Just remember," He directed a finger to my heart, *"there will always be a flicker of hope, even in the darkest of times."* Did Waha somehow know?

"Are you so blind to Alterra's truth that you don't have even the slightest inkling of her utmost desire?"

"You truly have no *idea why her desire led you here?"*

"No, I really don't." I chuckled. "Can't be too strange. I mean, she's a human."

"Curious..."

I furrowed my brow. "Are you saying that she's not?"

"You've answered our questions, so you may ask yours."

"Well, answer my last question. Is Alterra a human?"

"Yes, she is human."

"Okay..." I took another deep breath. "Where am I?"

"You're in a cavern."

I smiled with contempt. "Funny. I meant, what is this place? What's the deal with the web?" I gestured, using a hand to the space above me and felt the shadows tense as I grazed one accidentally.

"This is where we—"

"Also, who are you exactly?" I bit down on my tongue upon realizing I'd interrupted the shadow perched above me and winced at my own stupidity. But that was an important question I'd forgotten to ask first.

Seemingly sensing my regret, the shadow merely trudged onward, ignoring the interruption and instead answering the last question I posed.

"We are nothing but shadows but exist even so."

"We are the Keepers of the web; the Keepers of destiny."

"And you might say this place is our home or our prison. But nonetheless, we have been here, in this cavern, unable to leave since we were created an eternity ago."

"Why? Why can't you guys leave? Why do you look like spiders? Why—"

The web began trembling yet again.

"We only look like spiders in your mind."

What a comforting thought.

"*Truly we are of no form.*"

"*We can't leave because shadows can't survive in the light.*"

"But there's light in here from the lava…"

"*Yes, but its light isn't pure nor is it bright enough to have any effect upon the overwhelming darkness of our hollow.*"

"*Neither of us have desired to venture outside of the cavern.*"

"*We have eyes that can see all, be in all places.*"

"*We have no reason to leave.*"

I nodded, understanding their reasons only to some degree. If they could see *all* and be in *all* places, wouldn't at least one of the Keepers desire to be free? Wouldn't they eventually desire to tangibly experience the world that is just out of reach, taunting them with its beauty?

I shook my head, drawing my attention to the web above me once more. "You two still haven't told me about the web." It was shaking and clicking, and its movement evolved into something infinitesimal in the cavern above us.

"*Such a curious one…*"

I felt the shadow drift higher, then saw it hover over the golden web before the Keeper continued, "*This web unites us all.*"

"*And my dear, you've got it wrong.*"

"*There isn't just* one *web.*"

I cocked my head. "How many are there?"

"*We can't tell you that Sylver.*"

"*But know that each web controls a realm and that each web is connected to at least one other.*"

"*We have come to believe that* that's *how you were able to be in the middle of a bog one minute, and then in the middle of a desert in the next.*"

"How could that even happen?" I paused. "Don't you control the web?"

"*Mysterious.*"

"*We do control the web, and in turn the realms, but five years ago—*"

"*We lost our control for merely a second—*"

"*Not even—*"

"That's not of importance." The web began rattling again, more violently.

"What is of importance, though, is that your time in here is coming to an end."

"What are you talking about? You said that you'd answer my questions! Why is the web clicking?"

"We have Sylver. But you have yet to understand—"

One of the shadows interrupted, *"The clicking, the same clicking you heard out in the desert?"*

I nodded. "What does it mean?"

"That's the mechanism we have in place to protect us."

"And a way to keep those away who dare to venture to the Mount."

"Very few can survive the Dunes of Almalto." The voice spoke of them with a reverence one would muster when speaking of a god. "But the Dunes are the only way to enter the Mount's perimeter."

I pondered. "So the clicking is to scare people away…what's so bad about the other ways to the Mount?"

I'd never been told those stories as a guide.

"All you need to know, is that those who take those paths, never return from the Mount's shadow."

"But enough of that. You have to leave."

I couldn't just leave; I still had to get whatever it was that Alterra needed.

"Indeed you shall."

The furthest shadow vanished from sight for a second, then reappeared, dropping a black stone on the ground in front of where I stood.

I made to pick it up but was halted as the second Keeper blocked it from sight. *"Give this piece of obsidian to Alterra. It will ground her, and whoever else uses it."*

"However, when only she uses it, it won't just be herself that she grounds."

"In order for her to reach her final destination, she will have to first go to the mouth of the river of Aspitha, where it meets the *sea to the north. Then from there, she will have to use it as she would a knife, and slice through the air like so."*

The shadow who'd been speaking lifted a leg, shifted it into a razor-sharp scythe, then brought it down upon one of the golden threads, cleaving it in two.

I jumped back, alarmed. "What did you just do?" If that web held together the realms…

"My dear, it does. But don't fret over this itsy-bitsy tear. My sister and I can patch it up when the time is right, and it will be as if it never existed."

I exhaled through my nose, then stepped forward to the still shielded artifact and asked, "Why would she have to do that, Alterra I mean?"

I waited a moment for the shadows to tell me, but instead of answering me as they'd promised, the most distant shadow appeared in front of me, shrouding my body in darkness, and whispered, *"You might find yourself needing to use this artifact beforehand."*

The shadow ignored me, but I couldn't help myself and pilfered the bait it offered me instead. "Why would I need to?" My mission would supposedly be accomplished upon giving Al the stone.

"Moira and Alterra need you."

"What do you mean?" Their non-answers were seriously beginning to piss me off.

More clicking erupted around us. Someone was nearing the Mount. And if Al couldn't handle whatever their problem was on her own…I couldn't let myself ponder what that meant. I had to get out of here.

Moira needed me.

"They both will need you, but in due time."

"To save them, you can activate the relic by slicing your palm."

"To return to yourself, all that must be done is to remove your blood from the obsidian."

The shadow materialized away from the shard. It was exquisite, perhaps the size of my palm. It didn't look special amongst the other debris in the Mount, and when I picked it up, I couldn't sense any supernatural quality radiating from it. It appeared to just be a very light and very sharp shard of black glass.

"Sylver, not everything nor everyone with great power flaunts it to the world."

"Sometimes it's those who keep that great power hidden, those that no one would ever suspect, who prove to be the strongest when they're needed."

I brushed my fingers over the relic. "How do I get out of here?" I'd need an alternative escape from Mount Poyanjen. Swimming blind through the lava wasn't something I was physically capable of—let alone something I'd be able to survive again.

I glanced above to the shadow still gracing the web when it began plucking various golden threads. *"Sylver my dear, you will need to act decisively and quickly if you plan to save them both."* More plucking, then, *"Ah-ha! This one should do it."*

The leg scythed through yet another web, and I heard the Mount shudder in response.

The shadows vanished with the onset of the trembling, and they spoke in unison from the darkest corner of the cavern, *"It will all make sense with time."*

To my right, magma began spilling over the ledge into the grotto, and I turned to look back to the Keepers of the web—

Not a trace of them remained. Only the empty darkness I was first greeted by stared back.

I spun to the wall that had been to my back in an attempt to find a way out of the crumbling volcano and saw that a gaping hole, big enough for me to fit through, had now replaced it.

I rushed to the open gap and saw that the night sky and the sea stared back at me. This escape route faced the opposite side of Mount Poyanjen from that of which the three of us had climbed earlier.

The shaking of the Mount then halted, and I peeked over a shoulder, obsidian in-hand, and uttered a curt, "Thank you," before squeezing through the fissure for good. I dragged my empty hand through my hair then stared at the shard under the ruddy moonlight; it reflected back an almost flawless mirror of the sky above me.

The Mount shuddered again from behind me, so I stepped forward a few steps. Turning on a heel, I noted smoke spewing from Mount Poyanjen's main vent and the fusion of the Mount at its base; shutting the gap that had just enabled my escape from the volcano's heart. I watched as it sealed off in its entirety, then made to see what the shadows had warned me about. I didn't allow myself to sprint to the Mount's other side—if the shadows believed it that would be in my best interest to use the stone beforehand, it was best to know why the secrecy was needed.

I tiptoed as best I could around its left side, avoiding rocks and other pieces of volcanic debris all the while to stay quiet. The area around the Mount was silent, but as I rounded its far side, I began hearing voices.

Male voices.

I quickened my pace but kept on silent feet so as not to startle them.

Who could those men be?

Obviously, they weren't harboring good news if the shadows had made a point to warn me of their presence.

Leaning around a slight outcropping, the glow of a fire off the sand caught my attention. *We* didn't bring the supplies for a fire. I'd completely forgotten. How the fuck did I forget *that*. Some "guide" I was. I probably—no—*definitely* should have remembered at least some flint and something to light. I could remember *pigskin* for crying out loud for Alterra's injury but not— I shut down the thought. It was simply a miracle that neither of the girls managed to become hypothermic because of my *damned* stupidity.

I hurried my pace, keeping my body glued to the Mount itself for protection, when I finally glimpsed Alterra and Moira. I sighed with relief in establishing that they were both still alive; however, upon further examination they were clearly tied. Trapped. And three men sat opposite of them to the fire.

How'd *they* make it through the Keeper's safeguards?

Both of the girls were held captive off to the side—away from the fire—attached to some sort of motorbike I assumed the men had arrived on.

Silence would be my only ally if I wanted to continue my approach.

What made it so that Al couldn't fight them off?

And what in Dima's name made me so *sure* that Alterra could fight off three full-grown men after having just recovered from a wound that should have killed her.

A wound I'd intended *would* kill her.

I crouched and stalked forward.

Those men seemed familiar somehow…not their faces, per se, but maybe—it was their uniform; a slate-gray mirroring the dreary gray of storm clouds.

They were disciples.

Chapter 26

Moira

I GROUND MY TEETH at the motorcycle-thing I was now a part of—bound to. I hadn't thought it was possible to hate it here any *more* than I already did, but apparently, I was wrong.

Again.

I'd asked Alterra why they'd come, why the disciples had followed us out here, but she didn't answer me. Her only excuse was that she had no real time to. We'd barely enough time to grab her sword before their howling bikes became visible, and only seconds after that they'd practically screeched to a halt in front of where we stood. They'd merely sneered at us before one of the three brutes stepped forward, and Alterra cocked her head in return, a predator readying her attack.

I'd scowled at her. Her bullshit behavior back at the Forum and afterwards practically beckoned for the disciples to follow us. It was her own fault that they'd arrived. *Her* idiocy that put both of our lives in danger.

Perhaps even Sylver's life too.

"Kieran, we've found you at *long* last."

"Keeto." A pause as Alterra surveyed the grey men before her. "What brings you to the legendary Mount Poyanjen? I can't imagine the Messiah would send three of His most trusted disciples here just to talk to me..." She'd seamlessly stepped into her role as Kieran and didn't balk as the other two parked their bikes and strode to Keeto.

"I'd have thought you smarter than this, Kieran. It should be rather obvious why I'm here, and why the Messiah has ordered—not one—but three to do His bidding." Alterra yawned in response, and he seethed, "You're coming with us."

"Keeto, Kieran's a woman."

The man to Keeto's right interrupted his speech as he edged forward, and the other man followed suit. Eyes widened with shock as realization crept in, and I smiled to myself.

I wasn't the only one who had been fooled by Alterra in the darkness of the Forum.

She'd made fools of us all.

"Surprising. Huh. You've known me for a while now... To put it bluntly, I'd have thought you smarter than that, Keeto." She smirked as she spit his words right back at him with disdain. "At least Laqueres has some basic observation skills."

Keeto sniggered. "Oh but Kieran, the difference between Laqueres and I is the fact that I'm not stupid enough to acknowledge such a detail. I already thought you were useless and worthless before, but this newfound discovery has made it very clear to me that you're worth even less than I'd thought. You're nothing. If the Messiah only knew."

"If He was truly a Messiah, He would *already* know." Alterra whirled on a heel and threw me a look lined with desperation, the whites of her eyes clearly visible, as she casually fingered the hilt of the blade at her side.

What did she honestly expect me to do? She was the one responsible for getting us into this mess.

She read the reproach in my gaze, and visibly exhaled.

My own flicker shot fire down my spine, urging me, mutely screaming, *Just help her Moira! Do what she asks.* I ignored it. My little dancer clearly didn't understand that if I got myself involved, I could very well face their fury too. It lanced more flames down my back in reponse, and I winced as its silent voice grated my mind. *Moira, listen to me. If you don't help Alterra right now, it won't matter that you didn't step in. They will punish you too.*

I raised my eyebrows to Alterra, then turned around, facing the Mount once more. Smoke plumes floated into the sky high above its main vent, shifting the moonlight into an ominous, sanguine parody of the silver-blue hues I'd yearned to dance with time and time again throughout my existence.

Liquid fire dripped into my feet before coiling around my organs and tears noiselessly fell down my face.

I just wanted to go back home.

Hurry up Sylver.

"So, what exactly did the Messiah have in store for me?"

I didn't turn to face her as Alterra continued, and instead remained glaring at the shivering Mount.

Where was Sylver?

I began tapping a foot.

"We were instructed to return you to Him and to tell you that He has some very important questions to ask of you."

"Well, why can't you just tell Him that I don't want to return to Neosordess."

"You don't have a choice, Kieran."

"I've *always* had a choice."

The hiss of a blade as it was torn free of its sheathe, and then the subsequent snorting of men who evidently didn't seem to care echoed through the desert night.

"Doesn't that seem a little unfair Keeto? I'm just wielding a blade. Guns sort of seem like overkill, don't you think?" The uneasiness of her tone made me turn.

Each of the three men had guns. Two of which were directed at her, yet the other—the one belonging to the man I didn't yet know—pointed his at me.

A caress of flame as my flicker gloated, *I told you so*, and I ground my teeth once more.

I hated this world with a passion.

Chapter 27

Sylver

I WAITED IN THE DARKNESS beside the Mount as I planned their escape.

Al and Moira were bound with rope at both their hands and feet, and the three men holding them hostage carried weapons. Guns. I'd forgotten that only the disciples and the Messiah Himself were allowed to carry them in the city of Neosordess.

Their captors were passing around a bottle and I smiled quietly to myself. It was a stretch, but maybe if I waited long enough, perhaps I wouldn't even have to use the artifact to help the girls escape; the men would be too drunk and tired to care.

But what exactly led the disciples to capture Alterra and Moira in the first place?

For what seemed like minutes, I watched and I waited, trying to glean how I could possibly free them without screwing us all over in the meantime; I was failing. Even with the artifact—

Suddenly, one of the men rose from where he sat beside the fire and bellowed, "So, we found you Kieran, and the other girl He talked about." He took a step toward Al before demanding, "Where's the man the old merchant called, Sylver?"

Old merchant...did he mean *Waha*?

"Keeto, we were told not—"

"Just shut up. I don't care about the Messiah right now. I have questions of my own I'd like to ask."

What'd they do to Waha?

The man who'd spoken to Keeto recoiled momentarily, then returned to his drink seemingly without a second thought.

Now *he* was a coward if I'd ever seen one.

"Now where were we?" Keeto took another few steps to Alterra's bound feet, and when she didn't recoil at his approach, he merely grabbed her chin with a hand, and said, "Listen, this can go one of two ways..."

"I know the drill." Al's voice rang out clean through the desert. "After all, I was the leader of Sin's Forum for practically three years if you haven't forgotten."

Was she wanting to get herself killed?

I glanced to Moira, who was still tied to the (modified) motorcycle behind Alterra, and noticed that she didn't even bother looking at the man who spoke to Al. What was she thinking—did she for some reason think that she was *safe*?

I let my gaze shift to Al yet again, and I thought I saw the man glare at her before continuing, "We don't have to bring you back to the Messiah, you know. All we have to say is that you died in the desert of your own stupidity, and that would be that."

"I'm sure you'd like that, wouldn't you?" Al chortled. "The last thing you want to tell your boss is that for years He's been dealing with a *woman,* and that He didn't even catch on."

"I'm only going to ask one more time. Where is the man—"

"Sylver died back in the Dunes of Almalto. We tried going through them, but..." She took a deep breath, then looked at Keeto from beneath her lashes. "He didn't make it."

"I don't believe you." Keeto released Alterra's jaw then spit at her bound feet. "You just admitted to me that you've spent years lying to us—the disciples." He paused. "To the Messiah Himself."

"But I'm not—"

"Don't lie to me." He stepped around Alterra's confined form and started heading to...

Moira.

Moira didn't condescend to look Keeto in the face, but instead kept her head cast downward to the sand in front of her heels. He kicked the sand she'd been staring at in his attempt to startle her.

It didn't work.

She didn't flinch.

"You find that funny, eh?" Keeto seethed. "Well, I'll show you something hilarious next."

Moira only continued staring at the sand before her. She was so petite; a fiery little dancer...

I had to think.

Keeto didn't vacillate as he dropped low and began untying Moira's restraints. He ripped at the rope holding her legs together, then at her arms where she was still bound to one of their bikes. She remained staring at the ground in front of her, never shifting her gaze from that singular spot, even after being freed of all fetters by Keeto. His hand then latched onto her upper arm, and he hoisted her up.

Oh *no*.

But Moira didn't fight him as he dragged her to the campfire.

Alterra implored, "He's dead. You don't have to do anything to her. I am telling you the—"

"You mean this?" Keeto released Moira's arm, before grabbing a fistful of her hair and forcing her head to the flames leaping from the campfire mere inches away.

"*No*—DON'T!!" Alterra's scream shattered through the hush of the night.

Keeto cast a syrupy smile over a shoulder. "Just tell me the truth you sneaky wench, and I'll leave her be."

"But I'm telling you the truth! Sylver died back in the Dunes of Almalto."

Keeto inched Moira's face to the flames once more when Moira began sobbing. Unrelentless, wailing sobs. If she was in pain—was I somehow *wrong*? I had to move.

"I swear to you, Sylver is dead!" Alterra seethed. "Why can't you believe me?"

Keeto chuckled. "Would you trust the person lied to you for the entire time you've known them?" He stopped, seemingly waiting for a response from her, but when she fell short, he continued. "That's what I thought."

That was when he pushed Moira's face into the fire.

"She's telling the *truth!!!*" Moira's sobs turned into a scream that echoed out all around them, but Keeto held her there. Moira bucked against his hand, trying to escape the heat, but she didn't have the strength to succeed.

"Please Keeto, whatever discord there is between us—don't take it out on her. *Please.*" Alterra's plea was dismissed by Moira's still sobbing form,

"He died out in the Dunes. It was the lightning."

Keeto cursed before releasing Moira's head, and she fell backwards into the sand.

He shook out his hand, then gave Alterra a smile fortified with contempt. "Now *that* I can believe." He pointed to Moira who still seemed to be sobbing on the ground. "Foolish woman." Keeto chuckled, then added, "Foolish *man!* Any guide would know that everyone who goes there doesn't come back out." He hauled Moira back to the bike behind Alterra, binding her in cord again.

Moira let her hair fall over her face, casting it in complete darkness, and continued weeping so that Alterra wouldn't be able to see what had been done to her. Or lack thereof.

Hopefully.

Keeto then turned to the others and, without looking back, called out to their almost-drunk forms, "They know too much. We have to put them both down tonight."

Put down—like animals?

The fucking nerve of that man. First with what he'd already done to Moira, and now *this*. I took a deep breath. Waha would probably tell me not to let my temper get the better of me; he would be right. I needed to pull myself together and focus on what needed to be done. I was wasting all of the precious time the Keepers were so sure to lend me.

The man who had spoken up earlier slurred, "Why do it now? Can't we wait and have a bit of fun with them first?"

Keeto gave him what looked to be a warm smile in return before heading back to the men at the fire. He extended his arm, reaching for the bottle so he could take another a swig, and nodded. Their laughter inundated the world as they punched each other's arms, happy to congratulate themselves on their conquest.

I nearly choked. How could these men—these *monsters*— actually enjoy the thought of rape, or of anything else they'd planned? I doubted they wanted to play an actual game like the ones I'd introduced Moira to; the ones Waha had showed me as a form of entertainment in the keep.

I had to move fast.

Moira cast a pleading glance to Al, who was still staring at the man they called Keeto, before she began fidgeting with the restraints at her wrists.

I glanced down to the shard in my hand, then used it to slice a gouge across my palm.

Blood seeped from the wound, and I whispered, "Please, please...let me become a flame again." I would do anything for Moira, even if it meant returning to the wretched form. My lifeline began leaking from my still outstretched palm into the ground beneath my feet, and still I stood there, totally useless.

Those shadows were full of shit. Maybe if I—

Then I felt it.

I dropped the shard as a wave of weakness came over my entire being and I fell forward onto the small puddle of blood that had already oozed from my hand.

I couldn't move.

And though I wanted to, I couldn't allow myself to scream either.

I'd need the advantage of surprise on my side.

I trembled as I felt my human self fading away, and I let my eyes drift upwards to the night sky beckoning to the flame.

It was beautiful; stained with the Mount's haze, a falling star bisected it and the stars seemed to shine even brighter after its passing. If these were my final moments—if I were indeed to die here while trying to save them—I'd at least be able say that I enjoyed this little piece of peace after going to wherever we go after this life.

My convulsing ceased, and I was left on the sand, paralyzed.

I heard a shout from one of the men, and I tried to sit up against the invisible restraints endowed upon me by the relic, but I couldn't. I could no longer feel my body—but my eyes…they were still capable of movement. I dragged them down to where my legs should have been and saw that they were no longer there. I had no body; only silver fire danced and twined around my consciousness.

I'd become a flame once more.

Chapter 28

Alterra

THE CORD RESTRAINING MY ARMS made my wrists ache as it began tearing through my flesh. I could feel the familiar warmth of my blood as it dripped onto the rope, and I quarreled with the desire to quit trying altogether.

Sylver was dead. It was my fault. And now Moira was going to die and that too was going to be my fault.

I was the monster responsible for both of their deaths, just as I was the monster who had murdered close to two dozen people during the three years I'd been known as Kieran.

Nausea churned low in my gut as my mind pondered the fact that perhaps I was never meant to be happy. I would never see him again. We would never be able to do everything we'd desired to do together.

My breathing became laboured, and I gazed ahead, past the fire where Keeto, Laqueres, and Treian now sprawled, laughing, taking swigs from the bottle of hard liquor one of them had brought for this very purpose.

Thank the Messiah for this albeit temporary distraction.

I tore my gaze from them to Moira behind me, who was still sobbing, and whispered, "Moira, Moira, are you okay? I am so, so sorry."

Her exposed eye flicked to mine, and I could practically read the words she left unsaid.

This is your fault.

She wasn't wrong.

Her face contorted with agony again and I had to look away. Scars I'd caused would mar her beauty for the rest of her life, and there was nothing that could be done about it.

I closed my eyes and took a deep breath.

Everything will be okay in the end.

My mother had never been wrong before, but there was a first time for everything.

I braced myself for another pass of my wrists over the now slippery rope and didn't bother letting myself contemplate anything any further. I couldn't lose hope now, not after everything.

Chapter 29

Sylver

WHEN THE MEN HAD SETTLED IN, gathered together, taking swigs of their communal bottle of booze, I moved.

I drifted through the desert, barely casting a light. As a sliver flame, I was barely detectable in comparison to the blazing campfire mere feet away from them.

It was odd returning to this form. I still knew that I had to save the girls, but now the part of me, the part of me that yearned for Moira and for me to become something more, couldn't care less about her. As a flame, I didn't want her the way that *I* did. The flame didn't want anything. But I had to force myself.

I continued on my path to Moira and noticed that Al was wringing her hands. Blood slowly dripped from her restraints onto the bike, making the metal glisten, but it didn't stop her. Maybe she'd get free on her own.

I shielded myself in the dark; they couldn't know I was here. Not yet.

Alterra continued her struggle, tearing at her wrists with each pass, but still she didn't stop. Instead, her movements grew more fervent with each second the men seemingly forgot of their presence. Alterra must have known that if she was going to act, she'd have to do it while they were at least somewhat distracted.

Smart.

I continued on past and saw that Moira no longer fought against her restraints. Even as a flame, I couldn't fight the overwhelming pain that crashed over me.

Did she not think to continue fighting for herself?

To continue fighting for us?

To continue fighting for me?

I floated to her back pressed against the dirt bike and heard her quiet sobs.

"Moira." I wanted to comfort her. My poor, ardent flame. Her back tensed as her sobs came to a sudden halt. She'd heard me. She'd understood me.

"Moira, don't cry." My voice sounded like nothing of this world; popping embers and the hiss of fire. *"I need you to listen to me."*

Her head bobbed in a curt nod.

"I am going to burn through the rope. You're going to run to the Mount as fast as you can. Once that's accomplished, I'll tell you what needs to be done next." I didn't hesitate as I drifted to the rope binding her hands.

Her hair fell back over a shoulder, unveiling a face with no trace of the flames that had licked it minutes earlier. She *was* one of Dima's. It would be impossible to burn her. I went so far as to let my flame touch her skin while I gradually frayed the rope holding her captive. It withered away at my touch, whilst her skin remained as flawless and perfect as ever. The rope vanished in all of a minute, and I began my trek floating towards the Mount.

She'd have to unbind her feet and follow me if she wanted to escape with both her and Al's life intact.

I looked to the men who were still busy gloating over the two women they'd molest without any judgement, before focusing all my attention upon the Mount. Reaching it without getting caught was a challenge unto itself. Not like the men would suspect anything.

I'd forgotten I was no longer human, but rather a miniscule wisp, capable of escaping their judgement. But, still, drifting through the open desert air wasn't exactly a quick endeavor.

Moira caught up to my light within seconds and folded her hands around my flame, carrying my consciousness to the Mount's other side. She released me then muttered, "I expect a very thorough explanation when all of this is over with."

I'd have chuckled if I were able, but resorted to merely saying, *"As do I."*

I hated being a flame, but it'd served its purpose.

"Moira, there's a shard of obsidian on the ground nearby. I need you to grab it."

She sifted through the various pieces of debris on the ground around the Mount, before dragging her hand over some darker spots littering the rocks. "Why's this wet?" She brought her hands up to the dim light being cast by my form, then demanded, "Why is this spot soaked with *blood*?"

"That's not important. Grab the black shard beside you." Moira cast me a disapproving glare before leaning forward and grabbing the piece of debris that stood out amongst the other bloodied pieces. *"Yes. I need you wipe this shard clean. We can talk about what to do next after that."*

Moira brought the shard to her chest with a grimace, then wiped it a few times on the dress she wore. "It's too bad Alterra's wardrobe has gone to rat shit. I really did like it before I had to start using it as... Well, before using it for everything." Moira gestured to the gown, now smattered with my blood, before she said, "I guess it's too late now, so there's no point regretting it."

She finished wiping the obsidian clean with a couple more passes on the fabric, and I began feeling myself. My blood on the obsidian had bound me to misery—a life I never wanted to don again. I didn't feel so cold. My warmth, my *human* warmth was returning, and I almost heard a sigh from myself despite still being a flame.

Moira smiled, then watched as I slowly began materializing back my limbs as a white light shot from the flame twining around my mind; beginning first with my appendages in a few shaky, unsteady manoeuvres, then with everything else following suit quickly afterwards.

I made myself sit, not trusting my legs enough to keep my body upright without falling over, then took a gulp of fresh air. As a flame, I didn't need to breathe, but my body still felt starved of the oxygen it couldn't inhale. It was exhilarating to *feel* again, and I couldn't help but glance to Moira's eyes to see them flicker with the faintest hint of amusement. "What is it?" I smiled at her at last.

She was so stunning with her blue eyes, raven black hair, and porcelain skin still untouched by the kissing fire… Her eyes dropped to my groin. "So I guess that's what I missed the night we met."

I glanced to where she looked and nearly yelped. I was at attention, and I had nothing to cover up the evidence of my arousal. I'd completely forgotten that the magma had made quick work of the clothing I'd been wearing upon entering the vent.

Typical, horrible luck.

Instead of covering myself though, I left myself bare. Completely exposed for her. I'd thought myself dead merely hours before, and all I yearned for in the vent was to see her, to be with her. I didn't care if she saw how much she meant to me. She needed to know that I still desired her.

I desired Moira more than anything I'd ever encountered in my millennium of existence. Plus, I'd already seen her naked, so it was only fitting that she saw me naked too.

I smirked at her, then mumbled, "I wish we didn't have to save Al right away. I can think of a much more enjoyable way to spend our time..." I dared a glance to her chest, then saw her visibly swallow before licking her lips. It was obvious that she desired me too, but did she want me in the same way I wanted her?

She blushed, and her breathing became almost arduous as she whispered, "So what's the plan you were going to tell me, or have you forgotten it now that you're human again?"

"Forgotten?" Her eyes darted to my face, and I crossed my legs so she could focus, "You're going to need to slice your palm."

"What does that have to do with this?"

"Moira," I let her name sit on my tongue, "slice your palm with the obsidian, and you will go back to being a spirifae as you were back home."

Her eyebrows rose, "How is that going to work?"

I folded her hand over the shard still resting there, and whispered, "I'm not entirely sure, but you're smart. You don't have to know *how* it works, so long as it does. The plan is for you to get the men distracted enough for me to get through Al's restraints as well."

Moira beamed at me, before gazing down at the black shard. "If this works..." She dragged the shard over her palm in one swift movement.

"Well, for whatever reason, it worked for me already. Also, a professional tip, you should sit down before you fall over."

"You've only done this once Sylver; you're a far cry from being a professional already." Moira sat down beside me and tossed me a taunting grin as she reached her hand to stroke the leg closest to her when she began shaking. She convulsed in the sand, and her limbs jerked back and forth.

More seconds passed, and Moira continued thrashing. But as time progressed, I noticed her skin began taking on an incandescence of its own. Her eyes, still the brightest blue, also began to ignite, flickering just as her flame would.

Then, suddenly, she stopped and twisted her head to face me entirely. She lay there biting her lip, and I could see her eyes linger on where my legs remained crossed. "I would have thought this feeling would disappear..."

"Maybe its because you aren't quite a flame yet," I muttered.

She threw me a pleading glance, then stood up with otherworldly grace. "I know you have to save Alterra, but I also think you should watch." She chuckled quietly. "I'll make this show an interesting one, just for you." She tapped the end of my nose as she said it, then paused. "Actually, I'm doing this for me too. They don't deserve to live after what they've done to us. What my flicker sensed they wanted to do to us..." Her eyes banked infinitesimally in the moonlight, and I angled my head, eager for her to say something—anything. But before I could even ask, Moira winked at me, and casually strode off around the corner of the Mount.

I jumped to my feet, then followed her course.

She was a flame now. Moira in all likelihood wouldn't have the sense to remember whatever it was that made her react that way. And if she did, I doubted that she would feel like rehashing it.

I shut down my curiosity.

She had a mission to complete.

Damn. The whole proposition felt wrong; letting her waltz herself into harm's way almost felt criminal. She was so small and delicate and...if only I still had the freedom to choose who I could be while still holding onto some semblance of strength.

I shut down my worry too. I was certain that Moira could handle her own while in this form. Back home in this same form, she'd been forced to face monsters much deadlier than a few perverted men in the middle of a desert.

At night...

I nodded my head. She'd be fine.

But I still couldn't understand what was going through her mind. Why was she so eager to become a flame again? What *drove* her to join the circus? What *drove* her to help Kieran? Why did she simply give up?

I knew that if I was in her position, I would have never given up or in or anything else. There would have only been one thing they could do to me to halt me from breaking free to have a chance of rejoicing with her again.

I watched her from afar as she freely swaggered to the men at the campfire and brought my still-bloody palm to my hair. I was overthinking everything. There was no point in hyper-analyzing everything she did—she didn't need to lie to me. I was a flame too, and even though I no longer carried the gift she possessed, I knew that what we had was something special.

I swore I could see Alterra's eyes expand as she noticed Moira was now liberated from her restraints.

"If you wanted to fuck me, you should have done it when you still had the chance." Moira's voice was chilling, and it cut through the desert loud enough that the three men whipped their heads to her lithe, subtly glowing form standing before them.

"How'd that cunt escape?" Keeto reached for his gun, and the other men followed suit.

That was when she ran.

Chapter 30

Moira

THE SAND DID NOTHING TO HINDER my course as I bolted for the sea. I was free again and there was nothing on this planet that could keep me from enjoying every second of this temporary liberty.

Coarse granules bit into my feet as I pushed onward to the distant waves lapping in the distance, but I couldn't care less. I couldn't care less as I felt like myself for the first time in what seemed like a lifetime.

I'd forgotten the dulled senses that came with these past five years of torture. Now the reflexes I'd been blessed with for centuries seemed too quick, my eyesight too sharp.

As I ran, I could make out the individual blades of various types of grass littering the shoreline, and the rachis of each feather of some strange looking bird soaring over the open ocean before me.

I was alive.

And I was going to make the three disciples behind me desire to have never met me.

My legs didn't falter as I made them move faster.

Their panting breaths and raucous footfalls became a symphony as I practically flew over the sand, never deigning to glance behind or slow down. I wanted them to fear me. I wanted them to fear the monster that I'd missed for such a long time.

But even as I rushed for the shoreline, listening to the pounding beat of their footsteps, I couldn't help but wonder why I could still feel as I had while I was a human. Why did Sylver's face still make me want to melt into him? I'd never *once* felt these emotions as a spirifae.

I'd hoped they would fade away. I'd hoped that I'd have an excuse for not desiring to pursue anything further with him. I'd hoped that I would have been able to escape the memories that came with this world.

But now, would they ever go away?

Whatever.

I cast the thoughts aside as I'd done for the last five years as my feet struck the shoreline; the wet sand and slick rocks sharply contrasted with the dry, debris-laden terrain they'd just torn through, but still, they did not falter.

I refused to slow my course as I splashed into the waves and barreled through the water that tried restraining me. It failed. I was strong again and whole, and there was nothing that was going to stop me. Water sprayed and soaked me, and I dove in.

Nothing could stop me.

Chapter 31

Sylver

MOIRA WAS A STREAK OF FIRE as she bolted towards the sea, leaving both the men and Alterra gaping in her wake. Glowing and immortal, she was still the most magnificent of everything I'd ever seen in my own existence.

The other two men now grabbed their guns too, and they synchronously began their pursuit.

But it was useless.

Moira's skirt caught in its own wind as she sprinted to the shore. Only when she was just entering the water did I venture from the darkness to free Al from where she was left attached to the bike.

I hurried to her, and her eyes widened with shock yet again.

Shock, but something else lingered in her gaze.

She then smiled before saying, "Maybe while you're over there getting my blade, you can grab yourself something to cover up with." She indicated a spot to the left of where the men had been sitting, and I noted that her blade leaned against the third bike.

Seriously. I'd forgotten that I was still at attention.

I gave her an apologetic look, then rushed to the spot where her blade rested.

The disciples' sleeping bags were set up beside the motorcycle to be used for the night, so I quickly grabbed the one closest to me and used it as a wrap before returning to Alterra.

I went behind her and wedged her blade between where her wrists were and the rope. Her wrists dripped with blood, and it didn't appear that she'd made any progress in getting through the thick cord on her own.

She shook her hands free when she felt the rope drop and twisted to me after untying her bound feet. "What the fuck happened earlier? I thought you died. You jumped into a volcano for the Messiah's sake." She exhaled. "I would have left you for dead if it wasn't for Moira convincing me otherwise. And how is she completely fine after having her head shoved into the campfire?"

I shrugged. "I guess we have a lot to talk about when she's done."

"No fucking kidding. What's Moira doing?" Alterra squinted at the water.

I could see that Moira was swimming, further and further out to sea with each second, and that the men had only just reached the beach, now aiming their guns in her direction.

Then a bang.
And another.
And another.
And another.
Still, Moira kept swimming.

"Is she crazy?" Alterra made to run at the men with her sword drawn, but I halted her with an arm.

"Trust me Al, she's *anything* but."

Upon realizing they'd missed and that they'd each wasted their cannisters on the incandescent target, the men simply threw their guns to the sand, then launched themselves into the water after her.

Moira really was truly a beautiful sight to behold as the moon reflected back its strange light on her skin, and as her own intrinsic fire answered with its own, making her graceful movements visible even in the dark—even from the shore.

She swam and swam away from the coast, and the men, drunk on the idea of catching her and doing who knows what, continued their conquest.

They waded until the water became too deep to do so, then halted.

I squinted to look at the sea myself, then noticed the most stunning azure light ignite just an inch above the water's surface.

That could mean only one thing.

Moira was hunting.

Chapter 32

Moira

THE BRISK COLD OF THE SEA gnawed into my warmth as I swam forward. Gunfire popped behind me, and I chuckled to myself as I spied each of the spots their bullets penetrated the water. Diving deeper, I opened my eyes, glimpsing corals, and fish.

Then to my left, a much larger, more alarm-inducing creature poked its snout from behind a crop of rocks and I froze. A sharp fin rose high above it, and others worked in tandem to help the grey beast glide seamlessly through the open water. Its tail helped to propel itself past where I floated near the water's surface, and I couldn't help but exhale the breath I'd been holding as I noted that it charged directly for the three men wading almost two hundred feet away.

I had no idea what that *thing* was, but for whatever reason, perhaps the human instincts that still ceased to leave me, warned me not to get on its bad side. Those same instincts also warned me not to make any more sudden movements, as the beast seemed to be attracted to the splashing.

I wouldn't be able to swim. Fuck. Well, that wrecked the plan.

I smothered my annoyance and closed my eyes. I couldn't swim, but a flame wouldn't need to swim. My heart practically leapt out of my chest as the realization dawned upon me. I was finally able to do the one thing I'd desired to do so many times.

So, *so* many times.

Part of me still wondered if this was all a dream—if in the morning I would wake up in the midst of the desert yet again with Qasir, or instead beside some other man I'd only met the day before and was forced by Salvador to assist.

I opened my eyes and gazed star-ward. Twinkling lights and swirls of clouds and even some smoke still hung overhead, and I let myself ease into a feeling of restfulness, serenity, peace, home. The flame rested just under my skin, and I could feel its hesitancy to enter this foreign new world.

Creeping and skulking out of my pores, the blue fire of my soul consumed me, and I was left without my body; a deserted mind, hovering above the waves, finally free of the sentiments that had haunted my other half.

There was no delight as a flame—I barely recalled the desire I'd felt only seconds before to return to this feeling of nothingness. The numbness was all-consuming, and I fought against the urge to silently drift away.

But I had a job to do.

It may not have been an oath or a promise I'd made to Sylver, but I wouldn't break his faith in me, nonetheless. I turned my consciousness to the men striding deeper into the sea and forced myself to remain still.

Inches above the surface, I watched, and I waited, and I wordlessly vowed, the three disciples who had attacked Alterra and me, would never reach the shore again.

And I would be the one to do it.

Chapter 33

Sylver

I COULD HEAR THE MEN CURSE in a chorus of sorts, before hearing one yell louder than the rest, "She has a light!" He pointed to her radiant form before diving into the water's depths.

Little did they know that she *was* the light.

I glanced to Al and nudged for her to come closer to the water with me—hesitantly, she followed. Standing in silence, we wordlessly agreed to listen to the conversation the men closest the shore were having:

"Keeto knows I can't swim…"

"Keeto's a clown. I don't see why we can't just leave her and go back to the other one."

The man chuckled, then said, "It's funny, Kieran always seemed a bit feminine to me."

"I don't know. The revelation caught me off-guard."

"And the fact that she has such big knockers too…"

Alterra scoffed at my side before whispering conspiratorially, "Moira won't let those men live, will she?"

I gave her a small grin in exchange, and she returned the gesture.

Keeto called out from where he now floated on his back, "Are you two just going to leave this all up to me?"

"You know I can't even swim!"

"I don't care. You do what *I* tell you to do, and I am telling you to get your ass in the water!"

"You know what, fuck you, Keeto!" One of the men turned to face the shore, catching sight of both Al and I who were standing there, watching like a couple of fools. "Keeto!"

"Oh, shut up already! You told me to fuck off. Do you think I give a shit about what you want to tell me." Keeto began swimming out to Moira's luminescent form again.

The other man spoke up, "Kieran escaped Keeto; we've got to go back."

"Can't you see that I'm busy? I'll leave her up to you two."

The man gave the other one a grateful look, then went to move forward in the water but froze before demanding, "Did you feel that?"

"Feel what?"

He didn't respond for a moment then shrieked, "There! Something just brushed by my leg."

"You're imagining things now, Laqueres."

We watched as the man called Laqueres whipped his head to the left and pointed, "It's right there."

"What is?" The other man deigned to glance where Laqueres had pointed, then mocked him, "Laqueres, you're too bloody drunk."

"That doesn't even make sense! I am *not* drunk. Didn't you see that dark patch in the water?"

"It's all dark Laqueres; it's night for the Messiah's sake!" He grabbed Laqueres by the collar of his shirt and began dragging him back to shore, when Laqueres screamed.

His scream was one of the foulest sounds I'd heard, and he desperately made to grab at something in the water before he yelled, "*MY LEG!!!*"

The other man's eyes widened with what I could only describe as horror, as Laqueres was ripped from the man's grasp and pulled beneath the water's surface.

"Laqueres!"

"What's the problem with Laqueres now, Treian?" Keeto's voice echoed across the water from where he paused to float once more approximately thirty feet from Moira's light.

"He's—"

Laqueres erupted from the water, sputtering, screaming, blood dripping from where the moonlight highlighted that something had gouged a chunk out of his arm.

"Holy shit." Alterra whispered.

Treian splashed over to where Laqueres now thrashed for his life, further out in the water column. An eternity passed before Treian was within reaching distance of his fellow disciple—and it was only seconds afterward that Laqueres forced him under the water in an attempt to leverage himself. I could just see Treian's arms as they flailed from where he was held submerged, and then the bubbling of water from where he finally released his only breath.

Laqueres didn't even notice him in his blind panic.

Maybe Moira would only have the one to deal with.

She wouldn't be too happy to hear that.

Treian's hand twitched after a minute, then after another, his arms stopped splashing altogether, leaving Laqueres with nothing to help himself stay afloat.

The gouge that had been ripped from Laqueres' arm still bled, and I smirked as I knew that *that*, along with whatever had happened to his leg, would be a certain death sentence. He would never be able to step foot on the beach again. So he, too, sunk to the bottom of the sea, leaving not a trace of either of them behind.

In the distance, Keeto yelled behind him, "What's going on over there?! *Guys?!*" From a floating position he screamed their names, but neither of the men responded. I could almost see Keeto debating whether to continue out to where Moira remained perched above the water's surface as a flame, when Moira drifted inwards, towards the shore a few feet to entice him further.

And Keeto, taking her bait, swam forward.

Moira didn't shy from her position as he continued.

He swam and swam and swam—

Keeto was apparently determined to not give up on this particular conquest of his.

We could see an outline of his face as Keeto came within reaching distance of her flame, and he called out, "Guys, she has to be somewhere around here." He splashed the water under her light; gently illuminating the rippling water like she was a moon unto herself. He called out in victory, "She must have drowned! I can't find her anywhere!"

Still, no response could be heard from his drowned men.

Alterra shook her head fervently and grumbled, "It can't be. She must still be alive."

Moira then transformed back into her Fae form.

Chapter 34

Moira

THE MOMENT THE BUFFOON SHIFTED his head to the shoreline was the moment I forced myself to imagine Dima; to imagine her face as she herself uttered the words we'd been forced to utter thousands of times since to return us to our Fae form. *One cannot burn a flame, yet a flame can burn all those around. Shift.*

The tongue of the flames was nothing of this world; hissing campfires, popping logs—a symphony only a spirifae would dare listen to.

White light shot outwards from my mind, and my limbs quickly followed suit, lowering me near silently into the black water of the sea.

Keeto's human eyes finally adjusted, catching a glimpse of Alterra and Sylver standing on the beach, and he murmured, "I thought those idiots were supposed to do something about you two."

Keeto cursed again, then began swimming back to shore.

Not on my watch.

I allowed my body to flow seamlessly into the waves, soundless, even as the waves crested where I still broke the surface, and I smiled wholeheartedly as I stalked Keeto without being noticed. His strokes were choppy, sloppy, tired. Even if I were to have mistakenly made a sound in my haste, he wouldn't have been able to hear it.

Hell, he didn't even hear the commotion of his lackeys.

His foot came to graze my hand as it stretched forward, and my grin became grotesque when he withdrew it as if he'd been struck. I didn't hesitate as I lurched forward and seized his ankle in a hand, pulling him back into my embrace. His head whipped behind him to where I held him and something like fear lit his gaze.

"You're a ghost."

I leaned into his warmth, pulling him even closer, and whispered, "But I am not dead, Keeto."

Eyes widened and he sneered, "Then what in the Messiah's name *are* you?"

I didn't answer.

He didn't need to know anything about me. Not about me, or Sylver. Sure, Sylver had ventured to the Mount for Alterra, and I was still pissed with him, but after everything Keeto had done, and after everything my flicker sensed he *wanted* to do to the two of us, I wouldn't even let him have that. He was impossibly even worse than Qasir…

Seconds passed and Keeto thrashed against my touch before I let my mouth curl into a lupine smile. "Let me show you something hilarious."

Shock registered across his features as he recalled the words he'd spoken earlier, and I chuckled as I latched even tighter to his ankle before diving deep into the sea. The bright colours of the reef sailed by us as I dragged him even further, and he kicked and flailed behind me.

Pathetic.

Small sea creatures skittered away from the dark smear we became, and the grey beast that'd caught my attention minutes earlier charged towards where we now barrelled through the water, blood marring its snout, but I didn't care as I continued dragging Keeto deeper into the reef. Moonlight filtered down through the corals and seaweed, illuminating the path ahead, and I tightened my grip as he flailed and kicked at my grasp.

It was almost difficult keeping him restrained, and I silently cursed his burden. What the fuck was this prick eating on a regular basis? Even Qasir wouldn't have been such a pain in the ass to lug around.

More seconds passed, and Keeto's thrashing became an afterthought.

Perhaps the whale was finally starting to tucker itself out.

Whatever.

I twisted to face where he languidly floated behind me, and I paused as I noted his lack of movement.

His eyes were closed, mouth already parted, and no bubbles erupted from his lungs to indicate that he was still alive. Shit. I'd forgotten humans were so fragile. Liberating Keeto from my grip left him to peacefully drift deeper into his eternal sleep, and I watched as his body became enveloped by the sand that he disturbed upon crashing into the sea's bottom.

I smiled at his demise, then began the ascent back into the light of the night's sky, kicking my way back up to the surface. The grey blur swam past me, and I felt more than saw the water part beneath me for the brackish monster. I couldn't bother glancing behind even as Keeto's inky blood diffused past me.

At least I wouldn't have to deal with him any longer.

Chapter 35

Sylver

A BRIGHT LIGHT EXPLODED from behind Keeto, where she'd been floating above the water column, and I saw the glow of the flame she'd been transformed into in her striking blue eyes.

Al let out a gasp beside me. "What exactly is going on here?"

I'd forgotten that she still didn't know what Moira and I were.

Silent as the flicker she always spoke of, Moira trailed him in the water, then brought him into a lover's embrace before dragging him beneath the surface with her into a watery grave.

As a spirifae, she was more than capable of overpowering him.

The world held an eery quiet as Al and I watched where she lured him deeper into the reef.

I felt Alterra's prying eyes eating away my façade as she watched me, rather than the water ahead of us. I glanced back for only a moment when she murmured, "I must be crazy...Sylver, what are you guys?"

"Soon Al, sooner than you'll know, we'll tell you everything."

"Sure you will." Al took a deep breath, then twisted back to the too-still sea, nodding her head, where Moira suddenly propelled out of the water column with Keeto nowhere in sight. Catching our eyes, Moira shot a gleaming white smile to the shore, where Al and I still stood frozen.

Moira was so beautiful. I had to readjust my wrap as simply watching her kill her captor made me hard yet again. She mustn't have been in her Fae form for very long back in Laspiar—I would have remembered her...I *should* have remembered her.

Alterra gave me a knowing look but returned her stare to the sea where Moira was now swimming back. "When she gets back, you have to promise me that you'll give me some answers. I know you already said that you would; however, the fact is that I still don't trust you...not entirely anyway." A pause. "I mean, how could I?" She didn't tear her gaze from the water as she continued, "You've tried killing me more than once now, and you've been very clearly keeping some information from me."

She was right.

I still couldn't trust her after the stint she pulled as Kieran.

I pored over her expression; leery, full of scrutiny. "I promise that I will tell you everything you need to know, Al. Everything you need to or want to know..." I trailed off as I thought about what I was saying. What would she think upon learning the truth about Moira and me? She was a human; would that even make her capable of overcoming her fear, or would she try to kill the both of us?

I tucked a loose strand of hair behind an ear as I watched Moira wade her way back to shore. As she stepped out, she shot me another beaming smile that made the azure fire in her eyes burn brighter, burning away all the worries bothering me. I shifted my legs as her porcelain face and newfound confidence made me even hotter for her than I already was.

Then she was standing in front of me, clothed as she had been before she'd been engulfed by the flame. I made to embrace her, but Al held an arm in front, halting me, and demanded, "Tell me what the *fuck* is going on. Both of you."

Moira's eyes shimmered with Al's challenge as she said, "I'm me again, and if I'm not mistaken, I just saved your life."

Alterra rolled her eyes before splaying her arms. "Seriously Moira, that's it? Who are you exactly? What *are* the both of you?"

"Al, can't we just explain that on the way up north?" There was no point in wasting precious time and I was eager to get moving now that Moira was out of harm's way.

"Why do we have to go *north*?" Alterra sarcastically enunciated the last word, and I smirked.

Moira only angled her head and glanced to my groin yet again.

I fought against my arousal and spoke, "We have to go north, up the coastline so we can reach the mouth of the river of the Aspitha."

"And why do we have to do that exactly?" Alterra asked, folding her arms over her chest.

"Because that's where the Keepers said you can find your greatest desire." I held the shard of obsidian out towards her, and she took a step back. "You're supposed to use this and slice through the air like so." I demonstrated the action the spiders urged me to tell her to do.

"Are you sure?" She blinked, then squinted, confused. "What Keepers—the *Keepers* of what?"

"It's a long story…" I glanced to Moira, who still peered at me with her otherworldly eyes. "I made a promise, and I'm willing to tell you everything. Just have some patience."

"Fine. But we should rest soon." Alterra sighed. "You were in there for *hours* you know, and we weren't even able to sleep because, as you could see, tonight we were sort of busy."

"Why were those men here?" I'd forgotten to ask her directly. Perhaps she'd be able to explain that to me, and *a lot* more.

"I'll also tell you everything in due time, Sylver. But not now. I was serious when I said I'd like to rest first. Go through a few things if you know what I mean. Sort out my thoughts." She looked at both Moira and I with eyes that seemed far too knowledgeable before chuckling. "There's quite a lot to decipher it seems and I still need to wrap my head around it."

Moira smirked. "You aren't one to get scared easily, are you?"

My thoughts exactly.

Alterra scoffed. "Please. I've dealt with scarier things than you back at the Forum."

She then strode back to the campsite that those men had set up.

At least the disciples were good for one thing.

Chapter 36

Sylver

I COULD ONLY PRAY FOR ALTERRA to quickly fall asleep when Moira looped her arm through mine and began hauling me back to the other side of Mount Poyanjen. She was so much stronger as a flame than she'd been before.

I held the shard of obsidian in one hand and asked offhandedly, "Do you want me to wipe off the obsidian so that you can return to your other form before we do anything?"

I didn't exactly want to rush into whatever this was between her and me.

"Are you kidding me?" She halted mid-step and looked at me from under her thick lashes. "No. I have waited for *years* to be myself again…to be whole." Moira let her eyes drop to where the wrap still covered my groin, then slowly dragged them up my torso.

"I want to have everything I've ever wanted tonight, and I..." She began walking around the other side of the Mount without me. "I want you while I am strong and...not a pathetic circus act in need of someone stronger to save her. Don't ruin this for me."

Ruin it—where was this suddenly coming from? "Moira," I swallowed. "All I want is you, and I want you to be happy. I'm more than willing to give you what you want." I made to step forward but stopped myself, crossing my arms.

"What's the problem? You aren't scared of little old me, are you? If you want me to be happy—"

I shook my head, interrupting her, "I have a condition."

Not a *great* start.

"What is it?"

"If I give you what you want, you have to promise me one thing in return."

I was so fucking trusting.

Her glowing eyes flickered, offsetting her pale complexion. "Fuck Sylver, you just have to..." She paused, closing her eyes as she went to continue, "What is it?" She glanced down to her beautiful form. "I thought you wanted me..."

"Believe me, I do desire you, Moira." I took a step forward, opening my arms, "I just..."

I thought of the words that she left unsaid, *Fuck Sylver, you just have to...* Why couldn't she be forthright? We were the only two on this planet who would ever understand each other, but still she seemed so...taciturn with me. I peered at her from beneath my now lowered brows and inhaled before slowly releasing the breath. She was a fate, and it would be pointless to continue chasing, to continue yearning for her, if she was to be no more than a wisp of an impossible dream to me.

"Promise me," I pleaded. "Promise me, that this won't just be sex and that you will give *us* a chance."

Concern washed over her features and some of the flames winked out in her gaze. "Sylver, I—"

"Am I not good enough for you? What the fuck Moira?"

She furrowed her brow. "What?" She shook her head. "No, that's not it."

"Then what is it, Moira?" I was livid. She was so ready to use me; assumed I would just hand over this sacred piece of myself for her.

"When I'm a flame…" She smiled to herself. "I love not feeling. Being able to escape this…" She gestured to the space between us. "It used to be so easy and free." Pain washed over her features.

Free?

How could she *think*—

"But you're missing so much." I took another step her way. "Moira, feeling is not weakness. And when you're forced into a form in which you can't feel, are you really free? Are you really happy? This," I took yet another step towards her, "this might go to shit, and you may wish that it never happened, but there's always that chance. That chance that things won't go south."

She swallowed and her throat bobbed as I took yet another step.

"And if that's the case, you've waited long enough to be truly free. Truly happy." I eased a torturous breath. "Moira, please. Take this chance on me." My jaw clenched as I prepared for her rejection yet again. "Take a chance on us."

The silence between us became deafening, but I waited. I needed to hear her say something. I counted, seconds, then a minute passed. If this was it—fine. I took a step away from her, from the future I so desperately wanted with her. She wasn't going to give me…I shuddered. How could she live with herself—why couldn't she just *try*? Was *all* of this just another lovely piece of the ugly curse Dima conjured up to—

I heard a whisper from over a shoulder, "Yes."

I glanced to where she still stood, and she repeated, louder this time, "Yes; I want to risk it." She nearly closed the gap between us. "I want you too, Sylver, and you're right; I want to feel this." Moira cast me a smile that suggested sincerity, and I wanted to cede to her possible façade. But she'd taken *so* long—so long to deign to respond...to ease my pain.

I didn't want her pity.

But I still wanted her more than anything.

"You have to swear to me." I took the last step that sealed us together. "Swear to me—"

Her eyes glistened as she interrupted me, "It won't just be sex." She lifted a hand to my cheek before wrapping both arms around my neck and branding me with a kiss.

I couldn't back away from her. I didn't know if it was real, but I couldn't smother the kindle of hope those words had ignited in my soul. A tear spilt over onto my cheek. As a human, she was stunning, but as a flame...

I returned the kiss with everything I had and brushed my tongue over the roof of her mouth, trying to pull her in closer.

It wasn't enough.

Her scent of cloves washed over me, and I opened my eyes to gauge her reaction. She flicked her gaze up to mine and smiled before exposing her neck. I gripped the back of her head with one hand, felt the silky ink of her hair, then kissed her mouth again.

Harder.

I needed to *taste* her.

An eternity I'd waited for someone, anyone, that I could fathom spending the rest of existence with, and...and it was finally possible. She was finally here.

I began a trail, kissing first from her mouth, then down to her chin, then to the space just under her ear. She leaned into each touch, before murmuring a bit breathlessly, "More—I need more."

That was fine by me—I needed more too.

I moved my hands from her hair, letting them rove down her back until I found the hem of Alterra's blood-drenched attire, then heaved it over her head in a swift manoeuvre.

We were now bare chest to chest. She was so beautiful; skin illuminated by the no-longer-reddish moon overhead. I cupped her petite breast firmly with a palm, then made to kiss her neck again when she used her arm to yank my wrap off.

A feral part of me couldn't care less if I could only have her like this for one night. I threw the thought away. I wasn't going to ruin this for her, or for myself either.

I purred.

I glanced down to her hands which were no longer caught in my hair and saw her fiddling with the elastic of her skirt.

I knelt down onto my knees, slowly, making sure to drag my teeth over her exposed teat as I did so, and she thrust her hips towards me.

"*Please.*" Her voice was frantic.

I ripped through the fabric of her skirt, granting my mouth complete access to the awaiting buffet between her legs.

I glanced up at her from where I knelt below her naked form, and she shuddered. "I think this would be," I smiled, "*easier* for you if you came down here with me."

She practically threw herself to the ground, coating her naked form in the soot from the Mount, then breathed, "Don't hold back," before spreading her legs as wide as she possibly could.

I nearly climaxed at the sight.

I gave her a wicked grin. "*Moira,*" I hummed her name as her beautiful sex opened up before me. "I would never dream of it." My restraint was already wearing thin as I watched her chest rise and fall—as I watched her sex twitch.

But as she thrust herself towards me yet again, my restraint shattered entirely. I lunged forward, then brought my teeth to her core, grazing it just slightly.

She needed to enjoy this as much as I was.

And I needed to worship her; the faithful flame from another world who, as Waha had imagined, could very well be my fate. She moaned, and that was my cue to plunge my tongue deep inside her. She tasted like fire itself, and I *needed* it in my mouth. I swallowed, then lifted my head yet again only to suck on her clit.

She thrusted harder, and moaned my name, before grabbing the back of my head, forcing me to suck her harder, forcing me to taste every inch of her perfection.

I removed my head from her sex completely, then positioned myself over the top of her still writhing form. My hair fell onto her face as I leaned down to murmur, "You aren't allowed hold back from me either you know."

If this was to be the last time, I wanted her to give me *everything*.

I could still taste her on my lips, but I still needed *more*.

The feral, sex-addled piece of me practically begged to feast on her flesh *more*.

I lowered myself down slowly so I could guide myself into her when she decided to take my cock with her fist and thrust her hips upward.

A whimper escaped my lips as she nudged me inside of her and I exhaled as her smooth entrance came to envelope me, but not completely. I whispered, "Hold on Moira." Her hips continued thrusting up, desperate for the release to come, and I halted her bucking torso with a hand.

She whined. "Please, more. I can't—" Her breathing was laboured. "I need you inside me *now*."

Those were words I'd waited an eternity to hear.

I didn't dawdle as I plunged deep inside her and reached her innermost wall.

Moira screamed and thrust upward.

She was silk, and I could feel myself beginning to tingle in my lower spine. I ground my teeth. *Not yet*.

I plunged again, and she hoisted herself up to lick my neck.

Fuck.

I brought my head down as I plunged once again and began suckling one breast as I kneaded the other.

"Harder!" She screamed at me, and my eyes opened to see her own gazing at where I still suckled her teat, blazing with blue fire. I bit at her nipple as I did yet another faithful plunge, when I felt a distinct tightening around my cock, and knew she'd found her pleasure.

She moaned my name, then moaned it even louder as I felt her contract yet again.

I climaxed as she bowed backward and felt her velvety wall stroke me as she fell away.

I rolled over her still limp body and lay in the volcanic ash beside her.

She began laughing as she opened her exquisite eyes to gaze at me. "I'm *throbbing*." She paused, taking a breath. "I had no idea…"

"That was your first time?"

I took in a sharp breath. Fuck. I should have asked her beforehand…I could have hurt her. Did I hurt her?

"Yes." She smiled as she glanced down to her still swollen sex. "Was it any good?"

What kind of a question was that? She was more than perfection. I'd pumped myself more times than I could count, but never before had I felt like this.

I never could have imagined—

"Moira, you should have told me. I could have hurt you." She gave me an "as if" smirk, and I chuckled. "You're perfect. So, are you satisfied with yourself now?"

"Well, that depends…are you ready for another round?"

My mouth quirked to the side. "I will always be ready for you, Moira. But I'm still human, remember?"

Fiery delight quickly melted into disappointment on her beautiful face, so I leaned in to kiss her mouth yet again.

"But this human can taste you all night if you so wish."

Chapter 37

Sylver

I WOKE UP WITH THE DAWN, content to see that Moira still lay curled into my side. I brushed a stray strand of hair away from her face and played with a few locks, twirling them between my fingers as I watched her sleep. I quietly hummed the melody of the bog, the melody I'd sung for so many years in Laspiar and smiled as I recalled Dima's reaction to its peaceful rhythm. She'd said that I was too similar to my Fae brethren, dabbling in a diversion that would only ever make me grow restless and tired of the life I was crafted to follow. I smirked to myself as the memory faded; Dima had been right.

We didn't go back to the camp where Alterra slept after we'd exhausted ourselves last night. I was almost certain Al had heard us both at one point or another, and the thought of explaining it…

It also didn't help that we were too bloody tired to move there even if we'd wanted to.

"Hey Moira," I cooed into her ear, "I would love to lie here for forever with you; however, we still have some explaining to do for poor Al."

Moira grumbled and pulled herself closer to my chest.

I didn't let myself think of how many times I'd heard her make that same sound only hours ago. I shook my head; we had some serious things to do, and I couldn't let myself get distracted by the blue-eyed dancer at my side.

No matter how much I wanted her to distract me again.

"Come on my little flame." I continued stroking her cheek, then decided it would be beneficial for both of us for me to gift her with a few wake-up kisses—*solely* to motivate her out of my grasp. I began by pecking the seam of her lips, then kissed her slowly, deeply, as I felt her begin to revive with my touch.

She murmured, "*Sylver*, don't tease me—" as her eyes opened, albeit a bit groggily.

I pulled away as she leaned into the kiss more, and whispered, "I'm sorry, but we have to check to see how Al is doing."

"Ugh. Don't you mean check to see if she decided to abandon us in the middle of the night?" Moira shoved her head into the nape of my neck. "Can *you* at least do the whole explaining thing? I don't feel like talking. All I feel like doing is fucking." She sighed. "If we're legitimately a thing now, I'd love it if I don't have to explain myself to her."

I couldn't help the grin that became plastered on my face as she spoke of the two of us as a unit—as a *we*. Even after everything that she'd said the night before, I still questioned her authenticity. It was foolish, and I knew I was being paranoid—

I interrupted my train of thought. "But how about if she asks you something directly?"

"Just pretend I'm a mute."

"Moira, she knows you're not a mute…especially after last night."

"Fine. But if she doesn't ask a question to me directly, you'll do most of the talking for me, yes?"

"Sure thing." I eased out of her grip, then looked down to our clothes which were still tossed about in the soot around us. "What are you going to wear exactly?" I'd forgotten that I'd sort of completely destroyed her skirt.

"You could always let me use the wrap you used last night to cover yourself up…" Her eyes twinkled as they pondered the idea. "And you could be free, just as you were last night when you went to save Al in the first place. I'm sure she won't mind."

I nodded. "True, I could do that…but she'd probably think that I'm a creep if I choose to keep greeting her like that." I reached down to where my wrap had been thrown in the midst of our frenzy and threw it to her.

Moira had already donned her shirt, and was well on her way to replacing her skirt with the wrap, when she said, "I wonder what Alterra *actually* suspects?"

"I have no idea." I chuckled, shrugging as I turned to face the sea. "The Keepers said that she's human, so…I don't know what to think of what she thinks." But even still, I had to acknowledge that Alterra's reaction wasn't particularly *human*. A human would have taken one of the men's bikes when we were tossing about and rode far, *far* away from us.

Moira came to my side and gazed at the water, before nodding her head. "Let's not keep her waiting." I stayed behind her petite frame as there was a distinct possibility that Alterra too had woken at dawn's first light, yearning for answers from the two of us. But honestly, I prayed that she'd still be sleeping so that I could inconspicuously steal another sleeping roll and use it as a means of covering myself from her without her noticing.

When we eventually rounded the Mount, Alterra was already awake and seemed to be observing the dirt bike in front of her. Great. Perhaps upon thinking about it more, some human instincts had finally decided to click in.

"Good morning." She said this to the two of us without turning around. It didn't sound like she was having a particularly good morning herself.

"Morning," I mumbled. "Are you ready to head out yet?" We continued our approach, but still Alterra didn't bother turning around to face us. "Are you all good?"

She whirled from where she leaned over the bike and frowned at me. "I would be a lot better if you two didn't keep me up all night. How was that even possible?" She then jeered, "And why did you have to rip Moira's skirt? Cover yourself up for Messiah's sake." She brought a hand to one of her temples and began doing what I assumed to be soothing circles to calm herself.

I caught Moira glaring at me from the corner of my eye; she was obviously in agreement with Al.

I gave them both an apologetic look, then directed my gaze to Alterra, "I was sort of hoping you weren't going to be awake while I found something else to wear…" Moira and I reached the area where two more sleeping bags were strown about, and I quickly wrapped one as I had the night before. "So I take it you want to talk on the way as we discussed?"

"The sooner I reach my desire the better." Alterra grabbed a backpack which she'd seemingly already prepared, full of food and of at least a few jugs of water.

I followed suit and grabbed another one when Moira muttered from beside me, "Why do we have to walk? Three bikes are right there."

"Yes," Al answered before I could, "but when you're on a bike, you can't exactly talk because the engine swallows up all of the sound." She hesitated, then puffed. "Besides, I've already checked. There are no keys. The disciples must have brought them into the water when they went after you. I actually contemplated searching for them earlier, but I decided that I really didn't feel like hunting for them either, especially after you guys fucked all night and kept me up."

I gave Al an abashed look, then grinned to Moira who seemed to be on the verge of pouting, and asked, "Do you want me to carry you there?"

She rolled her eyes, "That won't be necessary. Thank you very much."

I smirked and watched her lips as she accentuated the last syllable, soundlessly reminiscing the feeling of those soft lips as they'd touched mine.

Alterra began walking off towards the coast.

Moira and I could only stride after her.

This was going to be fun.

"So, where do you want me to begin?" I waited a couple of seconds for her to respond before continuing, "Is there anywhere you want me to start?" Maybe in telling her the…truth of things first, she'd feel a bit less hostile towards us.

"Tell me why you survived for one. That's a good start."

Well Al certainly didn't waste any time, did she?

"I know that you noticed how Moira and I don't burn in the sunlight…" I hesitated, not really knowing how to explain it without freaking her out too horribly. "Okay, now imagine that that was the case all the time." I shifted on my feet. "We don't burn, period."

She hissed. "You think that's an explanation? Why can't the two of you two burn?"

I sighed, kicking a loose stone at my feet. "Moira and I aren't exactly from here—as in, we both originate from a realm outside of this one. We're from another world so to speak. Where we come from, we're called the spirifae." I grinned as I glanced to Moira, who was still glowing ever so slightly. "We're a race of flames, and no one and nothing can burn us."

"Another world?" Alterra spat. "Yeah, right. You're funny Sylver—I'll give you that—and you're also full of bullshit." She scoffed as she continued her pace. "What's the name of this *world* you speak of?" She wasn't convinced. She was a human; it wasn't like the name of our world would really matter to her. I let my voice carry across the dunes we now wandered past, "Laspiar."

Alterra twisted towards me mid-step and nearly fell over. "Say that again—*where*?"

I continued as we all came to a halt, "Moira and I come from the mire back in a place we call Laspiar. There, we're nothing but flickering flames. But we can also become Fae—humanoid creatures which are—"

"You're lying." She interrupted me, and her face reddened. "Stop fucking *lying* to me Sylver. You are *not* telling me the truth." Her eyes welled up, and she trembled. "You *can't* be." Regret hit me like one of the waves which perpetually assaulted the coast. This was too much for her. Our very *existence* was too much for her. But there was no point in taking it back—

We'd promised her the truth.

"We're not lying to you Alterra. The bodies we're in right now…I don't think they could fully contain our pure energy forms, so we took a bit of our power with us when we came here." I glanced to Moira, whose eyes still raged with caerulean fire. "That's why we still don't burn."

"When did you two come here?" Alterra cut Moira a contemplative glance. "Why would you two ever leave to come here?"

"We were ripped away five years—"

"Five years?" A sob tore out of Alterra's mouth.

I couldn't tell why she'd reacted that way. She'd wanted the truth, hadn't she?

"Yes, it was five years ago that we were ripped from our home and thrown here. This—"

"Shithole." Alterra finished my sentence and wiped at her eyes. "So you guys didn't come here willingly? You too were forced?"

We "too" were forced?

"What's that supposed to mean?" I shifted my gaze to Moira before letting my eyes settle on Alterra's weeping form yet again. The Keepers said she was human, but they didn't say that she'd *always* been human.

I cursed myself a fool as the realization dawned upon me.

"You're from Laspiar too."

Alterra only nodded, and murmured to herself more than anyone else, "It all makes sense now."

My voice was muffled to my own ears as I said, "It seems you have some more explaining to do yourself." I folded my arms over my chest and waited again for her to respond.

"Back home, you guys were only ever a legend to me." She chuckled and ran her hand through her cropped hair. "I should have known better though. The bog was always my go-to spot whenever I wanted to escape from everything and everyone else." She took a shaky breath. "I guess I should probably tell you guys my truth now, eh? On the way, though."

She twisted and began a more fervent pursuit up the coast.

"My full name is Alterra Iubi." She huffed on a breath. "Five years ago, I'd gone down to the bog to try and gain a different perspective about my very *complicated* life at the time in the middle of the night—it's so stupid to think about now. That's when I was taken—*ripped*—away as you'd described it and tossed in the midst of Neosordess, a city in which I was nothing, treated worse than garbage for simply being a woman." Alterra's breathing didn't falter as her steps quickened. "That didn't last long though because I, more than anything, wanted to go back home, to my Thyello. And I knew…" Another deep breath, "I knew, that no one would ever give me the information I needed on how I could possibly return home, unless I was someone people cared about. Specifically, someone people both feared and respected."

"That's when you decided to become Kieran?" Moira questioned Al with a nonchalance that could only be deciphered as being a direct consequence of the flame.

"Yes. That's when I adopted his persona…" She slowed down again. "So everything I did, it was because I didn't care if my reputation here was smeared with violence. I needed to return to him. I still do."

I cocked my head and made to adjust the wrap around my hips. "Thyello…" Why did that name sound so familiar?

"Thyello Ave. He's the one I've been searching for all of this time."

"The *prince*." My jaw dropped. A true descendant of Raifaer. If Alterra was royalty...I brought my hand to my mouth in an attempt to hold back the disgust that accompanied the thought. If Alterra was royalty, then I'd almost slaughtered one of the ones both Moira and I had sworn to protect upon our creation.

No wonder I'd been cursed.

"There's no need for you to look at me like that. I know what you're thinking; I'm not royalty." Alterra chortled. "But we were engaged before...you know."

"How can you not be royalty?" Each of the three royal families had decreed that only those with royal blood could marry into another royal family.

"Thyello isn't exactly the type of individual to follow tradition." Alterra smiled as she said his name, and I glanced to Moira. But Moira no longer winced as Al spoke of her betrothed.

Moira noted the shock that I was sure had spread across my features, and said, "I *am* the flicker now, so I don't feel her desire the same way I had. Now it's more of a pressing—a hand, urging me to go forward, to lead you." She looked to Al. "Besides, you already know very well that I would give you some serious shit if your thoughts set me into the same frenzy as they did before."

Alterra nodded and resumed her pace as she asked behind her, "How exactly do you two know of the royal family?"

Moira didn't hesitate, "We're their guardians. It is our solitary duty to protect them from the dangers that yearn to destroy everything they hold so dear."

I didn't want to elaborate. No need for Al to know that I'd already failed in my singular duty to shield the man she'd loved so dearly for my own selfish desires.

I changed the topic and asked a bit breathlessly, "So, why exactly did the disciples bother tormenting you last night?"

A smile crept into Al's voice as she explained. "*Apparently*, the Messiah didn't want me escaping Neosordess with His secrets. He entrusted them to me—to Kieran—and I guess he found out I'd left the city and had a few of his best men come looking for me." She sighed. "The only thing I can think though is that He thought I was going north to Aktearean—a place where the people still have rights I might add, and thought I would overthrow what He has built over these years after spilling the truth about who He truly is."

Her tone surprised me. "Would you have done that?"

"I mean..." Al shrugged awkwardly, trying to maintain the jog she'd started. "I don't think the people in Neosordess would do well if I did that."

Moira made to interrupt Alterra, "But, I could feel their—"

"Moira, you weren't there for five years." Al glanced at us over a shoulder. "What you saw...you simply don't know enough of the place. The people there haven't once protested against His rule, and I've asked them. One time I asked one of my workers a question along that same line, and she flat-out declined, saying that He was the *Messiah*, and who was she to halt the will of God or something like that."

I watched as abhorrence washed over Moira's features, even as she made to fix the makeshift skirt that now hung just below her navel. "How can they not see that they're suffering? I could feel it when I was there. It was awful."

Al's voice didn't falter as she continued, "Not awful enough for them to want change or revolt against Him. Really, I figure that when they're ready to do something about the Messiah, they'll go about and do it themselves. I'm not even from there, but if the people of Neosordess were ready, if they genuinely wanted to be free of His corruption, I'd have gladly gone and done just that." Al bobbed her head once. "I would have left Neosordess and travelled all the way to Aktearean, even though that would carry a death sentence for me."

I laughed and gave her a wicked grin when she turned to face us. "I can see why the prince wanted to marry you." I couldn't quite believe what I'd heard. I'd never have imagined that Kieran of all people would come to be another one of the lost.

Al didn't return the carefree gesture, and instead focused her gaze to the purple sky of the Dunes of Almalto which were now to our right.

A few more minutes of jogging passed, before I heard Al audibly swallow. She asked, "So what exactly happened to you, Sylver, when you went inside the volcano? Who are the *Keepers*?"

I smiled. "Well, I didn't quite realize how far down it was, nor how much just jumping into it would hurt, nor how difficult it would be to get into the lava."

"Did you manage to think *anything* through, Sylver?"

I ignored Moira's criticism and continued, "I also forgot that I still needed to have a source of air and a way to see when I fell into the pit, so those were all problems." My breathing was shallow, so I fought for air between gasps as I spoke, "After a while of trying and failing to get deeper, I felt something drag me in and I passed out. When I woke up, I was in an empty cavern, except there was a web stretched all above me. But it wasn't just one web—there were thousands of webs, stacked, interwoven, and connected to one another." I took a deep breath as I struggled to both tell the story and keep up with Alterra's accelerated pace. "Anyways, I'd heard voices while lying down with my eyes closed, pretending to be asleep. Spider-like shadows lurked in the darkness of the cavern, and they already knew who I was and who you two were, and they told me things once I told them my own truth. I thought I was hallucinating them."

"Okay, so did they know why we were taken away from Laspiar five years ago?" Al's voice was mixed with something like hope, and it almost broke my heart to tell her the truth.

"No."

She merely nodded her head as she continued, "Can you at least tell me what that shard of obsidian is supposed to do? What the Keepers said about it?"

In the distance, I could now see where the mouth of a river met the coast—the Aspitha. If we were to maintain the pace she'd set, we'd surely reach its banks in a few minutes. Glancing to my feet, I noted how the desert's sand began subtly shifting; patches of grass now littered the ground here and there, marking a boundary. I pointed to where the Aspitha met the sea and bowed over, desperate to catch my breath again before I continued. "I think that's it...that's where the shadows told me to tell you to use it."

It was as if Al had been walking this entire time; she used the grass at her feet to help her press forward, and it was all Moira and I could do to catch-up without losing our slack swathes of clothing.

Moira grumbled loud enough for me to hear, "I'm surprised she can still outrun me, even though I'm a flame again." I could only breath a bated laugh in exchange. We just had to make it there, and then Moira could be free of her oath and—

"*HURRY UP!!!*" Al yelled from where she now paced at Aspitha's mouth.

That was my cue. I felt like keeling over, and my lungs were raw by the time Moira and I made it to Al's side. We both still hadn't eaten anything all day, and we had had no rest the night before, although that was admittedly our own doing.

"So tell me, what did they say?" Al's eyes sparkled with curiosity, and it reminded me of one of the wood mosses back home. It was if her eyes glistened from dew left behind the night before.

I took a moment longer to catch my breath and tried to use the same ethereal tone the Keepers had used when they'd spoken. "*Give this piece of obsidian to Alterra—it will ground her, and whoever else uses it. However, when only she uses it, it won't just be herself that she grounds...*"

Alterra angled her head. "So you'd said before that I'd have to slice my palm, and then cut through the air like so?" She followed through precisely with the movement I'd demonstrated the night before.

"Exactly." I still didn't quite understand what the shadows were getting at. It wouldn't *just* be herself that she'd ground if she were to use it?

Moira's voice carved through the building tension. "It's obvious what it means."

A wicked grin crept over Alterra's features. "If I use the shard, I'll be able to go back home to Laspiar..."

"And we'd be forced to go back with you." Moira's radiant face was a beacon of hope, and I closed my eyes.

If there was *any* doubt that I was *in fact* cursed...

I couldn't take it.

I couldn't watch as their happiness oozed from them while I silently fell into despair.

I took a step back and grasped the shard with all my strength. "No," I said. This wasn't right. I'd just gotten what I'd wanted—*no*—what I'd *needed* my whole existence. I was now able to be myself *and* to be with the one I cared for. But now after I've finally tasted my hopes and dreams, I was just *expected* to give all of it up? "You can't do this to me." I bristled as I readied myself for what was to come. "I won't let you take me back."

"Why the fuck not?" Alterra screamed at me. "I've searched and searched for five fucking years, and finally, *finally*, when I'm given this way back home, you'll deny me it?" She reached for the blade hanging on a sheath at her side. "You don't think I won't use this on you if I have to? After *everything* I've done and after...just everything."

I felt my fist struggle to keep clamped on the shard, and hissed, "If I go back..." I took another step away from Al and Moira. "I'm *cursed*. I will never be allowed to be *me* again. I will only ever be a heartless, cold flame." I would rather go down fighting and die at Alterra's hand than go back to that void, miserable existence.

I'd only returned to that doom for Moira.

"What do you mean?" Anguish etched itself across Moira's ceramic features. "You're telling me *now* that you aren't a faithful flame?" I watched as she clamped down on her tongue, wincing as she probably drew blood. "Sylver, I don't know what it is you did, but Laspiar is my home, and it always will be."

"What does it matter, Moira?" I couldn't help that I'd been forged different than the spirifae to come after me. I couldn't help that I was a defective prototype. I couldn't help that whenever I'd been made to shift into a flame I'd felt hopeless, empty. Was I suddenly nothing to her now that she learned—

Was what I wanted nothing to her?

My jaw quivered as she cast me an imploring look. "Sylver, when I'm here, when I'm not under the will of the shard, I feel like I'm missing an intrinsic piece of who I am. I want to be with you, but I want to go back, and you want to stay here..."

Al intercepted me. "Wait. Maybe this doesn't have to be it. *Maybe* we can all..." She heaved another sigh. "My mother knows things, and I'm certain that she would know how to remove your curse. We'd all be able to get what we've wanted for a long, long time." She sheathed her blade and grinned.

Acid rose as I caught her in the lie. "Fae can't bestow nor remove curses."

"Who said anything about my mother being Fae?"

Moira asked the question before I could muster the words, "What exactly are *you* then?"

Alterra's smile was fraudulent as she responded, "I'm a mixed breed. My mother is a witch, and my father...he is Fae."

"You must be the only one of your kind." Moira's voice was grim as she spoke.

But if that was indeed the case, her mother would be more than capable of vanquishing this damned curse from me. I let a small smile reach my lips. "And you're sure that she'd do that for me? I mean, I can't exactly say that we've been on the best of terms with you thus far..."

"Pfft. That's an understatement. But, without you two, I would never have had this chance to see her and Thyello again. I think she'll just be grateful that you two helped me get back to her."

I looked to Moira who now pleaded and analyzed me as I joked, "You realize that you're going to have to carry me with you if you ever expect for us to go anywhere without taking a year, right?"

Relief and perhaps even weariness flooded her gaze. She bobbed her head. "I should be able to do that."

Maybe everything would be okay. I was just being paranoid again. Maybe Alterra was right—we could all get what we'd desired by the time this day was through.

I slowly loosened my grip on the stone, then said to Moira, "You might want to sit down again."

As soon as she did, I wiped the stone of her blood, using the wrap still around my waist to do so efficiently. Seconds passed before her otherworldly brightness began to fade, and she let out an unimpressed groan when I'd finished. "At least I won't be like this for very long."

I interjected at her defeated tone. "You're beautiful, Moira. You always will be to me, no matter what form you're in."

Sorrow lingered in her stare even though she curled her mouth into a grin. What was she hiding?

I shut out the thought as I handed the now shining obsidian to Alterra, who cradled it before gouging her own deep wound on her palm. It splashed into the sand at her feet, and she swallowed.

We all did.

Al then turned to both Moira and me, with fierce determination lighting her eyes. "A toast." She lifted the stone into the air like she would a glass of the finest wine, and let her voice peal, "To those who have lost, and to those who have so much left yet to gain." She then brought the shard up to her lips and kissed it—sanitary—causing blood to trickle down from where it'd touched. "I'll be with you soon my love." She closed her eyes and let the stone rest at her mouth as tears began streaming down her cheeks.

As if performing a ballet or a waltz, she then slashed through the air; graceful, elegant, trained. Blood splatter from the obsidian peppered the sand and grass in front of her, creating an arc mirroring the path the shard had taken in the air above it.

Instantaneously, the air itself transformed into a depthless black ink—ink that devoured worlds, a gap between realms. It was a vacuum, sucking us deeper into the eternal darkness, and I could just make out the glow of a golden string.

It was one of the gilded webs from the volcano.

It shot to us, spiraling out of the shadows, forging its own path through the darkness until it snapped out of the gap and wrapped itself first around Alterra.

Then Moira.

And then finally, me.

We couldn't fight the web's power as it tore us from where we stood in the sand.

If this was the end, and if the shadows had, in fact, lied to me, lied to us all, I had to say something to let Moira know that no matter what she thought, she would always be special to me. She was my future—Waha believed that to be true—even in death.

So as our feet left the earth and we felt the gap tear at everything we'd taken for granted the last five years, I fought for Moira's hand. Her panic-stricken face gazed into mine for possibly the last time, and I squeezed her hand once.

Time halted as I finally brushed my thumb over her skin and mouthed before we were sucked into a space without sound, without light. "I was fated to love you, Moira."

The golden thread of the realm's web tore us apart before she could respond.

She was my future, and she had been ripped away from me.

Chapter 38

The Prince
FIVE YEARS AGO

I AWOKE WITH AN URGENCY that seemed completely uncalled for. The moonlight trickled in through the curtains, illuminating my chambers just enough to see that it was too damned early to wake up.

Perhaps I couldn't sleep because of what I'd dreamt about...I wiped my hands over my eyes. It wasn't like I needed to sleep anyways. It wasn't like I'd been planning this big day for Alterra tomorrow for over a month.

She'd be turning twenty-three with the dawn.

I shook my head, trying to shake away the uneasiness of that damned dream. In it, she'd been taken from me. That was all I could remember.

I glanced to where she usually slept beside me and found her side of the bed bare.

That was fine; she'd often take off in the middle of the night to soothe herself by the mire. I'd never blamed her for it either, especially after how badly my parents had treated her tonight, when they'd noted she wasn't at her post like she'd been told to be. Even though, *I* was the one to "irresponsibly" drag her away from said post. Part of me yearned for the day in which I would tell them about how special she'd become in my life—just so I could see them both squirm. After what they'd said to her, they would deserve that much. And that day would be tomorrow.

Tomorrow they would learn *officially* that Ally was to be mine for the rest of our lives.

Ally didn't know *that* little detail yet. She hated the idea of conflict and I smiled to myself as I imagined her likely reaction tomorrow. But she was worth it.

I caressed the bed beside me to see just how long ago she'd left, and quickly found that her side of the bed had turned cold...

She'd definitely been gone long enough.

Where was she?

I shut my eyes against the light trickling through the curtains and let my mind drift to where I knew I'd be able to find her.

My staircase had always been a hard walkway of air with various coniferous trees lining the railing.

This place—I would always be in awe of what our love had crafted.

It transcended class and race.

Alterra was mine.

And I was hers.

I glanced ahead to the top of my staircase and halted mid-step.
It was blocked.
I was blocked from our dreamscape by what looked to be…
I rushed to the barrier.
Rock.
Cold earth cleaved my staircase in two.
No.
I screamed and pounded against the wall of stone, "ALTERRA!!!"
No response.
Something was wrong.
Something was terribly *wrong.*
I backed from the barrier slowly.
Where was Alterra?
Maybe my dream wasn't a dream after all, but a warning.

I snapped myself out of our realm and ripped the sheets off the bed.

I had to find her.

I began donning on some pants and reached for my sword, *Alas,* when I heard someone step through the doorway and approach from behind.

I sighed with relief. "I'm so grateful it's you."

I spun around to greet Ally, but…she was different. Her eyes, which had once reminded me of life and of the forest, now brought a different image to mind. Now they were like the cold soil one would carelessly dump over a rotting corpse. And her long, curled hair which only hours ago seemed warm, now seemed as cold as the corpse her eyes now reminded me of.

Something was off.

"You were missing me?" Her voice sounded the same, but the Ally I'd grown to love would never have responded that way. My

Alterra would have asked me what the problem was after analyzing everything I'd done in the moments she'd been gone.

I forced a smile onto the surface and edited the would-be-uneasiness from my tone. "Of course, my dear. You are my life. You're worth more to me than the earth I walk on." A test.

She laughed and took another step forward to me. "That's a little dramatic, don't you think?"

I feigned her carefree expression. She failed. This thing *looked* like Alterra, but this wasn't my Ally.

I tried again. "Are you excited for tomorrow?"

"Why would I be? What's tomorrow again?"

I felt a tempest brewing inside my soul. "It's nothing. Don't worry about it my dear."

My Alterra had been insistent—talking to me just a few hours earlier about how she didn't want anything for her birthday. She wouldn't have forgotten about it like some old party trick.

I subtly nudged my foot away from her and stated, "I hope you don't mind, but I have some business to attend to."

"At this time of night?"

"Yes." I reached for a shirt I'd worn earlier as I continued, "Just before you came, one of the servants informed me that I was to see my parents immediately."

She inclined her head. "Oh, well I guess I'll see you later?"

I could barely nod as blind panic came over me and cast her a line of a smile.

I had to get out of here.

The creature approached me, and I fought my urge to take a step away.

I had to play the role.

She made to kiss me, but I shrugged out of her grip. "It's urgent. Sorry Ally."

I did nothing short of bolting from the chambers.

I would do anything to find Alterra.

Just as I knew she would do anything to find me.

To be continued.

Pronunciation Guide

CHARACTERS

Moira: Moy-ruh
Qasir Rahat: Ka-seer Rah-hat
Alterra Iubi: Alt-air-ah You-be
Sylver: Sil-ver
Waha: Waw-hah
Dima: Dee-muh
Donovir: Dawn-oh-veer
Treian: Tree-an
Laqueres: Lack-eers
Thyello Ave: Thee-yel-low Av-ay

PLACES

Neosordess: Neo-sor-dess
Aktearean: Act-ear-ian
Meriyaet: Merry-yay-t
Laspiar: La-spee-ar
The Aspitha: The Asp-ee-thuh
Mount Poyanjen: Mount Poi-an-jenn
Masyron Sea: Massy-ron Sea

OTHER

Spirifae: Spear-if-fay
Pierserk: Pierre-serk

About the Author

QUINCY LEE CLARK is a young author, who according to those who know her best, is a bit of a work-a-holic. Having grown up as an only child in Northern Ontario, she may or may not have developed a slight obsession with self-improvement—at least, that's if you consider trying to learn eight languages on top of attaining a bachelor's degree in biology, whilst simultaneously minoring in psychology, all the while writing and painting and dreaming…an obsession.

But in all seriousness, writing has always held a special place in her heart—*my* heart. I've loved writing since I was a little girl, and the quarantine we all experienced with the COVID-19 pandemic allowed me to reinvigorate this true passion of mine. When I was supposed to be studying and focusing on the importance of stereochemistry—*blech*—I was instead reading, escaping into the worlds fabricated by some of the greats. Unfortunately, their worlds, as perfect as they were, were simply *not* enough. I wanted to be able to be forever lost in a world of my own…and now it exists.

Thank you so much for reading!

www.quincyleeclark.com
instagram.com/quincyleeclark

Acknowledgments

My most sincere gratitude and thanks to those who have helped to
make everything—even the impossible—possible:
my mother, Sunday,
my rock, my other half,
for an unconditional stream of love and support,
and for giving me the strength to follow my dreams;
my grandmother, Sandra,
my "swear-teacher"
for always testing my limits,
and for making even the dull days interesting;
my aunt, Melissa,
for the carefree music you spontaneously sing,
and for remaining true to yourself to spite adversity;
my cousin, Roderick,
for being the brother I never asked for,
and for being the brother I always wanted;
—my friends—
for supporting me on this journey,
for teaching me, for inspiring me,
and for the late-night drives to the middle-of-nowhere
so that we could escape the turmoil of our lives

Thank you so much for reading! Please add a short review on Amazon, and let me know what you thought!

Manufactured by Amazon.ca
Bolton, ON